EXERCISE IS MURDER

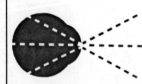

This Large Print Book carries the
Seal of Approval of N.A.V.H.

EXERCISE IS MURDER

JANIS PATTERSON

WHEELER PUBLISHING
A part of Gale, Cengage Learning

GALE
CENGAGE Learning·

Detroit • New York • San Francisco • New Haven, Conn • Waterville, Maine • London

GALE
CENGAGE Learning®

LIBRARY OF CONGRESS CATALOGING-IN-PUBLICATION DATA

Patterson, Janis.
    Exercise is murder / by Janis Patterson.
      pages ; cm. — (Wheeler Publishing large print cozy mystery)
    ISBN-13: 978-1-4104-5738-7 (softcover)
    ISBN-10: 1-4104-5738-9 (softcover)
    1. Ex-police officers—Fiction. 2. Women with disabilities—Fiction.
3. Antique dealers—Fiction. 4. Murder—Investigation—Fiction. 5. Large type
books. I. Title.
PS3563.A9418E94 2013
813'.54—dc23
                                           2012048834

Published in 2013 by arrangement with Janis Patterson

Printed in the United States of America
1 2 3 4 5   17 16 15 14 13

to Leslie and Steve Coker,
dear friends as well as beloved kin,
and
to CAPT Hiram M. Patterson,
USN/Ret,
the most wonderful man in the world

CHAPTER ONE

Elevators, thought Flora Melkiot with her usual lack of originality, *were sort of like surprise packages.* When the doors opened you never knew what you'd find.

On the other hand, she usually added with sour expectation, *very few surprises were nice.*

"Good morning, Mrs. Melkiot," chirruped the brainless blonde from the building office.

All teeth and legs, Flora had decided at their first meeting, and she had never had occasion to change her opinion.

"I'm so pleased we ran into you," the blonde went on, shepherding her charge onto the elevator. "This is Mrs. Laura Tyler. She's just taken number four-oh-six."

Taken, indeed. No one connected with the rarefied atmosphere of the Olympus House would ever use such a plebeian word as "buy." The entire subject of money was regarded as somewhat vulgar and, like body functions, finances, and other private matters, was never mentioned except between the most intimate of friends. It really didn't have to be; the fifteen spacious stories of marble and gilt on Dallas' tony Turtle Creek Boulevard housed more than enough real wealth to purchase a small European country or two.

The doors whooshed closed and the elevator slid silently down.

"Mrs. Tyler, this is Mrs. Flora Melkiot. She lives on the twelfth floor."

Flora didn't speak, but she did give a regally slow nod of acknowledgment. Already she had taken in the too-tight gray curls (Ramon would have a fit at the sight of that frizzy perm!) and the cheap-looking but probably quite expensive pink suit. An unhappy linen-poly blend, it still wouldn't have looked like much even if the plain little woman had worn it well.

The woman simply reeks of suburbia, Flora decided. If she tried, she knew she would probably be able to smell crabgrass and bicycles.

"It's such a pleasure to meet you." Laura Tyler spoke with such enthusiasm that her springy gray curls bobbed.

Flora took such pleasure at being met as

8

her due. After all, her great-grandmother had come from the Russian court, and Melkiot's was one of the largest jewelry store chains in the country. Flora even believed sometimes that she had been personally responsible for its success. After all, hadn't she been a good wife to Morris (God rest his soul) for over thirty-eight years, and if that wasn't a meaningful contribution, what was?

"Mrs. Tyler will be moving in on Friday," said the blonde, who — as far as Flora Melkiot was concerned — needed no further appellation.

"How nice," she allowed.

"Moving is such a trial," Laura Tyler said as if it were a profound new discovery. "Packing and throwing stuff away . . . I never dreamed I could have accumulated so much stuff in twenty years! When we bought the house, I didn't think we'd ever fill it. I mean, it was almost four thousand square feet. But now it's just stuffed, every nook and cranny —"

There were several things Flora could suggest be stuffed, but she kept her silence, merely noting with satisfaction that the blonde's overly made-up eyes were beginning to glaze around the edges.

"— and of course the children are squabbling over everything."

Children?

This suburban nothing had possessed the temerity to breed? Flora wondered.

Of course it was against the law to discriminate against selling to anyone with children — a very foolish law in Flora's opinion, now that her own two were grown and gone — but management still was very discouraging toward having children as residents. All the amenities of the Olympus House were selected with adults in mind, but there was no way to age-classify a swimming pool.

"— just because they want to live in big houses in Garland, well, actually they live in Allen and Plano, but it doesn't mean I have to stay in Garland, does it?"

Garland, Flora thought with revulsion, unjustly maligning that satellite city. *Dear God, what next? I'll bet she'll have hordes of noisy, bad-mannered grandchildren come visit her for days at a time!*

"But the grandkids are so excited that I've moved into a place with a pool. Here, I have some pictures."

Days at a time? More likely weeks, and of course they'll want to spend the entire summer with Grandma . . .

"Are you cold, Mrs. Melkiot?" the blonde

asked. "You're shivering."

Flora managed to shake her head.

"My grandmother would say that's someone walking over your grave," twittered Laura Tyler, all but diving into her overstuffed and shapeless handbag. "Isn't that just the silliest thing? Now where is that photo book?"

That, Flora thought balefully, *depended about exactly whose grave you were speaking.*

Fortunately for Flora's blood pressure and temper, the blonde took the garrulous new resident off at the lobby, even as she continued to scrabble in her trunk-sized bag for the promised pictures.

Flora sniffed. The Olympus House certainly was not what it used to be!

At least, she thought maliciously, *the encounter would give her something to talk about in the beauty shop.* For once that snide witch Isabel Orwell wouldn't be the first with the news.

In her heart Flora Melkiot knew she did not need to go to the luxurious emporium of beauty that sprawled over a great chunk of one of the Olympus House's several subterranean levels. She still wore her hair in the same sophisticated chignon she had since the late fifties. It was, Flora believed, the essence of elegance for a woman to find her own style and then stay with it. To do otherwise was to show an unflattering lack of self-confidence.

The beauty shop was, however, one of the best places in the building to keep abreast of what was going on. While disdaining to actually gossip, Flora did love to know what was going on and to share such bits of important news as came her way.

The other prime location for information was Madame Norina's Temple of Health on the mezzanine. While Flora felt no need to exercise — she truly believed her body had the same athletic firmness it had during her sports-filled twenties — she was a regular member of Madame's early morning "jewel" class.

Several members of that same elite group were now in the beauty salon, including, Flora noted with some distaste, that tramp-ish redhead Ginny Wylde, who chased all the men.

"Good morning, ladies," she said briskly. "You'll never believe what is moving into four-oh-six."

Isabel Orwell looked up from her half-done talons. Today they were scarlet. "Four-oh-six? That pokey little dump?"

"But it has no view except the top of the garage," said a startled Eleanor Anthony. "Even Miss Alicia couldn't sell that one."

Ramon, himself the finest advertisement for his art, raised a perfectly plucked eyebrow. "I had heard the management was going to make a storage area of it."

"Well, they didn't," Flora called from the changing room as she slipped into a soft pink cover-up with a gold-emblazoned R on the shoulder. The girlish color and cut were startling on her. "And just wait until you see what's taken it. I don't know what's gotten into management's head."

Awaiting her turn beneath Ramon's talented hands, Eleanor flipped listlessly through a magazine. Somehow she managed to make even that simple movement seem patrician. "The idea of selling four-oh-six, of course. It's been empty for over a year."

"And Lord knows," Isabel added, artlessly studying her nails, "they're letting just anything in the building now."

Ginny Wylde couldn't move; her flaming locks were tangled in Ramon's fingers as he twisted them into a flattering corona. As the newest tenant in this countrified dump, she knew Isabel's barb was meant for her, but Ginny really didn't care. She lived in one of the penthouses, while Isabel just had a meager three bedroom on the ninth floor.

If I had to live with that dumb husband of hers, I'd be jealous too, Ginny thought with rare charity. Besides, Isabel was stuck here in Dallas, and before long Ginny would be moving back to New York, where the really important things were going on.

Surely, she thought with an unwanted rush of desperation, *it couldn't take much longer to persuade Waldo to move back to civilization!*

"Perhaps they realized they needed some younger women in the place," Ginny said sweetly. Her spurts of charity never lasted very long.

Mrs. Peterson led Laura Tyler back across the marble magnificence of the Olympus' lobby, grateful that the elevator encounter had gone so well. Of all people, they would run into that gossipy old snob Melkiot!

"Now we'll just go back to the office and finalize everything. Shall I have some coffee sent in?"

"That would be very nice, Mrs. Peterson." It would never have occurred to Laura Tyler to call this nice blonde lady by anything but her name.

"Won't you sit down?" the nice blond lady asked, gesturing toward a chair. Small and tasteful, her office looked more like a private den than a place of business.

"Thank you, Mrs. Peterson," Laura said and sank down gratefully. She was more excited than she could ever remember being, at least since she was a very young girl. Little Laura Holman Tyler, who had grown up poor in the poorest white part of Oak Cliff, who had lived all her adult life in a tacky part of Garland, was now living in the same building with some of the biggest people in Dallas society. Now she had her own condo in the Olympus House on Turtle Creek!

The feeling gave her a tremendous rush. All her life Laura had been forced to cater to other people — her old-fashioned, working-class parents; all the customers at the shop; the children; and Edwin. Especially Edwin, who had hurt her so badly by being good to her.

Now that she was a resident of Olympus House, Laura realized, people would have to start catering to her!

In spite of her resolution to remain businesslike, she giggled from sheer happiness.

"Did you say something, Mrs. Tyler?"

"No, Mrs. Peterson," Laura said; then something awoke in her. At last she was in Olympus where she belonged and she

15

should expect to be treated commensurately. "And may we have some cookies to go with that coffee? I'm suddenly very hungry."

There was a gym, roughly the masculine equivalent of Madame Norina's Temple of Health, in the subterranean regions of the Olympus House, but Waldo Wylde never felt the call to darken its door. His strength was a strength of the mind — and of the wallet. Besides, the idea of sweating and grunting and making oneself tired did not appeal to him at all. It was much easier to live well, eat well (though he religiously skipped lunch as a part of his health regimen), and have new suits made every couple of months.

Ginny complained, but then Ginny complained about everything.

"Good afternoon, Mr. Wylde," said the blonde from the office. She looked harassed, but her voice was still smooth and calm.

As far as Waldo was concerned, she was nothing more than the blonde who worked in the building office, but his use of the appellation was completely different from Flora Melkiot's. He loved beautiful things for their own sakes, and by any scale the blonde was beautiful, whatever her name was.

"Good afternoon," he returned politely.

Talking to Waldo Wylde always unnerved Amanda Peterson. He was a remarkable looking man; as big as a mountain, over six feet tall and almost that wide, utterly bald and with the unblinking, intense stare of a curious snake. Add to that his being head of one of the most influential financial newsletters in the world, a radio personality, and a player, however much behind the scenes, in world economics, and he unnerved a number of people more sophisticated and powerful than the blonde in the office.

Another face appeared behind the blonde. Older. Sort of like a cartoon happy face surrounded by frizzy gray hair. A face he had not seen before.

"You're — you're — I know you!"

Waldo was not unaware of the effect he had on people. He cultivated it. He gave as courtly a bow as his girth would allow. "Waldo Wylde at your service, madam."

The happy face split wider. "Waldo Wylde! I knew I knew you! I'm Mrs. — I'm Laura Tyler."

The blonde gave a weak smile. The hours she had spent in Mrs. Tyler's company had been wearing. "Mrs. Tyler has just taken number four-oh-six."

"We'll be neighbors!" that lady exclaimed

delightedly. Not even moved in yet, and already she had met the publisher of *Wylde Times Financial Newsletter* and one, she was sure, of the most powerful men in the world!

"It is our gain, I'm sure," Waldo replied with habitual polish. In his world, a fifteenth floor penthouse was hardly neighbors with a small fourth floor flat, even if they were technically under the same roof. "Welcome to the Olympus House. Now if you will excuse me — ?"

Without waiting for an answer Waldo left, heading toward the elevators in his oddly dignified waddle.

Laura would have forgiven him anything. What a tale this would make for the Tuesday Afternoon Bridge Club, she thought before remembering that she had decided to let go of that part of her life. South Garland just didn't go with the Olympus House on Turtle Creek, but . . .

Maybe she could relent and go back a time or two, just so she could tell them of her triumphs.

Neighbors with *the* Waldo Wylde!

Laura grinned.

Waldo was grinning, too, but it had nothing to do with the funny little old woman he had just left and instantly forgotten. He was not a religious man or a believer in luck, but sometimes it did seem as if things did fall together most serendipitously.

"Good afternoon, Anthony," Waldo said. His bulk almost filled the elevator.

The brief look of distaste on C. Edward Anthony's thin, aristocratic features passed almost immediately, but he knew Wylde had seen it. He didn't care. He had told Wylde what he thought of him the first time they met, and his opinion had not changed.

The elevator glided silently upward.

"I have been waiting to hear from you."

"I gave you my answer the last time we met," Eddie Anthony replied easily, mopping his streaming face. He regularly frequented the gym, though he never put on a pound no matter what he ate.

"But now that you have had time to consider it . . ." Sure of himself, Waldo actually smiled.

Eddie thought the gesture grotesque, almost as grotesque as the offer itself. "I haven't changed my mind. And I don't intend to."

The smile vanished, replaced by a look so blank it seemed somehow charged with menace. Waldo Wylde was not accustomed to having his wishes denied.

"Are you sure that is wise?"

The doors whooshed open on the sixth floor. With the unconscious grace acquired only through generations of patrician breeding C. Edward Anthony turned to face the other man's ophidian stare.

"Perhaps not. But it is the only honorable course."

The doors slid shut, separating the men and cutting off any final attack Waldo might have made.

Except Waldo wouldn't, couldn't have made any. The famous scathing wit that made *Wylde Times* the most devastatingly entertaining show in talk radio was carefully scripted and rewritten until it had the hard, bright edge of a stiletto. In personal encounters Waldo relied more on gravity and an impressive appearance to underscore his words. He rarely encountered outright defiance on a personal level, and the actuality left him tongue-tied.

Waldo Wylde was still standing as immobile and vengeful as a pagan god when the elevator stopped at the tiny atrium separating the two penthouses. He fumbled in his cavernous pockets for the key; no use expecting Ginny to be home at this hour. Even less to expect her to understand what was going on.

But Anthony would.

Yes, Waldo would see to that.

It was time someone taught that overeducated snob how dangerous it was to cross Waldo Wylde!

CHAPTER TWO

"Und von und two. —"

Two was as far as Madame Norina could go. Puffing, she straightened up, put her hands on her ample hips, and looked over what pleased her most. Her kingdom.

Madame Norina's Temple of Health was just on the brink of fame — real fame, beyond the Olympus House, beyond Dallas, even beyond Texas. Visions of franchises and QVC shows and wealth — wonderful, fabulous *real* wealth — teased her. For once in her life she'd have the kind of income she deserved, and not one minute too soon, either.

"Und von und two. —" Making the supreme effort, she bent again. Flowing gauzy outfits could only do so much to hide her solid girth, more's the pity. Since Jane Fonda and those other damned toothpicks had taken over the health business, everyone expected the *maîtresse* to be a skinny twig.

Even though the exercise had been mild, Madame was still sweating.

Glowing. Horses sweated. Men perspired. Ladies glowed.

She knew she didn't look tousled and elegant like that ill-assorted trio of beauties in her jewel class. Compared to Eleanor Anthony, Isabel Orwell, or even that vicious little bitch Ginny Wylde, Madame looked like a field laborer. That was why she was always careful to do even her truncated workout alone.

The soft knock on the door gave her the excuse to quit the half-hearted exercise. It was about time!

"You're late," she snapped, unlocking the double salon doors to admit a burly, ill-dressed man. He looked oddly out of place in the gilded precincts of the Olympus House.

His heavy features didn't change. Chuck Jernigan prided himself on his stoicism, though he had probably never heard the word itself. He didn't even show his dislike at having to come to this pink and scented womanish place.

Chuck was careful to step in just enough for the door to shut. He found the atmosphere unpleasant in here, almost like walking into a glob of gooey cotton candy. He

23

wouldn't even have come this far if there had been any chance of being seen.

"Did you get it?"

Stupid woman. Would he come here if he hadn't? "Sure did."

"Well, give it to me." Imperiously.

"Uh-uh." Chuck shook his head, then pulled the flat sack a tantalizing bit out of his pocket. Just in case she might have misunderstood, he rubbed his fingertips together in the universal gesture.

"Peasant! You know I'm good for it."

He rubbed his fingertips together again. "You could always go down to the newsstand and get your own."

Of course she could, and what would it do to the reputation of her salon if the *maîtresse* of the Temple of Health were to be seen purchasing a racing form? As usual, it was just a trifling sum, but Madame had already started toward her office. Creatures like Jernigan always loved to flaunt any tiny bit of power they could over their betters.

Not moving from the door, Jernigan waited until she had counted the correct amount into his waiting palm. Then he counted it again, his oxlike concentration painful to see.

It really wasn't much money, but you never could tell. Especially after what Barstool Benny said. Stupid women were all alike; Jernigan knew they'd just as soon cheat a man as look at him. Jernigan didn't like women. Especially this sour-faced old biddy who acted like she owned the world.

"Thank you," he said with a politeness that bordered on the sarcastic and handed her the sack.

"I'll call you later this morning," Madame replied haughtily, the sack crinkling in her fingers. She was *the* Madame Norina, soon to be known worldwide; how dare this vulgar creature treat her so? She should order him out, report him to the police . . .

But she needed him. For just a little while longer, she needed him.

"Whenever."

Peeking carefully up and down the elegant hall to be sure it was empty, Jernigan left the salon with a speed that was astonishing for his ungainly bulk. It was never wise to advertise his movements; he had worked hard to get this far, and now he could lose a lot.

Besides, he thought uncomfortably, what would people think about a man — a real man like him — coming out of such a womanish place like he was some sort of queer?

■ ■ ■ ■

Laura Tyler turned the corner just as the big, rough-looking man scuttled away down the hall. A workman, obviously here temporarily; at least she hoped he was. Laura had seen enough of coarse laborers in dear Edwin's company over the years. She hoped she wouldn't have to deal with them here in the Olympus House!

Here she should meet only gentlemen; society men, famous men, not rough workers. It had to be that way, it just had to be! Waldo Wylde — *the* Waldo Wylde! — had welcomed her to the building himself.

The memory of that momentous meeting gave Laura an extra rush of confidence as she stepped through the carved doors into the expensive, famous, and overwhelmingly pink world of Madame Norina's Temple of Health. She was actually here, and now no one, not even Madame Norina herself, could tell her she didn't belong.

"Madame Norina?"

In the tiny alcove that was her office Madame swore under her breath and, jamming the recently acquired and eagerly anticipated papers inside, slammed the desk drawer shut.

Damnation! In her hurry she had forgotten to lock the door.

"Yes?" Madame forced herself to reply brightly. She recognized that soft, pushy voice. How quickly could she get rid of her? "Ah, Mrs. Tyler."

"Hello again, Madame." Laura smiled. This time she was full of confidence. "I have come to apply for your early morning exercise class. Your jewel class," she added as if afraid of being misunderstood.

"As I explained to you last time, Mrs. Tyler, membership in ze early morning class is restricted to residents ov Olympus House und carries on it a premium. Zere is a class on Thursday afternoon that is open to zed general public."

Laura's eyes sparkled as she dug in her purse. "But I am a resident. I have my copy of the sales agreement here somewhere. Of course, I probably won't get the actual deed for a while, but if you have to have it I can probably get a copy."

"No, no, zat will not be necessary," Madame said hastily. A resident of the Olympus House? This nothing of a woman? But rules were rules, and if it would get her out of here . . . there wasn't much time left.

"You do understand zere is a premium to join ze jewel class. It is my smallest und

27

most exclusive class, vhere every woman is personally counseled."

Laura Tyler shook her head until the gray curls bounced. "It doesn't matter. I'll pay whatever is necessary."

Whatever her personal feelings, money was and always had been Madame's first language. She smiled at the thought of what she could charge this creature. "Ve vill of course be delighted to haf you join us. Vhen did you vish to start?"

"Monday. Yes, I'll be moved in by Monday."

Madame blinked. "Wery vell. Monday. Ze doors open at seven twenty-five; ze class begins at seven thirty sharp. No one is admitted after ze class has begun."

"Because you lock the doors. Because you don't want your jewels' concentration disturbed." The old face was as eager as a child's who expects a gold star.

"Exactly." In spite of her desire to hurry, Madame could not help asking, "Vhere did you learn all this, may I ask?"

Suddenly shy, Laura knew she could never tell this forceful, famous woman of the magazine articles read during those stifling, boring days of her marriage and the endless final days of Edwin's life, or of how the elegant and fashionable world they showed

28

had always promised a brighter, better life. She had dreamed of an existence beyond Garland and the plumbing supply business and Tuesday afternoon bridge games for years After reading the article about Madame Norina and her jewel class, though, she had begun planning in earnest.

And now it was going to pay off.

"I just heard it somewhere." Offhandedly. "Someone must have told me."

"Wery vell, then. I vill begin a personalized regime for you. Vhat is your flat number?"

"Four-oh-six."

Ah. That explained a lot. It might be a residence in the Olympus House, but it was the smallest, most dismal one in the entire building, and disgustingly overpriced for what it was. Madame should know. She had thought of buying it herself, but thinking was as far as she could go. Now.

"Wery vell. Until Monday morning, then?"

Laura's face filled with distress. "Aren't you forgetting something?" Then, brightening, "Or is there a presentation Monday morning?"

A presentation? What was the woman jabbering about? Why didn't she just leave? What did she want? Madame regarded her with pure dislike.

Ever helpful, Laura pantomimed drinking.

"Oh. Ze glass."

"Yes."

Laura could hardly stand still. Her very own jewel glass. Symbol of a new beginning. A new world.

"Come. Ve vill get you von." With a disappointing lack of ceremony Madame opened a storage cabinet and pointed to a small clutch of heavy, vividly colored glasses. "Take your pick."

Purple, dark and ugly. Green, the color of rain-sodden grass. Burgundy, lifelessly muddy. Orange, as brilliant as if it had been plugged in. Screeching acid pink.

Laura's happiness crumpled and vanished. "There's no blue."

"Blue?" Madame was almost twitching. Time was passing, and this idiot female was wasting her time dithering, when in her desk — "Zere was only von blue, und it is taken. You may haf any von of these."

Had she been younger, or less conscious of her new status as a member of the jewel class, Laura's lower lip might have trembled even more obviously. She had bought an exercise suit — an expensive one, suitable for the Olympus House — in the strong sapphire blue that looked so well with the golden red her hair had once been. For weeks she had gone to sleep with the image of herself in that blue suit, holding a glass to match, talking to her new friends in the jewel class as they sipped Madame's famous mineral water.

Madame tensed, then let go in defeat as the seconds ticked by. Too late. Thanks to that oafish doorman the time had been short; now it was gone. There was nothing she could do except glare at her visitor.

"If you please, Mrs. Tyler . . ."

Laura held the green and purple glasses, one in each hand as if weighing them. "I just don't know. It's such an important decision, isn't it?"

Madame barely restrained a contemptuous snort. She had dug out the colored glasses, a cheap gift from a long-ago client, early one morning when the concierge had been difficult about sending some from the restaurant until her account was made current. The notion to keep the colored glasses just for the use of her elite early class had been a last minute, lightning-inspired stroke of genius. The idea had impressed her other classes much more than the instantly renamed "jewel" class.

Those in the class itself had simply grabbed a glass and tossed the unpleasant mineral water down as quickly as possible. For the first few sessions there had been confusion remembering whose color was what; each member having her own color had evolved gradually more from inertia than from any design of Madame's. Only the faddish Isabel Orwell had seemed to take any real interest in the idea, grabbing the mottled tortoiseshell glass — which Madame thought the ugliest of the bunch — and claiming it for her own.

And now this stupid cow dithered over choosing a color as if it were a life or death decision! Madame thought with disgust. Hopefully it wouldn't be too long before she would be powerful enough to rewrite the rules and accept only the clients she wanted!

"If there were just a blue one."

"I am desolated zat zere is not, Mrs. Tyler, but zose are ze only colors left."

Laura sighed and put back the purple one. *Green was a pretty color,* she thought, *and not too different from blue.*

"This one."

"A lovely choice."

"Now do I get to put it on the rack with the others?"

Bowing, Madame made a sarcastically exaggerated gesture of permission. The woman had to be mad. That was the only solution to her peculiar behavior.

Glowing as if from a religious experience, Laura Tyler used both hands to place the thick glass with all the other jewel glasses on the shelf above the water cooler. She put it in the middle, between the ruby-colored one and the tortoise shell one, then stared at it with a raptness usually reserved for saints and icons.

Finally! After everything she had gone through, her own glass was really there! Monday couldn't come fast enough.

Definitely a loony, Madame thought. She was going to have to do something about this.

"A most pleasing arrangement," she said when it appeared the loony might spend the rest of the day staring at a shelf of cheap colored glasses. "Now if you do not mind, Mrs. Tyler, I do haf vork to do."

Reluctantly Laura pulled herself back to the present. She had work to do, too, a lot of it if she were to be moved in and ready for the new world Monday would bring. But this was such a special moment. If only dear Edwin could see her. On the other hand, if Edwin were here, she couldn't have been. And Edwin had never understood. Never.

33

"Of course, Madame. I will see you Monday."

She really must do something about her admission policy, Madame thought, and almost rushed her newest client out the door.

This time she didn't forget to lock it.

Isabel Orwell studied her colorless reflection and sighed. Another wrinkle; no matter how skillfully Katia at Ramon's had done her job, it didn't disguise that she had a new wrinkle.

It just wasn't fair! She was only thirty-six!

In actuality, Isabel was really forty-seven and had two daughters in college, but she had been lying about her age for so long that she had truly forgotten the actual figure, which was just fine with her. To believe oneself thirty-six in a world of younger, more beautiful women — shameless, younger, more beautiful women — was bad enough.

Did she dare think about another facelift? It had only been two years since her last one; Dr. Satterwaithe had said unequivocally that he wouldn't think about cutting on her face again for at least five years. Finding another doctor wouldn't be difficult, but Roland would be livid. He hadn't liked the idea of her last facelift, and her exploratory inquiries about a tummy tuck had brought on an argument that had lasted for days.

It wasn't natural for a woman to have herself cut to size like a suit, he had raged — he, whose head turned like a swivel whenever some bright sassy tramp sashayed by, he who . . .

Isabel forced her mind away. If she kept thinking that way, she'd start to cry. Crying always made her face so dark and puffy, and the pretty make-up job Katia had put on her would melt and run. There was no way she'd go to that damned party tonight looking like a clown!

She really didn't want to go at all, not to that party of all places, but Roland was determined, and there was no way she would let him walk into that apartment alone!

It was time to get ready. Isabel swept the crumpled tissues into the wastebasket, then made sure everything on her delicate little dressing table was in its proper place. One last look in the mirror, which was a ghastly mistake. She looked old, aged, and drained and ugly. And she knew whose fault that was!

Pushing away from the unkind mirror, Isabel lethargically pulled on the pantyhose, slip, and dress Lina had laid out for her. Tea length and almost completely covered with a profusion of beads and sequins, the dress was too formal for a simple cocktail party, but it was one of Roland's favorites. Once he had said she looked like a ray of morning sunshine in the golden creation.

Tonight she had to look her best. She was Mrs. Roland Orwell, wife of one of Dallas' foremost bankers, and there was no way she was going to lose her husband or her position to some cheap, white-trash tramp!

C. Edward Anthony looked at his wife and again thought how lucky he was. Eleanor was the most beautiful, the most talented, the most desirable woman in the world. He could never understand why she had settled for a shy, weedy-looking fellow like him.

Cynics, including most of his own family, had tried to convince him that the hundred and forty-three billion (as of the end of the last fiscal year) dollars his family possessed just might have influenced her, but Eddie didn't believe that. Money didn't mean that much to Eleanor; she probably could have had several other men with much more personal wealth than he, but she chose him. Their life together was quiet and calm. Eddie had never been so happy.

"What are you thinking about?"

Even to people who weren't in love with her, Eleanor Anthony was a strikingly beautiful woman. Fine, aristocratic features, a wealth of chestnut hair casually styled, and a slim figure made her a person to remember even before she exercised her considerable intelligence and charm.

Eddie couldn't say that he had been mooning about his own wife, not even to her. After five years of marriage, that was just too sophomoric. "I was wondering," he improvised, "if you'd had second thoughts about that party tonight."

"You must be kidding. We'd have to get all dressed up and I'm too comfortable." For emphasis she crossed her long, slender legs and put them both in his lap. The white of her shorts contrasted pleasingly with her slight tan. "You know I don't like standing around at parties, holding a weak drink and talking a bunch of inane drivel to people I either don't know or don't like."

"The women from your exercise class will be there. Don't you like them?" Eddie ran a hand, still hesitant after all their time together, up her smooth calf. Next to her, the pieces in his art gallery were the merest daubs.

"Not particularly. They're so — so —" she floundered. "Oh, I can't think of a word, but believe me, darling, five mornings a week and an occasional run-in at Ramon's are more than enough. Are you having second thoughts? I thought you didn't like Waldo Wylde."

"He's a disgusting creature. Did I tell you we rode up in the elevator this afternoon? Fat pig half filled the thing. He even had the nerve to ask me if I had changed my mind!" He was so indignant that he didn't see the subtle hardening that made his wife's classic features so much more like the classic marble statues he sold.

"And what did you tell him?"

"I turned him down, of course. The man's a liberal fool. We need less governmental control, not more. Besides that, my family has been Republican for years. I don't know why he thought he could convince me to run under his banner."

"You'd be a good congressman, Eddie. You're sensible and caring and honest."

"You idealize me, my dear. Unless . . . have you changed your mind? Would you like to go to Washington?"

Eleanor shook her head vehemently. She had been to Washington once. For business. A business she wished she could forget. It

38

was not a happy memory.

"No. Your being in Congress would completely change our life." *To say nothing of the campaign,* she thought with a shudder. "And we're so comfortable here, aren't we? I really don't want a thing to change." Smiling, she tickled him intimately with her bare toe.

C. Edward Anthony promptly forgot all about the party, Congress, and everything else in the world save his beautiful wife.

CHAPTER THREE

"Is everything ready?" Peering through his round glasses, Waldo Wylde looked like a querulous owl as he inspected the buffet.

"How should I know?" his wife replied petulantly. "Ask the caterer. He set it up."

Ginny Wylde was sulky. She had gone beyond expecting her husband to appreciate her. She had gone all out to make this a nice party, even hiring the most expensive caterer in Dallas. Then she had spent all day making herself look the way Waldo expected his wife to look, but had he bothered to give her one word of thanks or a single compliment? Of course not; all he had done was question her about the arrangements!

"And you hired the caterer. You should oversee him," Waldo replied mildly. "It isn't good policy to give hired help free rein."

He really didn't care much about how the party looked. Whatever her shortcomings,

Ginny would never let anything around her be tacky or second-rate, and even if she should slip, the caterer was a good one. He should catch any egregious errors. Each person doing what he or she did best to form a harmonious whole, with no surprises, no disasters. It was a system that fit in very well with Waldo's view of the way things should be run.

Standing in front of the entry mirror, Ginny made useless adjustments to her dress, which seemed to be made primarily of strategically placed black straps. Waldo hadn't even told her how pretty she looked, the selfish bastard! Well, Texas certainly had more than its share of drawbacks, but thank heavens it was simply full of men who appreciated a good-looking woman.

Ginny licked her lips.

"Were there any more acceptances?"

"No, not since we talked. I never did hear from the Anthonys."

"The Anthonys," Waldo replied tightly, "are not coming."

So that nerdy little weirdo turned Waldo down! Ginny thought with a surprising burst of satisfaction. Waldo never deigned to discuss his business with her, but she had figured out that for some reason he wanted an arrangement with C. Edward Anthony very much. Why, she couldn't figure; his family had as much money as God, but C. Edward seemed content to piddle around with his art gallery. He and his stuck-up wife lived in a tacky little two bedroom down on the sixth floor and never seemed to go out or give any interesting parties.

Dear, sticky-sweet Eleanor might have married money, Ginny thought, *but she was sure having to earn it!*

"So that makes twenty-six. I invited someone."

"Who?"

"Flora Melkiot. From my exercise class." Ginny hadn't really invited her; she didn't even like the woman, but it had been one of those things where you couldn't not invite her without being downright rude. The nosy old bitch was the worst gossip in the building, and Ginny didn't want Flora Melkiot's attention focused on her. It really wasn't too bad, though; Flora would home in on Waldo and her attention would make Waldo livid. He positively hated the old biddy.

A ripple of distaste passed over Waldo's fleshy features. He knew the ugly old crone all too well. Twice she'd had the temerity to trap him in the elevator and proceed to lecture him about how his politics were all wrong. Only his dislike for scandal had kept him from a childish retaliation. Not that he could hurt her much, either socially or financially. Unfortunately she was not at risk, as were most of his victims, and that put her beyond his reach, a situation that offended his sense of the way things should be. As a consequence, he had tried to put her out of his mind, convincing himself that she was too small a fish to bother with.

"I hope she will behave herself. She can be an obnoxious creature. I know you invited her only to irritate me."

"Waldo, my darling, would I do that to you?" Ginny replied with a wicked sparkle.

Waldo would have answered truthfully, but fortunately for his wife the doorbell rang to announce their first guests.

Miss Alicia Carruthers listened to the commotion of people coming and going on the landing, then checked her watch. Apparently everyone was being surprisingly prompt. Of course, in certain circles of power an invitation from Waldo Wylde was tantamount to a royal command. Because of that alone Miss Alicia would have gone, even though attending parties had long been part of her job. Make an entrance when the party was at its height, circulate, hand out business cards, then leave, generally within thirty minutes of arrival; she had followed the routine for years and garnered a surprising number of sales from it.

Now admitting to seventy and actually being close to a decade older, Miss Alicia Carruthers was an institution in Dallas real estate, secondary only to the legendary Ebby Halliday. Raised in an age when spinsterhood had been a thing to be ashamed of, she had defiantly made the hated title "Miss" so much a part of her name that even in these liberated and unmannerly days everyone called her Miss Alicia. She still kept a pace that awed the business community and left her employees gasping in an attempt to keep up with her.

Once, several generations before, Miss Alicia had complained that her teaching job simply did not bring in enough money. A colleague showed her an article about a man who had made a small fortune in one real-estate transaction and jokingly told her to try it.

Even in those days Miss Alicia did not joke. She threw herself into the real-estate business at a time when there were only one or two women in it and had proceeded in her own methodical way to make a great deal of money. Now she had twenty-three branch offices in six cities and was very seriously considering offering franchises all across the country.

Miss Alicia's only concession to advancing years was that she now appeared at the office between ten-thirty and eleven instead of seven, a small weakness for which her employees were intensely grateful. She still made it a point of pride to sell a minimum of one house a month, whatever her schedule was, but to everyone's amazement and relief, she had categorically refused to work on Tuesdays or Wednesdays for as long as anyone could remember.

Time to go to the party. Miss Alicia drew herself up to her full five feet and no inches, smoothed the skirt of her peach-colored silk cocktail suit, and marched across the ten feet of marble that separated their front doors.

"Good evening, Mrs. Wylde," Miss Alicia said, her eyes all but popping at the vulgar outfit Ginny was almost wearing. The woman's naked skin was visible through the sizable gaps of her dress.

"Good evening, Miss Alicia," Ginny returned with fair grace. She had hoped the starchy old bitch wouldn't come. "Won't you come in? The bar is over there, and the buffet is in the den."

"Thank you, my dear." Miss Alicia gave

her the nod due a hostess and marched into the room, smiling and greeting people with the aplomb of a queen.

What a pity, she thought, *that a man with such a logical mind and a clear view of the world's possibilities should be saddled with a little whore like Ginny for a wife.* Of course, men always thought with their glands instead of their heads when it came to the women in their personal lives, but it did seem that a great man like Waldo Wylde should have chosen a little more wisely.

The great man stood by the buffet, making a mental note to tell Ginny not to use this caterer again. The meatballs were bland and the shrimps overly iced, killing their flavor. It was an embarrassment, though probably no one but he noticed. That ever-vigilant attention to detail was what made him different from other people. It was a quality he cultivated constantly.

"Mr. Wylde, I heard your editorial today. It was superb."

Waldo gave the diminutive Miss Alicia as much of a bow as he could. "Thank you, dear lady."

At the urging of his fans, Waldo had begun doing a fifteen minute editorial every day on nationally syndicated radio. Each segment was carefully written to show the devastating Wylde wit and then pre-recorded on a machine in Waldo's office. Waldo himself had never entered a radio station.

"I quite agree with your ideas about the benefits of a guaranteed income. Such a safety net would be a boon to most people." *And the housing market would go through the roof,* she added mentally. The condominium principle made affordable to even the lowest classes would mean whoever built and sold them would make a fortune. Miss Alicia made a mental note to investigate construction costs.

"You are a charitable and far-sighted lady. It is only after we can assure an equal basis to all of our citizens that we can really begin to grow both fiscally and morally as a nation. I believe that once a man is free of the fear of failure and of losing everything, he can then feel free to try whatever his fancy chooses. Who knows what man can achieve then?"

"A police state, most likely." Roland Orwell smiled and raised his glass to his host. There was no malice in his tone; they'd had this discussion many times. "Remove the fear of failure from most of the population and you take away all incentive. Guarantee an income and you'll create a race of zombies who are incapable of doing anything

47

except voting for those who guarantee to continue their dole."

"That's a horrible thing to say!" Miss Alicia said. "You make it sound like Mr. Wylde is trying to control people."

He is, Orwell thought, but had enough sense to keep his mouth shut. He didn't want to antagonize Wylde too much — Wylde could create too much trouble if riled.

"I believe you know each other, Miss Alicia Carruthers, Roland Orwell." Ever the proper host, Waldo grinned indulgently. "Still a hard-line cynic, Roland?"

"Nope, just a sensible businessman. The government has no business taking money from those who earn it just so they can give it to those who don't pull their weight. People are worth what they earn, no more and no less. Everyone is responsible for their own actions."

It was the first thing he had said of which Miss Alicia approved. "Indeed they are. That's why society must be tightened. Everything today is licentious and indecent. There are no morals, and that will be the downfall of this country! Unrestrained sex —"

The sexual opinions of an aged old maid known for her puritanical ideas didn't interest either man.

Waldo sipped delicately at his diet ginger ale, one of his few concessions to attempted weight control. "How dreadful that you have such a dreary opinion of the human spirit, Orwell."

"Not an opinion, a fact. Have you taken a good look at the welfare system lately?"

"Immorality and sensuality —" began Miss Alicia, but they ignored her.

"An unfair comparison. When you take away a person's dignity —"

"Recipients of charity —"

"Waldo! Roland!" Her dress gaping alarmingly, Ginny insinuated herself between the two men. "Now I know how you love to disagree, but I will not have you two starting a fight in the middle of my party! Roland, there's a man over there I promised I would introduce to you, so I'm going to take you away. You and Waldo will just have to save your fights for private."

"I shall always be happy to try and convince Mr. Orwell of the correctness of my opinion," Waldo purred urbanely. This was his stock answer, but he meant it. Roland Orwell was a man he could and would use.

"And I will always be happy to resist," Roland replied. He meant it, too. Wylde's vision of an enforced, universal welfare state made his capitalist blood run cold.

Miss Alicia watched the pair weave their way through the crush. Someone wanting to meet Roland Orwell. Humph! Someone wanted Roland Orwell, but if what was buzzing in the building were true, it was Mrs. Ginny Wylde herself!

Well, Miss Alicia thought with a righteous sniff, *if a man picked a tootsie for a wife, he shouldn't be surprised when she behaved like one!*

The party was crowded, but that didn't stop several pairs of eyes from watching as Ginny led Roland Orwell's lanky, balding form across the room toward the kitchen. Several of those eyes narrowed in disapproval as they were deprived of their spectacle when the couple was intercepted by a jolly fat fellow in an expensive suit. Ginny was not a good enough actress to conceal her pique, but she put on her brightest hostess smile and, abandoning Roland to his fate, went to answer the doorbell.

Miss Alicia approved; it was a pure example of Divine intervention squashing incipient immorality.

"Good evening, Ginny." Flora Melkiot breezed into the room and struck a pose worthy of Joan Crawford at her peak. "I hope I'm not late."

Ginny's smile froze. She had been hoping the old harpy had forgotten. "Of course you're not. Come in," she added belatedly, but it was too late. Flora had already swept past her.

"Looks like you've an interesting crowd," Flora said, staring at the group.

Some stared back. Attired as usual in black, Flora resembled a rusty crow in a colorful garden — a very gaudy crow.

Mistaking Ginny's stunned look for one of speechless admiration, Flora stroked her enormous bib of coral and gold with withered fingertips. There was a brooch and a hair ornament to match, and similar bracelets encircled her scrawny wrists.

"Do you like my parure? It's English, early eighteen-fifties. Paid a fortune for it, but it was in mint condition and had documentation back to its manufacture." Flora looked down at it fondly. "Had it for ages, but just recently found a pair of earrings to match. A crippled woman with a shop down near the Quadrangle got them for me. Should be delivered Monday. They're particularly good specimens, especially . . ."

Ginny's eyes were glazing. Was this woman sent specifically to drive her mad? She could drone on for hours about that damned ugly old jewelry she was always collecting and, unfortunately, wearing.

"The buffet's in the den," Ginny said desperately, "and the bar's over there. If you'll excuse me?"

Flora looked after her hostess with a mild expression of annoyance. Really, these new people had no manners at all! Then she saw Miss Alicia and just knew she would be delighted to hear about the new antique shop she had found.

The party was winding down. After heaping more compliments on her host and passing out a number of her business cards, Miss Alicia departed. Her leaving started an almost domino effect, and within thirty minutes half the guests had gone.

"Disgraceful, isn't it?" Flora asked when she realized that Isabel Orwell was watching their hostess more than she was listening to her.

"What?"

"Ginny's dress. Isn't it hideous? Almost indecent. What people are wearing these days!"

Isabel had been looking more at the woman than the dress. Flora was sure Isabel had heard the gossip regarding their hostess and her husband. At least, she hoped she had. If Isabel hadn't, she was just about the only one in the building.

Being one of the first to realize that some extramarital canoodling was going on, Flora had informed just a friend or two, making sure that Isabel would hear. *It was,* she thought delicately, *so déclassé to tell the wronged wife directly.*

"Yes," Isabel said through clenched jaws. "Terrible."

"I notice that Eleanor and that funny little husband of hers didn't make it." Flora poked at the remains of the cheese tray. A gigantic cluster of Bohemian garnets on her finger looked like a splatter of blood. "Weren't they asked?"

"Declined. He refused to come." Isabel made Mr. Anthony's action sound heroic.

Flora's ears pricked. "A tiff?"

"More than that. Roland says Waldo wants Eddie Anthony to run for Congress under his guidance. Eddie doesn't want to."

"Never thought that inbred shrimp had so much good sense. Wylde is a positive menace. Worse than a Communist, if there are still such abominations around. Someone should do something about him."

Someone, Isabel thought bleakly, *should do something about the whole Wylde family!*

Across the room, Ginny was artfully ambling into the library. Isabel had watched her husband amble in there just as artfully not two minutes before.

"Did anyone see you?" Roland Orwell asked urgently. Bankers were supposed to be moral and circumspect, but somehow all those rules had gone out the window when Ginny Wylde had started flirting with him. Even now, as risky as this meeting was, Roland's body aroused painfully at the sight of Ginny.

"Of course not, darling. I don't want anyone to see you but me." Tantalizingly Ginny pulled one precariously placed strap aside just enough to show one pouting, carefully rouged nipple. "Especially not like this . . ."

"Ginny," Roland moaned. Though he saw his wife's naked body almost every day, Ginny's uncovered nipple reduced him to a groveling, babbling schoolboy, just as she had planned.

Ginny liked having a man desire her and beg for her favors. Getting Roland's attention had taken a long time, but now she had him and her conquest was worth it. Those boring moments of conversation, the stupid love notes, the snatched kisses in the elevator — thank goodness all the romantic crap was over! Now Ginny could concentrate on getting what she wanted, which was straight sex, and lots of it.

"You like it?" she purred. "You want me, don't you?"

Reduced to an inarticulate mass of rampaging male hormones, Roland could only nod.

Slouching forward, Ginny reached out and grabbed his distended trousers front. It was just as she thought.

"Yes, you do want me, don't you, darling?" Taking his assent for granted, she deep-kissed him with a hunger, rubbing her body against his like a cat.

The library door flew open, hitting the paneled wall with a bang. One of Waldo's treasured Waterford goblets exploded against the wall above the entangled lovers. It sounded like a pistol shot.

"Stop it!" Isabel screamed. Her face was contorted with rage, but the faces behind her, most notably Flora Melkiot's, were filled with curiosity.

"Isabel," Roland gurgled, but his wife wasn't looking at him.

"Stop it, you damned bitch! He's mine! Let go of him or I'll kill you!"

CHAPTER FOUR

The automatic's muzzle erupted into a dragon's tongue of flame. There should be a noise, but she couldn't hear it. She could only feel the white hot pain exploding in her left thigh and then she was flying . . . floating . . . falling onto the dirty, rain-slick street.

Jesse!

Jesse was falling, too, but his fall was different. Even then, even there, she could tell he was dead before his loose-limbed body hit the sidewalk. Jesse was dead, and she was dying and it was all because of Frank.

Thrusting herself from the grip of nightmare, Rebecca Cloudwebb gasped for breath and sat up abruptly in bed. She pushed a fringe of sweat-soaked hair out of her eyes and tried to quiet her racing heart with the familiarity of her dimly lit bedroom.

That had been a bad one, the worst in a

long time. Served her right for turning over onto her left side; when her bad leg cramped she always dreamed. Even in sleep she should know better.

Swinging her legs over the side of the bed, Rebecca grimly began to massage her left leg back to a state of relative normality. The pain made her grimace, but even it couldn't erase the lingering horror of the old dream.

Almost a year had passed since she'd last had it, four since the shootout had killed her partner and ended her own promising police career, and like a fool she'd brought the whole sorry mess up again by carelessly sleeping on her left side.

It was 4:36 by her alarm clock. She ran clawed fingers through her short crop, trying to bring some sort of order to the mop of brown curls. Did she dare try to go back to sleep and risk the dream again, or should she give up and try to stay awake? She didn't really need to be up early; not like her days on the police force when it seemed she always had to be out and somewhere at some god-awful hour.

Monday. Officially the shop was closed, but she had promised to deliver those Victorian earrings to Flora Melkiot over at the Olympus House as soon as they had come in. Sort of. Dan had brought them over on Saturday afternoon, but Mrs. Melkiot had specifically requested that they be delivered only during her exercise class.

The old showoff.

Rebecca was supposed to be there at eight. There was time to go back to sleep for a while.

And risk dreaming yet again of betrayal and gunfire and death? No, thank you!

Making a sour face, Rebecca went down the hall in search of coffee, limping heavily to favor her scarred left leg.

Isabel Orwell opened her eyes slowly, trying to sense if the other side of the big bed were occupied before actually looking.

The sheets were as pristine as they had been when she went to sleep.

As pristine as they had been since Saturday night. It was now Monday morning.

His cell phone, his lifeline, lay on the dresser where he had put it before going to the party.

Isabel closed her eyes again. She felt more than slightly sick.

Where was Roland? Did he intend to avoid her forever?

If she could only talk to him, tell him how much she loved him, how much she wanted to save their marriage. (Why should *she* be the one to have to save it? *He* was the one who was whoring around!) That was why she had acted in the first place! Surely he could see she had acted only from love?

So where had he been since Saturday night?

With that damned gray-haired bitch?

No, if that had happened she would have heard. Flora Melkiot would have forced her way in and delighted in telling her all the ghoulish details.

What would she do if he didn't come back?

Isabel choked back a sob. She had no skills, no training. The only real job she had ever held was as a bank teller. She hadn't been very good at it, but she had only worked there a couple of weeks when she and Roland met, and then they had married not long after that. He had loved her then.

She couldn't go back to that, working in a teller's cage where all of her friends could come and snicker at her misfortune! She'd die first!

The thought of her own death distracted Isabel. If she were dead, he'd be sorry. Then he'd know how much she loved him.

Lot of good that would do her!

The sound of the front door lock turning

over was almost like thunder to Isabel's straining ears. Almost immediately all thoughts of love vanished from her heart.

"Where have you been?"

Grim-faced and haggard, Roland Orwell entered the bedroom and mechanically began stripping off his crumpled clothes. His condition was almost an affront in the icily perfect order of their bedroom. He did not look at his wife. A faint reek of stale liquor surrounded him. "I have to see Madame Norina before your class starts. Business."

"Where have you been?" Isabel repeated, crumpling the sheets with her clinching fists. "I've been going crazy."

"I got a motel room."

"A motel room? You went to a motel and let me worry myself sick about you?" Then, more quietly and much more deadly, "Were you with her?"

"Don't, Isabel."

"Don't? You disappear for days without a word and all you can say to me is 'don't'?"

Roland hung his head wearily. He was not an impressive man to begin with, but now with unshaven jowls and bleary eyes he looked positively haggard.

"You're impossible, Isabel."

"I'm impossible? All I've done is be a good

wife to you and you say I'm impossible? Thank God the girls aren't home to see your shame!" Her voice rose to a shriek. Unable to remain still, she began to pace with angry stomps around the monochromatic blue bedroom. "You're having an affair with that cheap whore."

"Shut up!" Roland roared in a voice his wife had never heard before. Now he too was standing. Suddenly he was a very impressive figure, every inch one of Dallas' biggest financial men in spite of being half-dressed and unshaven.

"Roland —"

"I will not have you speaking about Ginny like that! She is a decent, caring, wonderful woman and I will not allow you to call her names!"

Isabel could only stare in amazement.

"Ginny is the sweetest woman I ever met," Roland was almost reverent. "She loves to talk to me. Just talk. She's really interested in me. In what I do and what I think. She wants to know how I feel about things."

"You never said you wanted to talk," Isabel murmured stupidly.

"I never knew I did until Ginny. She brings out things in me — I feel like a new man with her. She's more interested in me than in keeping things perfect. She really

61

cares about me."

"About you and a couple of hundred other guys!" Isabel exploded. "Your precious, caring Ginny has slept with at least half the men in the building and God only knows how many out of it. I just wish you could hear her brag about it!"

"Shut up!"

"Do you know they had to fire two of the valet parking boys because they were spending more time in your wonderful Ginny's bed than in the garage?"

"I'm warning you —"

"Or that a couple on the seventh floor divorced because of her? Or that once he was free she dropped him flat?"

"Shut up, Isabel!"

"You should hear her in class. She talks about her lovers as if they were trophies! Don't you wonder what she's going to say about you?"

Roland's features congealed. Even in these days bankers had to be more careful than most about their reputations.

"What is between Ginny and me is different."

"Sure, sure." Isabel made a rude sound. "You can believe any kind of romantic hogwash you want, as long as you believe that I will never let you divorce me. Do you hear that?"

"If Ginny wants —"

"I don't give a damn what Ginny wants. I am your wife and it's what I want that counts. Your *wife!* The one who signed all those papers that kept your name out of that stock scandal a couple of years ago, remember?"

Roland looked as surprised as if she had suddenly turned and bitten him. "Isabel, you wouldn't."

"You'll go to prison if I do, so you had better realize that we are going to stay married, Roland Orwell."

"But I love Ginny. And Ginny loves me. We deserve to be together. I deserve to be happy."

"More pity for you, then, but just remember I am your wife and I am going to stay your wife. Forever."

Any thoughts of Roland Orwell far from her mind, Ginny Wylde stretched luxuriously. Her body felt almost deliciously sore. She and Waldo had scarcely been out of bed since that delightfully disastrous party.

Normally Waldo Wylde was not a man of erotic appetite. Like all other skills he considered important for self-advancement, though, he had mastered the art of love-making as a young man. Ginny had found that if she kept her eyes shut and didn't have to look at his obscenely gross nakedness he could satisfy her as no other man ever had. The trick was getting him interested.

Ginny rolled over on her back and stared at the ceiling. She must arrange more scenes like the one that had ended their party.

I really should thank that silly fool Isabel, she thought.

After a mortified Roland had dragged his wife away, Waldo had all but thrown the rest of the guests out, barely waiting until the door was closed before ripping off his wife's clothes. Ginny had never dreamed her bored dabbling with Roland Orwell (of all the dull people!) could have had such spectacular results. Waldo was seldom, if ever, interested in making love. He had barely blinked an eye when, returning early from an extended European trip, he had found her in bed with two handsome young men she had picked up the night before.

The dressing room door opened. Today Waldo had chosen a suit of dark gray with the hint of a paler pinstripe. Owlishly he looked down at his naked wife, who was spread lasciviously over the bed.

"Excess always has been one of your biggest failings," he said blandly, then closed the bedroom door behind him

Just because old blubber-butt had declared fun-time over didn't mean Ginny couldn't enjoy herself. She'd go to class at Madame Norina's and see what was happening there. If Isabel Orwell dared show her face, she could have some fun teasing her; who would have ever thought she'd really fight for her husband — as if Ginny would really want to keep boring old Roland!

Laura Tyler puffed as she pulled on her pretty new blue exercise suit, then critically inspected the result in the mirror. The elasticized fabric showed she had kept her figure well enough for a woman of sixty-eight.

Edwin would have been scandalized. But then, Laura rationalized, Edwin had been scandalized by almost everything. His viewpoint on the world had been neither tolerant nor charitable.

He would have been horrified by the scene at the Wyldes' party. Laura was heartsick that she had missed it. If she only could have been here a week earlier! That nice Mr. Wylde certainly would have invited her; he had known she was moving in this weekend and probably thought she was too busy.

Any faint hopes Roland Orwell might have had of keeping the matter quiet wouldn't have lasted as long as the party. Even if the few remaining guests had exercised superhuman restraint over their tongues (which, of course, they didn't) there were the people from the caterer's. They worked most of the season's "society" parties and knew everyone almost as well as if they were friends. The *Dallas Morning News* didn't have a real society gossip column, not for the scandalous stuff, but by Monday morning the story was all over the part of town that mattered as thoroughly as if there had been a front-page story.

Laura had heard it from a talkative old woman in the elevator. She lived on the fourteenth floor and had heard some of the shouting in her own bedroom. Though she didn't doubt the information, Laura was unimpressed with the messenger. The woman appeared just plain common, hardly the kind of person one would expect to find in residence at the Olympus House.

Just think! Something like that going on just a few floors above her own apartment, Laura mourned, and she had been as remote from it as if she were still stifling in Edwin's big house in Garland.

Her mood lightened; she might have

missed this event, but she had been preparing. This morning she'd be in the jewel class! She wondered if Isabel Orwell or Ginny Wylde would come.

What if both of them did?

The prospect was so delicious, Laura Tyler giggled.

Laura Holman Tyler of Garland, Texas, one of Madame Norina's jewels! The idea still thrilled Laura. When she had first applied, Madame herself had told her that only Olympus House residents did not have to pass through a much-scrutinized waiting list. That, Madame had emphasized, insured that only the crème de la crème could attend. Such a policy would, she stated, keep out the jumped-up little nobodies from the suburbs.

Laura had nodded in complete agreement, the not-too-subtle insult going right over her curly gray head.

"Crème de la crème," Laura repeated happily, rolling the words on her tongue like candy. *Crème de la crème;* now she was one of them, those beautiful social leaders of Dallas, and she'd do whatever it took to stay there.

Deep in a dream of successfully robbing the Tower of London Jewel House, Flora Melkiot at first thought the alarm clock's metallic shrill was a call for the police.

"Drat," she growled sleepily. "I almost had them."

Having long ago accepted that she would never get her hands on those shining treasures in reality, Flora was more than a little put out she couldn't have them in her dreams.

Then she remembered.

They were rubbish compared to the Crown Jewels, of course, but today she would finally get those coral and diamond earrings. That nice crippled woman from the antique shop was going to deliver them, right in the middle of exercise class.

They wouldn't make the splash they would have last week, not when the whole town was still reeling over the catfight between Ginny and Isabel. It still astonished Flora that such a dry stick as Roland Orwell could get one woman to care about him, let alone two.

Care about him or his money?

Flora gave a knowing laugh and then, more importantly, wondered why it had taken almost a week just to check the prongs and fix a catch. She would have to ask . . . Cloudwebb. Rebecca Cloudwebb. That was the name. An odd one, as odd as the woman herself, but she and that Negro woman who worked for her certainly ran a nice shop.

Sophie Mandelbaum had found C & L Antiques, Sophie with her positively unhealthy passion for old Limoges. She had dragged a reluctant Flora there on the rumor of a particularly fine chocolate set. The set had disappointed, but Flora had found a collection of decorated hair combs, all made no later than 1850 and all in perfect condition. Since then the Cloudwebb woman had standing orders to notify Flora of all good Victorian jewelry, the earlier the better.

Flora hauled herself out of bed and into a hot shower. Her bones were old and stiff and they needed warming before Madame Norina put her through the mill.

Could what she had heard from Eleanor Anthony be true? That jumped-up suburban nothing What's-her-name had actually been allowed in her exercise class? Flora would have to have a little talk with Madame Norina. She shouldn't be allowing just anybody in the early morning residents' class, even if they did live in the building.

Tyler. That was the name. Mrs. Tyler's jewelry — Flora's personal yardstick — was undoubtedly real and obviously expensive, but it was commonplace. That was the worst possible sin.

The fact that her Morris had built a small empire selling great quantities of expensive but commonplace jewelry didn't bother Flora at all. Neither did she appreciate the inconsistency.

Well, she would be the same open and charitable woman she had always been and give that obnoxious little social climber the benefit of the doubt, but Flora was sure she wouldn't like her. If her suspicions were right, she'd just have to do something about it.

Someone had to uphold proper standards these days!

"Zat is impossible," Madame Norina said firmly. Everything was going wrong this morning. First of all her jewel glasses had not been delivered from their nightly washing when promised and she had been forced to call the kitchen and complain. Then practically on the heels of the surly young man who brought them came this pig of a banker with his ridiculous demands. "Utterly impossible."

Roland Orwell looked at the pudgy, homely woman opposite him and felt an unfamiliar urge toward physical violence. Was ever a man so cursed? Roland felt as if the entire female sex was out to drive him completely crazy. Harpies, all of them!

Except Ginny. Sweet, desirable Ginny. Even now the thought of her soft voice talking to him — not a little augmented by the soft curves of her lovely little body — made him tremble with love.

Damn Isabel! he thought with vehemence, hating his wife and her dirty thoughts. *Ginny does love me.*

He said, "Madame, here are the records of your account. We are totally within our rights in demanding immediate and full restitution. It is over three months since we have had any kind of a payment from you. Now, as I personally authorized the loan in spite of your being grossly under-collateralized, I think I am due an explanation."

Collateral? she had asked those many months ago. Her eyes had been fiery and her voice thrilling. What you need is here! she had cried and touched her head. Here! Not chairs and tables and machines!

Three months behind? How had it gotten to be that long? And her other debts . . .

Madame swallowed heavily. Her mouth was dry. She longed for a drink, but the only thing in the salon was the mineral water.

71

Her special, famous mineral water; how ironic.

"Times haf not been good, as you know," she began, her mind working frantically.

"I know what my wife pays for her classes, Madame, and I know how many pupils you have." His anger was exacerbated by the fact that it had been Isabel who had convinced him to finance the Temple of Health in the first place.

Madame felt all the harshness in his voice directed specifically at her. She swallowed again. Surely she could get herself out of this, if she could just think for a moment.

"Zere have been — problems. Small ones, but annoying. I need some time."

"You have had three months, Madame."

"Und surely you realize you haf un great deal to lose," Madame wheedled. "Mightn't I have chust a little more time?"

Roland caught the note of supplication, and it made him feel better. As long as she knew her situation and his power over her, he could afford to be kind. Besides, everything in this damned pink dump wouldn't cover half the outstanding balance. His anger with Isabel rose.

"Thirty days. And that's to bring the account current."

Madame's broad smile almost covered the

terror inside. Where could she come up with such a sum in just thirty days? How unfair that the bank should start dunning her now, especially now when she had other, more pressing, more frightening obligations?

"Thirty days," she repeated. "Yes, ov course. Thank you, Mr. Orwell."

Roland hesitated. He should leave now, but if he stayed he might have a chance to see Ginny.

He might also risk running into Isabel.

"I'll keep in touch," he said, majestically nodding his head and stalking out the door.

"Pig," Madame muttered under her breath. She could not believe that he and Ginny Wylde were lovers as the building grapevine insisted, but she could think of no two more unpleasant people, nor two who deserved each other so much. Spitefully she hoped that, along with each other, they both would get everything they deserved.

CHAPTER FIVE

C & L Antiques was closed on Mondays, but Esther Longfellow came in anyway. Quarterly taxes were coming due, and she could get so much more work done when she didn't have to be constantly alert for the door buzzer.

The shop had originally been an elegant mansion. Close to downtown and the fashionable Quadrangle shopping center, it had now been restored to some of its former glory. The ground floor was the shop, with a tiny office nestled in what had been the butler's pantry. Rebecca had converted most of the second floor into a flat. The rest, including the vast attic, was storage.

Some days, after fighting the glutinously slow traffic on Central Expressway down from Richardson, Esther envied Rebecca. Then she remembered why she lived in the suburbs and was content. JJ was already in middle school; before long he would be in college. Then she could move closer in.

"Good morning."

"Good morning yourself," Esther said with some surprise. Her partner was an avowed night owl. "You're up early."

"So are you, especially for a day we're supposed to be closed."

"JJ had an early track practice, so I thought I'd come on down and get some bookwork done. You?"

Rebecca poured another cup of coffee — real coffee, not the flavored stuff Esther preferred. She felt her partner's bright brown eyes scrutinizing her, making her uncomfortably aware that Esther Longfellow knew her better than anybody else in the world. Except one.

"Delivery. Those Victorian earrings to Mrs. Melkiot at the Olympus House."

So that was why Rebecca was wearing her good tan pantsuit instead of her customary t-shirt and slacks.

"The ones that look like chandeliers? Why this early?"

Rebecca's expression was wry. "I'm to interrupt her exercise class as if these had just come in for her and I couldn't wait for her to have them."

"Lucky you. You get to deliver and act all at once."

"You want to do it?"

Although similar in age and size, the two women could not have been more different in appearance. Where Rebecca looked like the embodiment of the old stereotype of the All-American girl, Esther was both exotic and beautiful. More than once, her chocolate-colored skin and almond-shaped eyes had drawn comparisons to some of the better examples of ancient Egyptian art. She had not found the resemblance particularly flattering.

"Uh-uh." Esther shook her head until her soft black curls danced. "No way. Mrs. Melkiot's your customer; she doesn't like dealing with the colored help. And," she added quickly before the righteous fire in her partner's face turned to words, "I don't want to. I came down to have a long, uninterrupted session with the quarterly taxes."

"And you want to do them."

"I have to do them. I don't have to do Mrs. Melkiot. You do."

"Lucky me."

Esther watched her partner's face carefully. Now Rebecca was being her usual offhand self, but when she had first come in, Esther had been alarmed. Rebecca's face had held the same hard, unreadable quality that it had for months after the shooting.

Catching herself, Esther consciously forced down the rush of grief that still hovered around her heart. Would she ever stop missing Jesse? He had been her life, her love, her husband, and the father of her child. And now he was gone. When he had become a policeman she had convinced herself she could handle anything that might happen. So far she had, but without him, living was still a day-to-day struggle.

She would have lost Jesse's partner and friend, Rebecca, too, if she hadn't been determined not to lose any more. Esther fought for Rebecca's life as she would have for Jesse's and, eventually, when even the dourest of the doctors grudgingly admitted that Rebecca was going to live, her survival seemed little less than a miracle. The bullet wounds alone had been enough to kill, but when compounded by that bastard's treachery . . .

The thought of Frank Titus still made Esther furious. A dirty cop was a loathsome enough creature, but a dirty cop who would sacrifice a longtime friend and his own lover for his own gain! There weren't holes in hell deep enough for such a man.

Not even the most optimistic of the doctors had given much hope of Rebecca ever walking again. There had been too much damage to bone and muscle and nerve, they said; the struggle for mere survival had taken too much of a toll on her strength. Like so many criminals — and so many of her fellow policemen — had done before, they'd underestimated Rebecca Cloudwebb.

It had taken a year, a year of pain and frustration and sheer nerve. Now, a little over four years from The Day, Rebecca not only walked, albeit with a cane more often than not, but with Esther's constant, prodding help, she had built herself an entirely new life.

Now that bleak look, the hardened mouth, the empty eyes, were back. Equally bad, Rebecca's cane leaned against the edge of the desk. She had been using it less and less lately, and Esther had begun to hope that she was going to quit using it altogether.

"Bad night?"

Rebecca considered lying, but it was never any use to lie to Esther. Jesse had told her that a long time ago. "Yeah. I dreamed again."

Esther didn't need to ask what dream. As far as both of them were concerned there was only one dream; the only difference was Rebecca dreamed it from memory and Esther only from secondhand accounts. There was no way to measure which was worse.

"I'm sorry."

"Nothing to be sorry about. I knew it was just a matter of time." *We don't get out of our private hells that easily,* Rebecca thought. She said, "Looks about time for my entrance. I better go."

Still unquiet, Esther asked, "Be gone long?"

Rebecca shook her head. "I'll just drop off the earrings and come right back. Shouldn't be a thing to hold me up."

Madame didn't get a minute to think about her new problem. As Roland Orwell left, Eleanor Anthony came in. She walked past him with the curtest of nods, she who was always so gracious and friendly. Roland knew then that there was no hope of keeping things quiet; reluctantly he went to his office with no real idea of what to do now.

It was not unusual for Eleanor to come in early for a short warm-up session before class. Normally Madame was glad to see her. Of all her pupils, she actually liked Eleanor, with her aristocratic ways and gracious manner. Eleanor was easily the most adept in all of Madame's classes, but she stood out even more against the wealthy lumps in the jewel class. Only she ever came in to work out on her own, only she seemed to care more about her body than the dazzle of smoke and mirrors Madame had been at such pains to create — or the continual hotbed of gossip the jewel class had become. From her movements and her dedication, it was easy to see she had once been a serious dancer.

Today Madame's greeting was ragged, but Eleanor didn't notice. She shed her peach-colored wrap to reveal a form-fitting yellow exercise suit, then placed her foot on the barre and stretched. Even though she exercised every day, it was not as easy as it had been a couple of years ago, another proof that she was aging. She leaned into her warm-up exercise, working at replacing extension with grace.

Madame forced her mind to the present. She had thirty days. Surely her luck would change in thirty days. Maybe her jewels — ? It was a thought. Her voice became warm.

"Goot, my jewel, goot. Perhaps a little more lift with ze arm. You are coming sideways rather zan over."

Eleanor nodded and did it again, ignoring the dull pain in her shoulder. "Like this, Madame?"

"Yes, yes. You are reaching for zomething

zat is always out of reach, something beautiful."

It was the story of her life, Eleanor thought sadly. Something beautiful just out of reach. Suddenly the exercise didn't seem so enticing any more.

"Is zomething wrong, my dear Eleanor?"

"I'm just tired, Madame." Then, as that seemed a silly statement to make so early in the morning, she added, "Eddie and I went bike riding yesterday."

How lovely to have the time to go bike riding, Madame thought with a sudden burst of anger. *Of course, she has a rich husband who gives her the moon and the stars, so she doesn't have to worry about paying debts without any money or keeping a roof over her head!*

Now was as good a time as any to start. In for a penny, in for a pound.

"Zat sounds most pleasant. Tell me, my dear, have you ever thought of making any investments?"

Her stretches finished, Eleanor pulled the cotton wrap back on. "Investments? Eddie handles all that kind of thing."

"Ah, but don't you believe a woman should have her own little nest egg? Something zat she can nurture und protect all by herself? It gives such self-satisfaction."

Madame was starting to believe herself, which gave her voice an added richness. "I have decided zat before my big expansion I should show my gratitude to my earliest students by allowing zem to become part of it."

"It's a very generous offer, Madame, but I've never had a head for business . . ."

No! Madame's mind screamed. *She has so much, and I have so many needs.*

"I was only thinking," she said slowly, "that vith your husband's standing in the community you might vish to invest —"

To Madame's astonishment Eleanor Anthony's face went papery white, then, just as she feared she might faint, flushed a dull, ugly red. Eleanor picked at a fingernail, carefully avoiding looking directly at the other woman.

"And just how much do you think I should invest, Madame?"

"Not too much." Madame had been prepared to fight and scream, push and cajole; Eleanor's quiet acceptance startled her into naming a figure approximately twice what she would have ordinarily dared.

Eleanor nodded slowly. "And how often would I be expected to make this . . . investment?"

Madame blinked. "How often? I don't

under—. As often as you like. It depends on you. It is a guaranteed thing."

"I'm sure." Harshly. "I assume this afternoon will be soon enough?"

"Ov course."

Madame was amazed Eleanor gave no resistance, asked no questions. This was too good to be true! Could she be one of those who couldn't say no, then allowed her husband to pull her back? It made no difference; it was really a good thing and Madame was determined that Eleanor would profit for her trust. But why did she look so hard and so angry?

"Are you all right, my dear? I do assure you it is a wery safe arrangement."

"It had better be," Eleanor said angrily. "How — ?"

The pink double doors opened with a whoosh and before Madame could think about Eleanor's hate-filled look, Ginny Wylde made a defiant entrance. A little disappointed at the sparse audience, she unconsciously struck a pose and, with a glowing smile, said, "Good morning, ladies. What do we have going this morning?"

Timing, Edwin had said. Timing is everything. He had said it repeatedly, especially before expanding into another store. As he had always made lots of money, Laura had acknowledged the statement with much more grace than she had his toilet jokes.

Good advice, however, was good advice, so while finishing her move she had thought a great deal about timing her entrance. Not that there had been much real moving to be done; most everything she had now was as new as her apartment. The things she and Edwin had shared were either parceled out to the children or disposed of. *A new life,* Laura had said repeatedly, *deserved new things.*

Now wearing her new blue exercise suit and cover-up, waiting across the hall from the pink double doors of Madame Norina's Temple of Health, Laura Tyler felt as if her new life were really about to begin. She was almost to the millisecond halfway between the time the doors were opened and when they were locked.

"Hello. Are you lost?"

Laura looked up and her heart gave a leap as she recognized the two arriving women immediately. This was Miss Alicia Carruthers, whose face had beamed down from innumerable billboards for as long as Laura could remember. The other woman was none other than Isabel Orwell. Inwardly Laura applauded what she coyly called a display of intestinal fortitude on Isabel's part. Such gallant behavior was indeed the mark of a true lady. Laura had wondered if she would have the courage to appear.

"I'm going to my new exercise class at Madame Norina's," Laura answered proudly.

"Well, it's right there." Miss Alicia made an impatient gesture toward the pink doors, then followed Isabel through them into the elegant anteroom.

Without any of the grace or élan of which she had dreamed, Laura stumbled puppy-like after them.

"I'm Laura Tyler. I just bought number four-oh-six."

"Indeed." Miss Alicia's tone was almost frosty. "I'm sorry my company wasn't able to help you purchase your new home." It was a standard line for anyone who had been foolish enough to buy without using one of Miss Alicia's offices.

"I was, too," Laura said with real regret. It would have been so perfect to come into the jewel class and the Olympus House under the formidable protection of Miss Alicia Carruthers. In Laura's daydreams Miss Alicia had always taken care of her personally, of course. "I called two different offices, because I wanted to buy through you because I knew you lived here, but neither one of them knew anything about a vacancy in the Olympus House, so I just called the Olympus House direct."

Miss Alicia stopped in her tracks. "You mean you tried to buy through one of my offices?"

"Two," Laura replied artlessly.

"Two," Miss Alicia repeated. Her expression boded no good for any of her sales associates who had managed to let a customer slip through their fingers.

Emboldened by the lady's personal interest in her dealings, Laura went on. "I really wanted you to help me, because I knew you lived here, but you are a very hard woman to get a hold of and I know you work very hard, so I just called your office."

"Two of them."

"Yes. But it really doesn't matter now, does it?" Laura smiled happily. "I've got my place, and we're in the same class and it's all worked out right in the end."

That speech made absolutely no sense to Miss Alicia. She frowned, thinking how lax things had become since she had eased off a little. Now she would have to live with this woman under her feet as a constant reminder that not only one but two of her offices had broken the cardinal rule — never let a customer get away. Someone would pay for that!

"And you're Isabel Orwell," Laura went on, riding the crest of her good luck. "I saw your picture from last year's Crystal Charity Ball."

Distracted, Isabel focused on the newcomer's face as if returning from a place far away. "You're new here?"

"Yes," Laura repeated patiently. "I'm Laura Tyler. I live in four-oh-six."

"They're about ready to start," Miss Alicia announced briskly. "We'd best go in."

Squaring her shoulders as if going to her own execution, Isabel stalked into the exercise room. The air seemed to crackle with a life of its own and without really knowing why, every woman there held her breath. Standing almost in opposite corners of the room, Isabel and Ginny saw each other at the same moment. For a moment there was the metaphoric smell of blood in the air.

Isabel broke the spell. After a long cold look at Ginny, she turned and nodded her head toward Madame Norina.

"Good morning, Madame," she said in cultured tones and carefully hung her cover-up on a hanger before taking her place on the mat.

For once that morning Madame did not spare a thought for Laura Tyler, a fact that was to haunt her later.

CHAPTER SIX

Today was going to be a good day. Waldo just knew it. Of course, as far as he was concerned, every day was a good day when he got what he wanted, but today was special.

Today he would show everyone who was in control.

How foolish people were to stand against him.

High above the city in his glass-walled office, Waldo looked out over the sprawling city as a king might his kingdom. Unlike Ginny, he didn't miss New York at all. In New York people had too many options, too many avenues of escape. It was better here, where he was definitely the big fish. When he was powerful enough that no one could challenge his will or his vision, he would go back East as a conqueror instead of just a scribe.

That might be sooner than expected. He

listened with pleasure to Roland Orwell's slight gasp as he announced himself. The man must be in a state to give so much away over the telephone. All the better.

"I need you, Orwell," Waldo said bluntly. "I'm going to be backing some candidates in the next election, and I want you to be treasurer of their campaigns." Might as well sweeten the pill. Waldo's voice became silky. "Your joining the cause will boost their credibility immensely."

Roland swallowed hard. He had told Wylde before that he was nothing but a pocket Fascist. Why was the man coming back at him?

"I think we have always agreed that our politics differ," Roland said as politely as possible.

All pretense of civility dropped away and Waldo rasped, "Not since you started balling my wife. That makes us bedmates in more ways than one. I wonder how your board of directors would take the news. Especially if I decide to be uncooperative about keeping silent."

Roland cringed. He could just imagine how Waldo Wylde would make the situation sound. Plus, with his leverage in the financial world he was quite capable of making sure that Roland Orwell would never work again.

"Ginny . . ."

"There's nothing you can tell me about Ginny," Waldo went on more easily. "I don't even care if you go on balling her. I want you to be happy, dear boy. That's why I would hate to have to tell certain people about certain papers involved with Sun-TimeLand and their late stock difficulties . . ."

All of Roland's blood pooled in a gelatinous mass around his heart. How could Wylde know? How could he have found out about that? He and his partners had been so careful in hiding the paper trail! Could Isabel . . . ? No, she wouldn't try to ruin him; not after what she had said this morning. She wanted to keep him around and alive and miserable without endangering her own comfort.

"Are you still there, dear boy?" Waldo purred.

"I'm here."

"Now I think we need to talk about this. You'll have to start whatever paperwork is necessary."

"Wylde, I appeal to you — I've been active in the Republican party for years."

"I don't think you heard me, Orwell. I will

91

have your help and your support for the candidates I choose, and you will be enthusiastic and sincere about your participation. Do I have to tell you what happens if you don't cooperate?"

"No," Roland said in a very small voice. "What must I do?"

"Come to my office today at three. We'll start work on the campaign financial strategy."

Smiling broadly, Waldo hung up and rocked back and forth in his especially made and reinforced leather chair. This was indeed a red-letter day. This was the beginning of a new life not only for him, but for all the world. Oh, life was good, and under his benevolent guidance it was going to be better for everyone.

He punched the sleek new intercom with a fat forefinger. "Get C. Edward Anthony on the phone."

Nestled on a shady block of Routh Street, The Anthony Gallery was not very far from C & L Antiques by distance, but miles different in ambiance. C & L was a joyous hodgepodge of true antiques and charming but merely old stuff jumbled together in an invitation to happy searching. Austere and spacious, The Anthony Gallery was often mistaken for an exquisite little museum. Each piece in the cool, monochromatic gray space was especially mounted and lighted to best advantage, and nothing was allowed in the doors without guaranteed provenance and authenticity.

His insistence on such niceties had several times cost Eddie Anthony a tidy sum, but on occasion it had saved him from scandal. The gallery had a top reputation and was gaining respect among museums looking to expand their collections with indubitably genuine pieces. In a good year the gallery just about paid its expenses; however, it kept Eddie occupied and out of the varied family businesses, a situation with which his brothers and sister were quite content.

"Mr. Waldo Wylde for you, Mr. Anthony," said Jamie Durbin, Eddie's weedy and intense young assistant.

Eddie grimaced. Would the man never give up?

"I don't want to talk to him."

"He said to tell you it concerned your wife."

An ugly knot, hard as black granite, formed in Eddie's stomach.

"Anthony, we need to talk," Waldo said without preamble the moment Eddie was on the line. "I have offered you the senate candidacy several times."

"And I have turned you down each time," Eddie replied smoothly.

"Which is very foolish of you. I need your name and position and you need my backing."

"I have no desire to go into politics."

"You have made that abundantly clear, but we are not talking about your desires, we are talking about what the country needs. America is going down the toilet, my friend. Foreigners, welfare abuse, disregard of law, homosexuality, every little upstart thinking he is as good as those of us who have worked to make this country great, illegal immigration, rampant crime — you cannot say you are in favor of those, can you?" Waldo went right on without waiting for a reply. "It is time for men like us, you and me, to take over and put things aright. Now with your family name recognition —"

"I do not want to run for the Senate. I don't know anything about politics." There was a desperate tone in Eddie's voice.

"I am not asking you to know anything about politics," the older man went on relentlessly. "I will help you there. I merely need you to run and win."

"No."

There was silence. To his disgust Eddie

could hear Waldo breathing; he sounded like a broken tin whistle.

"I wonder how your wife would feel about that answer."

"How my wife feels is none of your concern!"

Waldo's voice took on an unmistakable edge. "What you do now affects your wife and her future."

Eddie's insides turned to water and he struggled to keep his voice calm. There was no way Waldo could know. "I don't know what you're talking about."

Waldo chuckled. It was a chilling sound. "I think you do. Please don't make me spell out all the ugly particulars. Just believe me when I say certain people in Nevada have long memories. You know what could happen if I decided to be a good citizen and tell what I know, don't you?"

"You wouldn't." The protest sounded weak, even to Eddie's ears. Of course he would. Once his mind was made up, Waldo Wylde would stop at nothing.

"It would grieve me, but the fate of a single woman is nothing compared to the fate of the country. I will expect you in my office at two o'clock. There are certain legalities we must discuss." Without waiting for a reply Waldo hung up the phone. He stared at it for a moment, then began to chuckle again with great satisfaction.

Puffing from her climb up the short hill to the door, Rebecca leaned heavily on her cane. She hadn't realized it was such a hike up from visitor parking, especially in the broiling heat of a Dallas summer day with a highly polished marble wall to one side and mica-sparkled concrete under her feet. She felt uncomfortably like a grilled cheese sandwich.

Next time, she vowed, she'd use their valet service. The automatic doors whooshed open, letting the chilled air of the secured entry area wash over her like a flood of cool water.

"Are you all right, ma'am?" the guard asked through the window.

Rebecca ignored the burning in her bad leg and the sweat in her eyes and nodded. "Fine."

"What can I do for you?"

He was almost a head taller than she and as heavily built as a wrestler. On his imposing form the red, braid-drenched doorman's uniform looked almost silly, like a stage costume. It appeared especially anachronistic against the electronic paraphernalia of a modern security station — television monitors, panels of blinking lights, lots of gray metal boxes, and impressive-looking cables.

Looking up, Rebecca really saw his blunt, ugly face for the first time and fought down a faint flicker of recognition. No more of that! She had consciously given up trying to place faces. It was a disconcerting habit, a hangover from her police days. After all her years on the force, Rebecca rationalized, everyone looked familiar to her whether she'd ever seen them or not.

"Can I help you find your destination?" His voice didn't match the carefully memorized words.

"I'm here to see Mrs. Melkiot. My name is Rebecca Cloudwebb."

Chuck Jernigan's heavy face registered a hastily hidden flash of recognition. He knew that name all too well. He fumbled with the computer screen, scrolling down the list of expected visitors. "Miss Cloudwebb. Yes."

"Mrs. Melkiot is expecting me to come up to her exercise class. Where is that?"

"Madame Norina's Temple of Health is on the lower mezzanine," he said quickly, pushing the release button. The security area door yelped and slid open, revealing the elegantly appointed lobby. "The elevators are down the hall to your left."

Well, well, well, he thought as she limped

through the lobby. *A famous ex-cop; what would Madame Norina think about that?*

Rebecca didn't want to go. She didn't want to watch an exercise class in Madame Norina's Temple of Health or anywhere else. The emotion was so deep she hadn't even mentioned it to Esther, but she didn't want to watch all those women with their healthy, unscarred bodies moving in ways that were impossible for her now, didn't want to have them looking at her limp and her stick with pitying eyes.

The double doors were a dreadful shade of pink and quite tightly locked. Rebecca knocked and, after waiting a time and feeling profoundly foolish, knocked again as instructed, this time more forcefully and using her cane. From now on Flora Melkiot would just have to pick up her purchases at the shop!

"Come in," a pudgy older woman in unflattering green draperies said ungraciously, opening the door just enough to admit Rebecca and locking the door behind her.

Rebecca entered reluctantly, following Madame through a small, living-room-like antechamber into the exercise area. The Temple of Health was a big place full of exercise mats and a few machines, all in the same sickly variation of Pepto-Bismol pink.

Even if her mood had been better Rebecca would have hated it.

"Miss Cloudwebb!" Flora Melkiot cried. Today she was attired in an exercise suit of aggressive blue instead of her habitual black. It was not an improvement. She dashed forward, eyes squirrel-bright in her mud-fence face. "You brought my earrings!"

She tore into the small white box like a child, then triumphantly held up one gaudy dangle for admiration. In spite of themselves, the women milled around Flora for a better look.

"My God," Ginny Wylde drawled. "Are you buying Christmas tree ornaments already?"

Flora glared. "Miss Cloudwebb has an antique shop," she said to the others, "and she's always looking for special things for me."

"It certainly is a wonderful example of Victorian design," Eleanor said quickly. She had seen the wicked expression rising on Ginny's face.

"They look," pronounced Laura Tyler, unconsciously winning her first kind thought from Flora, "like they belonged to a fairy princess."

Remembering the elderly man from whom she had bought them, Rebecca decided the old lady was at least half right.

"Do you know old jewelry?" Flora asked Eleanor.

"Not really. Just a few basics. I do like old ivory, though. Where is your shop, Miss Cloudwebb?"

Rebecca told them and, as they approved of its location, the others began to list their own passions in collecting when Madame cut them short by a sharp clap of her hands. Displeased at having her class interrupted and attention drawn from the select desirability of her spa, she spoke more harshly than usual.

"Ladies! Ve do not vish our bodies to cool down too much, do ve, my jewels? Let us use zis time to drink our Vater of Health und zen return to finish our stretches."

There was a universal grumbling, but the women trooped obediently over to a large stoneware cooler and grabbed for their glasses. After a moment's struggle, even Flora responded to the *maîtresse's* order, reluctantly handing the box with her earrings back to Rebecca before reaching for her glass of brilliant, ugly blue.

The cooler gurgled unpleasantly as the ladies filled their glasses one by one. Most of the women wore grimaces of apprehension, Rebecca noted with faint curiosity, but while she waited her turn, the little gray-haired woman in a bright blue exercise suit she shouldn't be wearing was chattering happily on about how healthy exercise made her feel and how excited she was to finally be in the jewel class. The deep green of her glass clashed unhappily with her suit.

Her authority painlessly restored, Madame Norina could afford to feel a little charity toward the pretty woman with the cane. "Are you familiar vith my Vater of Health, Miss — ?"

"Cloudwebb. No, I'm not."

"Zen you should be. It is a special mineral water, brought from a spring long known to have great healing properties."

"And it tastes like shit," Ginny Wylde said bluntly, looking at hers with distaste. In her ruby-colored glass the water looked positively muddy.

The famous Miss Alicia Carruthers, the only person in the place Rebecca recognized besides Flora Melkiot, looked almost as pained at Ginny's language as at the prospect of drinking the water. "There is no need to be vulgar, Mrs. Wylde."

"Yeah," muttered Isabel Orwell so low that only Rebecca heard it. "There aren't any men here to impress."

"Well," Ginny said, her eyes alight with

101

mischief, "it really does taste like shit. Real, down-home, Texas shit."

"Vat is good for us is not always pleasant," Madame Norina returned with a hint of suppressed disapproval. "You must try my Vater of Health, Miss Cloudwebb. It has been known to vork vonders on all forms of physical difficulties." Madame Norina fluttered away into her office.

Even on bullet scars? Rebecca wondered with a sense of disgust as she watched the older woman go. Early in her career she had done a turn with the bunco squad, working undercover to nail a gang of gypsies running a curse-removal scam. This woman's set-up was a lot cleaner and much more sophisticated, but otherwise it sounded like the same old game.

"Ze jewel glasses belong to ze class members," Madame Norina explained, returning with a coffee cup bearing the Olympus House crest, then filled it from the cooler. Rebecca took it reluctantly. At least the cup wasn't pink, but the whiteness of the porcelain emphasized the murky sepia tinge of the water.

"Now, ladies, drink it all up, und remember, it is good for you. Von, two, three!"

Obediently the class upended their glasses and began to chug-a-lug with unladylike speed and noise. One cautious sip told Rebecca why. As bad as the water looked, it tasted worse. She quietly put her cup down on the marble table behind her. She wasn't paying for this nonsense, so she didn't have to drink the foul stuff.

Someone was gagging. *Understandable,* Rebecca thought before the sounds of incipient retching turned to something much more primal. Enthusiasm gone, the gray-haired woman in the blue suit dropped her glass and staggered forward, clutching at her throat. Her eyes, bulging and terror-stricken, begged wildly for help from the boiling mass her face had become. As she reached hysterically for the others, they drew back in instinctual fear.

Two steps later Laura Tyler's body convulsed. She stumbled and sprawled like a blue slash across the pink mat, her eyes fluttering sightlessly toward the ceiling.

Even that movement had stopped by the time Rebecca got to her knees and pressed shaking fingers against the left side of the crêpey throat. For a moment there was a thin thread of pulse beneath Rebecca's fingertips, then nothing.

Not trusting her legs — either the good one or the bad one — to lift her up, Rebecca sank back into a sitting position, her hand falling helplessly to her side. Someone, several someones, were screaming, but she didn't know who. She couldn't take her eyes away from the red and white bubbling horror that had been Laura Tyler's mouth.

Responding to training and instinct, Rebecca fumbled in her pocket for her cell phone.

"She's dead," Rebecca said at last to no one in particular as she punched in 911.

CHAPTER SEVEN

A murder in the rarified precincts of the Olympus House was news, so almost immediately a group of reporters had taken up a noisy vigil in front of the building. Almost as immediately Chuck Jernigan, aided by the emergency addition of several gardeners and maintenance personnel, had taken great delight in throwing them off the property, though it disappointed him that he could not break a few heads or legs in the process. They could not, however, make the intruders vanish completely, so the entire bunch huddled uncomfortably on the small median between the sidewalk and the street. That, the outraged inquisitors protested, was city property. The protectors of the Olympus House did not care; it was at least twenty yards from them to the nearest entrance, a twenty yards rigorously patrolled by hastily called security.

John Ashdown had to force the car

through the living wall of the press, the windows kept tightly shut against shouted questions. Microphones and camera lenses banged against the glass, seeking entry.

"What do they think we can tell them?" Gus Spencer asked. Ashdown's partner for over a year, he was marking time until his retirement. The fact that it was at least ten years away made no difference. "We just got the call ourselves."

Ashdown hadn't wanted it. A murder, a spectacularly dirty murder in a snooty place like the Olympus House . . . It could be a career killer. Rich people didn't like the police nosing about in their business, even if a murder had been committed. Especially if a murder had been committed.

He stopped the car under the jutting awning in direct defiance of the "No Parking" sign and got out. Today all rules were off. The front-door lock buzzed open without him even having to look toward the security office.

"All the doors sealed?" he asked the uniformed officer in the front lobby.

The young man nodded. "There's been an officer posted on every door since the call first came in."

"Everyone upstairs?" Gus asked.

"No, sir." The uniformed officer took a

deep breath. "The ladies were all shaken up, sir. Some were hysterical . . . totally losing it. Someone called a doctor who lives here, and he sent two of them back to their apartments." The officer looked as if he were going to be blamed personally. He was young enough to be worried about such things.

It probably was the young officer's fault, but Ashdown said nothing. These people were accustomed to making their own rules and probably would have done the same thing even if he himself had been right there. No wonder he hated these high-flying assignments. Give him a good pimp-stabbing or gang shootout any day!

"Get their names and apartment numbers?" he asked. "Including the doctor?"

"Yes, sir."

"Are you two with the police?"

Ashdown blinked. A blond woman — a young, pretty, shapely blond woman — was clicking across the marble lobby toward him. How did these young women manage to keep their balance in heels that high? He didn't really care; they looked good doing it and that was all that mattered to him. Gus was getting an eyeful, too. If he weren't careful, he'd start drooling.

She was, Ashdown noticed, wearing a

wedding ring with a diamond approximately the same size as a peanut.

"Yes, ma'am. I'm Detective John Ashdown, Dallas Police. This is my partner, Detective Gus Spencer. Can we help you?"

She was short; standing next to him she barely cleared his shoulder, even with the boost of those absurd heels.

"Well, I certainly hope so! I'm Mrs. Peterson, the building coordinator. You're here because of Mrs. Tyler's death, I suppose. Before you go up, though, I want you to do something about them!" She made an extravagant gesture that could have included the entire southern half of the planet.

"Them? The press, you mean?" Gus looked confused.

"Of course. Make them go away."

"They're on a public right of way, Mrs. Peterson," Ashdown said slowly. "They have every right to be there."

Amanda Peterson frowned and suddenly she wasn't so pretty any more. "But they're drawing attention to the building. The Olympus House prides itself on its decorum and they're turning it into a circus. It will take months for us to live this down. Make them leave!"

Ashdown's views on the press were well-known and usually couched in words unfit for use in polite society, but he merely said, "They're doing their job, Mrs. Peterson, and I am going to do mine. If you'll excuse us, we're going to the murder scene."

The blonde gasped at such bluntness. Or maybe it was the fact that she had given a direct order that was being ignored. Ashdown didn't know and he didn't really care.

He turned to the uniformed officer. "Where?"

"Madame Norina's Temple of Health," the young officer said, not quite managing to say it without a grin. "Lower mezzanine. Pink doors. Some of the crew's already here. Elevator is over there."

"Thanks. Keep the place locked down. No one in or out until I say so."

"And you aren't going to do anything about them?" Amanda Peterson screeched. "I'm going to call your supervisor."

"That's your right, ma'am." Ashdown started across the vast marble expanse. "Captain William Talbot. And his boss is Deputy Chief Charles Cloudwebb."

And they both would make mincemeat of her, he thought, with a vague flicker of satisfaction. Old-time cops both, and not given to coddling prima donnas.

Whatever shred of lighthearted mood he'd had evaporated when the doors opened.

Enormous pink double doors stood open just down from the elevator. There was the bustle of crime scene techs and the indoor lightning from a flash, but no matter how much he expected it, a death scene always got to him.

Gulping, Ashdown walked in. The place was pink. Overwhelmingly so, except for a sprawled heap of blue that had once been a human being.

Gus swore softly.

Ashdown took one look at the face, then swore himself, and looked away.

"Corrosive of some sort, obviously taken by mouth," said the medical examiner. "Death almost instantaneous. That's all I can tell you now."

"Witnesses?"

"In the ballroom next door. Didn't see why they should have to stay in here with this. Two of them have already gone up," said another officer, his face a delicate green in spite of his prolonged study of the opposite wall.

"I know. Hysterics. Keep me updated," Ashdown said and went next door, Gus following like a shadow.

The ballroom was an enormous space. At the far end were stacks and stacks of metal chairs and flattened round tables. Half a dozen chairs had been brought nearer the door. The size of the all but empty room diminished both the chairs and their occupants.

Ashdown regarded them with a skillful eye. The older woman he recognized at once as the real-estate tycoon, though he couldn't recall her name. He would have bet the hard-faced woman with the turban and floating draperies was Madame Norina. She looked like the type who would own such a salon.

He had no guesses about the shocked-looking middle-aged woman or the angular old one with the dyed hair, save that they were class members because they wore brightly colored exercise suits. The other woman, clad in street clothes and sitting quietly, her cane in her hands, just as obviously wasn't. For a moment there was almost a flicker of recognition, but he couldn't place her. A partner of Madame Norina's, perhaps?

"You start with the real-estate lady," he muttered to Gus. "I'll take the civilian."

"Well, it's about time you got here," said the crow in a painfully electric blue exercise suit. She didn't have the figure for an exercise suit. She didn't have much of a figure at all. "What are you doing to solve

111

the case?"

"And you are . . . ?"

"Flora Melkiot. Mrs. Morris Melkiot, and don't try to change the subject. Don't you know we're all in danger?"

Ashdown grabbed one of the empty chairs and put it in front of Mrs. Melkiot. "What makes you say that, ma'am?"

"Well, it's obvious. Someone killed that little nonentity, didn't they? Why would anyone want to kill her? She's brand-new here, and I don't mind telling you, if nothing else, that shows how much the standards of this building are slipping, so it's obvious that she was done in by accident. The killer had to be trying for one of us."

Inwardly Ashdown groaned. "Mrs. Melkiot, did you see anything unusual in your class today?"

Aged eyes flashed. "Besides that woman dying, you mean?"

"Mrs. Melkiot —" Ashdown drew a deep breath. "Before that. Start with everything you saw."

"I got to exercise class at my regular time. Keeping to a schedule is such an important thing, don't you agree? Madame, Eleanor Anthony, and Ginny Wylde were there. Miss Alicia Carruthers, Isabel Orwell, and that Tyler woman came in a few minutes later."

"Did any of them go near the glasses?"

Flora gave him a stone-hard look. "Believe me, none of us go near those glasses until it's time to take that ghastly water." She gave a little shudder.

That didn't prove anything to Ashdown; the water cooler and the shelf were close to the middle of the room. The room wasn't that big. With all those women milling around, it wouldn't have been difficult for one of them to dump something into a glass.

If it were one of them. Whatever it was could have been in the glass all night. Or longer.

"Then?"

"Then we started our stretching exercises. That Tyler woman was yammering about how she had wanted to join the jewel class ever since she first heard of it. Heaven only knows why. She was practically weeping that she couldn't have the blue glass."

"All the glasses are different colors?"

"Yes."

"And you always have the same glasses?"

"Yes."

"What color was her glass?"

"I don't know. I didn't look."

"What color is your glass?"

"Blue."

"What happened then?"

"We began our stretches. Then Miss Cloudwebb knocked at the door. She brought my earrings." Flora whirled around with an agility that belied her years. "You still have my earrings, don't you, Miss Cloudwebb?"

The drab-looking civilian looked up and blinked, as if pulled from a long distance away. "What? Your earrings? I think they're on the table by the door in the exercise room."

Flora fixed Ashdown with a glare that had made three generations of maitres d' quake in their patent slippers. "And they had better be there when all this is over," she snapped. "I've looked for a pair like that for many years."

Ignoring her totally, Ashdown stood and walked until he practically loomed over the woman with the cane. "Cloudwebb?"

Rebecca had been expecting it. "He's my brother."

Ashdown gulped. The deputy chief's sister. He had heard the story, of course, about how she and her partner had been trying to bust a drug ring, only to end up in a firefight caused by a dirty cop named Frank Titus. A dirty cop who, by some accounts, had also been her lover and who had apparently vanished off the face of the earth since then. Her partner had been killed; she had nearly been and had ended up being invalided out of the force.

"Did you see anything?"

She shook her head. "Nothing out of the ordinary. I gave Mrs. Melkiot her earrings and everyone was looking at them and talking about what they collected. I have an antique shop, you see. Then the owner said they mustn't cool down too much and it was time for them to take their water. Everyone grabbed a glass — I've heard they each have their own — and got some water. The owner brought me some in a coffee cup. I didn't drink it. Just a sip."

"Bad?"

"Horrible. Then I heard someone gagging. Thought it a thoroughly logical reaction to that stuff. Then the victim fell over and her face . . ." The woman's lips trembled, but she went on calmly. "She was dead almost instantly."

"And you didn't see anyone near the glasses."

Rebecca shook her head, making her brown curls dance. "No. Not until they each grabbed their own. I'd like to go now, if you don't mind." She fumbled in her pocket for a card and handed it to him. "You can reach me here at just about any time. And I'm not planning to leave town."

Ashdown nodded, extending a hand that she ignored as she struggled to her feet. He watched her until she left the room, walking slowly and leaning heavily on her cane. The deputy chief's sister. A former detective herself. A trained witness who saw nothing.

This case was going to be a bitch.

With a sigh he turned back to Flora Melkiot.

Upstairs Ginny Wilde slept after being sedated for hysterics, which were perhaps the most genuine emotion she had experienced in at least a decade, while Waldo sat and pondered the situation.

He was more than a little testy at having been called from the office to attend to his wife's fits and starts. Surely she would have enough attention from the police and those women in her class without bothering him. The fact that the police had tried to stop him at the entrance of his own building had not improved his temper.

It was a matter of supreme indifference to Waldo Wylde that an old lady's life had ended. There was a glut of old ladies, and it was a basic marketing principle that a glut of anything was a drag on the market. If there were any kind of need for old ladies, anyway. He could not conceive of any, beyond investing and voting as he told them was best. No, the only truly important thing about this situation was how he could use it.

The masses were regrettably sentimental, Waldo mused. Might he turn this atrocity — a good word; he must remember that — into a botched attack against him? Yes, an attempt to harm him through his wife. That was good; he could use that. Waldo Wylde, the good and loving husband; of course, it would put Ginny in an unfortunate position of notice, which would delight her overactive ego, but the potential gains were worth more than her preenings and tantrums.

Purposefully he picked up his brand-new Conway Stewart fountain pen, reveling again in the intricate Arabian Nights design. Perhaps a little over twenty thousand might be considered somewhat extravagant for one pen, but it was a beauty and considering that the words he wrote with it were destined to save the American nation, he thought it money well spent. Uncapping his new treasure, he took up one of the leather folders that awaited his muse in every room and began to write on the prosaic yellow legal pad inside.

Several floors down it was a different situation.

"But why didn't you call me?" C. Edward Anthony asked his wife for the umpteenth time. "You know they don't give names on the radio, and when they said there had been a murder in Madame Norina's exercise class —"

Eleanor looked bleakly at her husband. Eddie never had been the most handsome of men on the outside, but now he looked positively haggard. He had been truly frightened and, like most men, he wasn't good at dealing with crises. It was all her fault. She should have called him.

Indeed she should have called him, but her mind had been on other things. As horrible as it had been, Laura Tyler's death was just an overlay.

"I'm sorry."

Eddie took her cold hands in his. At least she was all right. He could stand anything if she was all right. He hadn't known she was close enough to the old lady — what was her name? — to be so affected by her death.

To Eddie's loving eyes, his beautiful Eleanor looked like living death. Her skin was gray and stretched so tightly over her bones it looked as if it might split. He had only seen her this distraught once before, the

118

night he had proposed marriage. It had been beastly of him to take advantage of her situation like that, but he was a man in love and it had worked out all right, hadn't it? He would have sworn that she was happy.

"Darling," he pleaded.

With a visible effort Eleanor tried to pull herself together and failed. "I'm sorry," she said again.

"I didn't know you knew this woman. What's her name again?"

It took Eleanor a moment to understand him. "I didn't know her. This was her first day in class."

"It must have been just horrible, watching her die." Eddie's voice faded. Eleanor was upset, but not about the old woman's death. Normally murder would have traumatized the gentle soul of his wife; now she barely seemed to remember that it had happened. "What is it?"

Eleanor shook her head. This had been her doing; she was not going to burden her husband, not again. If all it took was money, she had money.

Reluctantly Eddie stood up. Seeing her like this distressed him, but he knew there was no moving her if she didn't want to tell. She was an exceptionally strong-willed woman.

"I hate this, but I have to go out. Will you be all right?"

Eleanor's nod might mean yes, but her eyes, wide and blank and haunted, said no. "Are you going back to the gallery?"

"No." Eddie hadn't meant to tell her. She had borne enough, but he couldn't let her think he was just going back to work as if this were an ordinary day. Besides, what he was about to do affected her, too. "I have a meeting with Waldo Wylde."

Something flickered in those bottomless eyes, something hidden and fearful. "Wylde! What about?"

"Nothing."

"But you hate him. Why?"

"He wants to talk to me about running for the Senate. Again."

"But you've told him no."

Eddie let out a deep breath. "Yes, and I'm going to tell him so again. It's just that —"

"Me? He's talked about me?"

"Yes. But there's no way he can know, darling. He's fishing. I just know it." Fishing? If he knew about Nevada? Possibly, possibly, but Eddie didn't believe it. Waldo Wylde knew enough to destroy both him and Eleanor.

A blaze of anger transformed Eleanor's face. "He can too know. Why not? Madame

120

Norina does."

It was Eddie's turn to be blank-faced. "Madame Norina? In the exercise class? How could she?"

"I don't know, but she gave me a good shakedown this morning. Oh, it was very civilized and very polite, couched in the terms of an investment that would reap me great benefits, but it was a shakedown, all right."

"Did you pay her?"

Eleanor shook her head miserably. "I said I would. It's not all that much, just a couple of thousand. I didn't want to risk her mentioning anything to anybody. I didn't want you to know. I . . ."

Fear, in the guise of great oily tears, welled up in Eleanor's eyes. She had always known that she wasn't good enough for Eddie, that someday he would tire of her, or that someone would find out, that someday. . . . Someday? Today . . .

"Eleanor! Darling — we could have handled — I love you."

Weeping, Eleanor allowed herself to be held and comforted, but even as they embraced, both of them knew that if Madame Norina had discovered their secret, there was no reason to think that Waldo Wylde had not done so too.

CHAPTER EIGHT

Esther was annoyed. "It's about time you got back —" She stopped mid-word at the sight of her partner's face. "What on earth happened?"

Rebecca limped heavily across the shop floor, not even trying to disguise how much she was leaning on her cane. So much for trying to get anything past Esther.

"Rebecca, talk to me. What happened?"

"I saw a woman die. She was murdered."

"Oh, my God! Wait a minute." Esther flew to the front door and locked it, flipping the embroidered placard to "Closed" without a thought. Then she grabbed Rebecca's flaccid arm and steered her toward the back room. "Come on. Let's get some coffee."

Rebecca's very docility aroused the worst of fears in Esther's mind. Rebecca was not docile; contentious, arrogant, hardheaded, yes, but never docile. Just during those first weeks after the shooting, when she seemed more inclined to fade away than to recover. Esther's blood went cold.

Esther waited until they were sitting at the tiny kitchen table. "So tell me," she said, pouring them each a mug of coffee. Chocolate raspberry today. Esther adored flavored coffees. Rebecca didn't. Normally Rebecca would have made some sort of acerbic comment on "candy coffees." When she didn't, Esther's alarm increased.

Slowly, Rebecca gave her the facts, as concisely and unemotionally as if she had been writing a police report. Esther could tell she glossed over the actual death, but didn't know which of them it was to spare.

"Then, after they told us we couldn't use our phones or tell anyone what had happened, we had to wait and wait and wait for the crime scene people," Rebecca said, showing the first signs of emotion, "then we had to talk to the detectives, one by one."

"That must have been a change for you."

"And how." A shudder of anguish ran across Rebecca's face. "I must have done dozens of interviews like that. Dozens! And I never thought . . . Jesse and I used to get so mad with witnesses who didn't see, didn't notice, can't remember."

"Yeah," Esther said finally, after Rebecca's voice had trailed away and the silence thickened. "Jesse used to bitch about that all the time."

"Well, I was there. I saw everything. And I didn't see anything! I saw this woman when she was alive and healthy. I was there when she got her glass off the shelf. I was there when she got her water out of the cooler. I was there when she died. My God, she died right in front of my eyes!" Rebecca's voice was a rising crescendo of emotion. "And I didn't see a thing! Nothing! Someone committed murder right in front of me, and I didn't see a thing!"

Explosive sobs burst from Rebecca. Coffee forgotten, she covered her face and wailed, rocking back and forth as if buffeted by unseen winds, while Esther, in spite of all, sent up a small prayer of thanks. It was the first time Rebecca had cried since the shooting, and Esther was profoundly grateful. Finally the ice dam had broken, and Rebecca could feel again.

Miss Alicia Carruthers had seldom been so insulted or upset in her life. It was bad enough that she should have had to witness such a horror as that poor woman's dreadful death. Miss Alicia was enough of a pragmatist to realize she was no longer a young woman and her heart was deteriorating rapidly; she shouldn't have to suffer such shocks.

No one should have to suffer a shock like that. She staggered into the living room and sat heavily in one of the large, overstuffed chairs that looked so much better than they felt. Like most of her furniture, the chairs had come from a model home closeout sale. They looked good, and it wasn't as if she ever entertained much, and — best of all — they had been ridiculously cheap.

What was almost as upsetting, though, was that she — she! Miss Alicia Carruthers! — should have been subjected to a police grilling and then ordered not to leave town as if she had been nothing more than a waiter or a secretary. Of course she hadn't seen anything; she didn't even know the woman, except that she had tried to buy her condo through two — two! — of Miss Alicia's offices and had been allowed to slip through both.

That was more upsetting to Miss Alicia than the fact of the woman's death. She had been hoping to slack off a little, but now it seemed more imperative than ever that she keep a tight rein on her little empire. Sloth! Weakness! All the things that Miss Alicia had fought all her life.

Well, she couldn't slow down now, not so

close to the end. This was her last chance to earn money, money that was desperately needed, and she would have to take it. That meant she should go to the office now. This was Monday. She was always in the office on Monday.

Her anger waxed again. The police had even told her not to leave town. As if she might be a suspect! Ridiculous! They would never have said anything like that to her arch-rival Ebby Halliday. Miss Alicia Carruthers was a good, law-abiding citizen, but there was no need for her to follow ridiculous strictures like that. Tomorrow was Tuesday, and she would follow the same routine she had every Tuesday and Wednesday for most of her adult lifetime. It was no one's business but her own, and the police had no right to tell her what she could and could not do as if she were some sort of criminal!

For the first time, Miss Alicia almost regretted that she had decided against the expense of full-time help. It would have been so easy to call for a glass of water and her pills. Today wasn't even the day for her weekly cleaning woman, a luxury she had allowed herself only after her sixtieth birthday.

With mixed emotions Miss Alicia sat and

waited for her heart to stop its tumultuous beating, then rose slowly and went to the kitchen for her pills. She would shower, she would dress, she would go to the office and personally fire both employees who had let that woman slip through their fingers. That should straighten things up for a while.

She almost smiled at the prospect.

Isabel Orwell let herself into the condo and leaned weakly against the door. She felt sick and unsteady and feared she might fall into little pieces on the floor. The cool, pale monochrome of the pristine living room wrapped around her like a safety blanket. What a horrible morning! Seeing that poor woman . . .

Maybe a drink would make her feel better. It was early. She had never had a drink this early in her life, but she needed something to calm her down, to dull the memory of that woman falling forward, the bottom half of her face dissolving into a froth of red and white.

Why couldn't it have been Ginny Wylde? That tramp deserved such a gruesome end. A rueful smile teased at Isabel's thin lips even as her stomach heaved. Ginny dying like that would have solved so many problems.

Isabel was distressed she couldn't even remember the poor dead woman's name, if she had ever heard it. One of the policemen must have said it, when they were interrogating her. Interrogating her, questioning her, all but accusing her . . . as if she would deliberately kill someone she didn't even know!

At least they had had the decency to have an officer escort her to her door because she was so weak and shaky. Even now getting to the bar across the living room was all she could do. She didn't even stop to put to rights a pillow that was off square on the couch or straighten the magazines on the coffee table. There was no ice, of course, but she didn't even think of that. Getting a goodly splash of bourbon into a glass was just about all she could manage. She didn't even like bourbon particularly, but it was the bottle in front.

Isabel's mouth twisted bitterly and not from the sweetish taste of the liquor. That tramp Ginny hadn't had to be escorted by an officer; she hadn't even been questioned! No, she just started crying and that fat monstrosity of a husband of hers rushed home to hold her hand. Even Eleanor Anderson had escaped, and Isabel would bet that her husband had been there in minutes to look after her.

Roland wouldn't come for her. He'd have gone to Ginny if given half a chance, but he wouldn't bother to come home for his wife! Maybe he was hoping that it was she who had been murdered.

If she had been murdered, Isabel thought bleakly, he would have come to Ginny to comfort her for having to watch! But his wife? Ginny had a husband. What did she want with hers?

But Isabel didn't have a husband any more. All she had was a maid.

"Lina!"

Her voice was absorbed into the unnatural stillness of the apartment.

"Lina!"

Nothing. No sound. Usually when Lina was around there was something — a vacuum cleaner, the rush of water, a muted radio set to one of the burgeoning number of Spanish language stations.

Nothing.

"Lina!" Isabel called yet again, an edge creeping into her tone. "Where are you?"

Starkly pale against the dark wood, an envelope sat on the dining-room table.

Isabel's stomach clenched. It was Roland's stationery, heavy and deckle-edged. Her name was written on the envelope — Isabel. Just Isabel, not Isabel Orwell. It was as if he was distancing her even from his name. Her name.

She took out the single sheet with shaking fingers.

Isabel —
You must be looking for Lina. I have fired her. She will not be back. Don't worry about her — I have given her a generous severance gift and a sterling reference from me. She has done nothing wrong and will not suffer. Things will change here, and this is the first. From now on whatever happens in or to this apartment or to you is your responsibility. I have decided to stay in the bank's corporate apartment for the foreseeable future.

R

Isabel read the short note three times and each time her brain refused to accept its meaning. What did he mean, firing Lina? How could he do that? Isabel needed Lina. She had trained her herself. There was no way she could manage without her and he knew that. This was torture, pure and simple.

With a cry of rage, Isabel crumpled the note and flung it as far as she could. The paper was heavy; it went clear across the dining room and well into the living room.

How was she going to manage?

Weeping, Isabel sank to the floor and bawled, even as a part of her mind knew this latest outrage was only one more thing to put at Ginny Wylde's door.

Flora Melkiot was conflicted. She let herself into her apartment and waited until the door was safely locked behind her before her iron control broke and she sank into the first available chair. It was an Oriental antique designed more for show than for use, and carved dragons poked out in uncomfortable places. Flora didn't notice.

Never in her life had she ever seen such a horror. She hadn't liked the poor woman who died and whose name she couldn't remember, but not liking someone was no reason to wish them dead. Especially like that. No one should have a death like that.

And no one should have to watch one.

Flora shivered. At her age — the real figure was a carefully kept secret, but anyone with eyes could tell that she wasn't a spring chicken any more — death was a very real possibility and its inevitability a reality of life. Death, a clean death in a lovely bed, surrounded by her children and grandchildren, a peaceful going off to sleep . . . that held no real terror for Flora Melkiot, though she wasn't looking forward to it any time soon.

Death like today, violent and raw and ugly — and induced — gave her the horrors.

Deliberately she unfolded her fingers from the small white box, opening it to look at her new earrings. Doing so helped calm her jangling nerves. It had taken a great deal of energy and no small amount of threats to get these beauties back into her possession. The stupid uniformed policeman had objected to her removing anything from the crime scene, even if they were her own property! She had given him the rough side of her tongue until that idiot detective had finally rescued the poor man and let her take them.

Flora had triumphed, because the earrings were hers and she should have them, but she didn't know if she could ever wear them.

Why had that woman wanted to change glasses with her?

Surely it couldn't have been just because she wanted a blue glass. That was too silly.

Had Flora been the intended victim? Had that woman wanted to kill her?

But if that were true, surely that woman — what was her name? — would not have drunk from the green glass knowing what the result would be. No, she had to be ignorant of what was in the glass, whatever it was.

But had it been intended for her, or for Flora?

Flora shuddered and for a moment felt faint, as if it were her own face that was blistering and bubbling and bleeding. No. It couldn't be possible. There were people who disliked her, yes; everyone of stature had people who disliked them; it was part of being a memorable person.

But who would dislike her so much that they would go to such lengths to see her dead?

There couldn't be any such person.

But to prove that to herself — and to ever feel safe again — Flora knew what she was going to have to do. She would have to solve the murder herself. She always knew she could have been a great detective if she really wanted to.

And she knew just who was going to have to help her do it.

CHAPTER NINE

"You're here. Finally."

Flora Melkiot yanked Rebecca into the apartment and slammed the door behind her.

"I came as soon as I got the call. You did tell Esther that it was urgent."

"Esther?" Flora blinked, then remembered. "Oh, your colored girl. Seems to be a smart one. Have you had her long?"

Remembering Esther's tolerance, Rebecca bit her tongue. "Esther is my business partner," she replied in a tight voice. *And so much more,* she thought. *She saved my life.*

"Yes, I know you have to say that these days, don't you? Not like it used to be, but that's no matter. We've got work to do."

"Work? If there is some problem with the earrings . . ."

Flora looked annoyed. "My earrings? What about my earrings?"

"I don't know. You called this morning

and told Esther I had to come right now. I supposed —" Rebecca was beginning to become a little annoyed herself. There was work to do at the shop. Tuesdays were fairly busy days. She didn't like calling on customers, especially here, especially after yesterday's horror, but Esther had said Mrs. Melkiot had been insistent.

"No, of course I didn't call about my earrings! I called about that Laura Tyler woman."

Death and a bubbling horror of a mouth . . .

"Laura Tyler? The dead woman?"

"Yes. Since she was one of my dearest friends, that nice policeman asked me to look through her things." Seeing an objection rising in Rebecca's eyes, she went on quickly. "I know they've already done it, but he wanted me to look again, maybe see some things he hadn't. Now come along."

"But why me? I never even met the woman!"

"But you were a policewoman. A very good detective, I hear."

Rebecca gulped. She had never made any secret of her past, but she never mentioned it either, preferring to compartmentalize her life. Now and then. Police and civilian. Healthy and cripple. Everything, Esther had once said, but before Frank Titus and after Frank Titus, and that was basically what it came down to.

"You had no right to go digging in my private life."

"I had every right!" Flora snapped. "I was spending a great deal of money with you and I like to know what kind of a person I'm dealing with. Now, are you going to help me or not?"

Grasping her cane tightly, Rebecca started toward the door. "I am not."

"Look here, Miss Cloudwebb —"

"No." Rebecca stopped so quickly she almost toppled. Her face was tight. She had thought she would like Flora Melkiot, but it wasn't the first time she had been wrong about something. "You look. I was a policewoman, but that was a long time ago. Now I am an antique dealer and nothing more."

Flora was silent until Rebecca got her hand on the door.

"For now."

"That sounded remarkably like a threat, Mrs. Melkiot."

"It was." Flora smiled seraphically. "I am not unknown in Dallas, especially as a connoisseur of antique jewelry. How long do you think your business will last once I start telling everyone the earrings you sold me were fakes?"

"Those earrings are genuine!"

"Of course they are. I accepted them. Do you think I'm so stupid I can't tell the real thing at a glance? I asked what would happen if I start *telling* everyone."

"I heard you the first time." Rebecca had heard stories about the outrageous Flora Melkiot and had dismissed them as fanciful gossip. It appeared they hadn't told the entire story.

Tall, scrawny, and sublimely ugly, Flora was dressed in an uncomfortable echo of 1940s chic to the point of eccentricity, even though she could not have been more than a girl during that decade. In spite of everything, though, she had presence, an almost regal sense of self that was accentuated, not diminished, by the girlish sparkle of mischief in her eyes.

"You are a horrible old woman." Rebecca's intended scorn sounded more like amusement.

Flora nodded complacently. "Have been for years, and a couple of wars back I was counted a horrible young woman. But I get what I want, and that's all that matters. Come on. We need to get started."

"Mrs. Melkiot —"

The old woman swept past Rebecca and

opened the door as if no word had been said. "I wasn't looking forward to doing this by myself."

For a moment Rebecca wavered, then tried to convince herself it was only because she couldn't risk offending a lucrative client.

Flora read her face before she could speak. She had intended it to turn out this way, but as always triumph gave her a thrill of excitement. All to the good; she had few enough pleasant thrills or excitement these days.

Which was why she didn't intend to miss out on an iota of this. She hustled her reluctant partner onto the elevator down to the fourth floor. If her luck held, all the dratted snoops who infested this building and had nothing better to do with their time than pry into other people's business would be somewhere else.

There was nothing to distinguish Laura Tyler's door. The yellow barrier tape printed with "Police — Do Not Enter" was gone. The new lock was still just-unwrapped shiny, but it turned sweetly to the master key copy Flora had bullied from one of the less stout-hearted maintenance men several years before.

Although she had had no doubts about

the success of her adventure, Flora breathed more easily once the door was shut behind them. "Not much of a decorator, was she? Some people just have no taste."

Perhaps they didn't, Rebecca thought, *but they still should have done better than this.* The room was perfect in a bland and very expensive way, but it was almost totally impersonal. Rebecca had seen more human rooms in store displays. Only three small, ornately framed photographs of very plain-looking people — her family? — showed that it wasn't a commercial set-up. This was a room for looking at, not for living in.

And she hadn't lived in it, Rebecca realized with a shock. Not really. Laura Tyler had only moved into the Olympus House a few days before.

"I wonder why she bought all new stuff?" Rebecca murmured, her curiosity activated in spite of herself. "Even when they redecorate, people usually hang onto one or two special things. Everything here is brand-new."

"And so boring." Flora's lips curled contemptuously. "Come on. It's in the bedroom."

The apartment was very small. All of it would have fit in a corner of Rebecca's sprawling place, but it was so full of big, puffy furniture that walking through it was difficult. Rebecca grimaced when she banged her leg yet again. Who would have thought such conspicuously overstuffed furniture could have so many hard edges?

"What's in the bedroom, Mrs. Melkiot?"

Already in the far corner, Flora shoved aside a surprisingly fragile looking table. Then, slowly, painfully, she knelt, her joints sounding like popcorn.

"Mrs. Melkiot?"

"The hidey-hole," she said, pointing to the seemingly innocent wainscot. "All the apartments have them somewhere."

This was the tricky part. If the key didn't fit, she'd look like a fool, an unfamiliar situation for Flora Melkiot.

Set at the floor line, the keyhole was almost invisible unless one were looking for it. The key turned halfway, then jammed. To have come so far and this! Flora muttered something under her breath that Rebecca was just as glad she didn't catch, then jiggled the key and turned it again.

The lock gave and the square of wainscot opened out on hidden hinges to reveal a cubbyhole about two feet square. There were two shelves and both were packed.

"Bingo!" said Flora Melkiot.

They spread the contents of the hidey-hole over the bed. In spite of herself, Rebecca was intrigued. Scrapbooks, a dozen or more; some were cheap store-bought ones, while the rest were obviously homemade. There were a few small, purse-sized notebooks and a handful of file folders, grubby from much handling.

There was also a photograph of Laura Tyler, a portrait in a heavy and very expensive silver frame. It took a second look for Rebecca to recognize the ordinary little woman she had seen alive so briefly. Laura's silver hair had been teased and added to and tortured into a memorable construction of curls and braids. She wore an evening gown and so much make-up and fake jewelry she looked like an old tart who had made good. Where besides a costume party would anyone wear such a get-up?

Rebecca had no memory of ever seeing the image before, but there was still a hint of familiarity to it, which annoyed her. Who could forget such a picture?

"Look at this."

Flora peered down her nose at the picture. "Cinderella went to the ball and left her taste at home."

The front doorknob turned.

Flora struggled wildly to her feet and lurched into the living room. Puzzled, Rebecca followed.

"What the hell are you two doing in here?"

"Good afternoon, Detective Ashdown," Flora replied coolly in spite of her racing heart. "Shouldn't the question be, what are you doing here?"

He regarded them both with a chilly gaze, but responded affably enough. "I wanted to talk to Miss Cloudwebb, and her partner said she came over here after you called. No one answered at your apartment, so I thought I would come by here. When I saw the tape was missing —"

"What's going on, Mrs. Melkiot?" Rebecca asked. All of a sudden she knew she had been made a sucker of, just like a rookie, and the knowledge didn't make her happy.

"I'm waiting, Mrs. Melkiot," Ashdown said in a voice that had been known to make hardened criminals break down, all affability suddenly gone. To his dismay it didn't seem to faze this crow-like woman.

A great deal more affected than she let on, Flora drew a deep breath. The weight of two disapproving stares felt almost physical. She tried to make her expression into one of helpful innocence. She didn't do a very good job of it.

"You aren't an old lady —" she began.

142

"Obviously."

"And I'm not either, really, but being closer to it than you —"

Ashdown cut her off with a single glare. "How'd she get you involved, Miss Cloudwebb? Or are you almost an old lady, too?"

"She told me you had asked her to look through her dear friend Laura's things to see if she could find anything that you might have overlooked." Rebecca's voice was hard. She disliked being played for a fool. The guys on the force would have a picnic with this!

"And you fell for that?"

"She threatened to start rumors that my shop sold fakes."

"I never!"

"Then she pulled just enough of an emotional act to make me believe it was all true."

Inwardly Flora preened. She had always been convinced that she could have been a magnificent actress if she had chosen.

"And," Rebecca went on flintily, "I saw the crime scene tape gone from the door."

"Ah, yes, the crime scene tape," Ashdown took a menacing step towards Flora. "When did you take that down, Mrs. Melkiot?"

"Tape?" she began, then realized it was no use. Two against one; it just wasn't fair. "A few minutes before she came."

143

"Why?"

"Why? Why not? Your bunch doesn't seem to be doing such a bang-up job of solving this case, so I decided I had to help," Flora snapped. "I should think you'd be glad of my assistance!"

"How did you get in?"

"I have a key. Obviously."

"Given to you by your 'dear friend Laura'?" Rebecca asked.

"Hand it over," Ashdown demanded.

After only a moment's hesitation Flora sulkily slapped the key into his outstretched palm.

"Your statement says you barely knew the victim." His voice took on an edge sharp enough to cut steel. "So either you lied then or you're lying now. Where did you get this key?"

Rebecca could have told him authoritarianism was not the way to get this autocratic old woman to talk. Flattery, cajolery, a little admiration of her cleverness and the outrageous old woman would probably brag the whole thing out.

"I think you had better cooperate," she murmured and was rewarded with a glance that would have withered greenery.

"That key is *my* property. I don't have to explain myself to him!"

Ashdown was comparing it to his. "This looks like a master."

"How on earth did you get a master key, Mrs. Melkiot?"

"I have my methods," she replied archly.

"Maybe we should send you over to Burglary and see if they're interested in you."

"I never stole anything in my life!" Flora watched as Ashdown slipped the key in his pocket. "And that is my property!"

"If that's true, it will be returned. Now I'm more interested in why you used it to get in here."

"I'm not a thief, if that's what you mean, and I find it most impertinent of you to question me so!"

"You do, do you? I don't, since we already have you for extortion against Miss Cloudwebb, criminal mischief, hindrance of an investigation, illegal entry, and, after finding you in here . . ." Ashdown paused for a suitably ominous effect. ". . . you have just become the prime suspect in Laura Tyler's murder."

All the flesh of pride and self-will melted away from Flora Melkiot, leaving behind only the stark bone of fear. She had no color at all and her mouth was a fluid, formless hole as she gasped for breath.

"Mrs. Melkiot! Here, sit down." Alarmed,

Rebecca folded the unresisting body onto the couch. It was like handling a bundle of dry old twigs. "That was stupid," she snapped at Ashdown. "See what you've done?"

"Kindly stay out of this, *Miss* Cloudwebb! Now, Mrs. Melkiot, why did you kill Laura Tyler?"

"But I didn't." The worst of the shock was over. Flora's cadaverous face had gone from bleached white to an only slightly less alarming putty color. "You just said I barely knew the woman!"

"Then why are you here, if you aren't trying to hide evidence? What didn't you want us to find?"

An ugly connection arced in Rebecca's brain.

"Come here. There's something I think you should see."

Ashdown followed Rebecca into the bedroom and, not wanting to miss anything, Flora was right behind him. He saw the gaping hidey-hole at once.

"What's that?"

"A hidey-hole cabinet," Flora said airily. "All the units have them."

Ashdown knelt and touched the lock. "And you just happened to have a master key for this, too?"

146

"I didn't need one. The locks are all the same. Unless the owner has it changed, of course." Her hand, clawlike and taloned in red, clutched at her key ring, then dramatically dropped it down the front of her dress. "And this is my key! For my hidey-hole!"

Muttering, the policeman obviously thought better of his first impulse, for which Rebecca was very glad.

"Take a look at these," she said mildly.

Laura's scrapbooks were almost like history. Age-marked and greasy along the edges from much handling, they began in the early sixties. The last entry was barely three weeks old.

"What is this crap?" Ashdown asked, flipping through first one book and then another. "There's nothing here. Just a lot of clippings. There's no rhyme or reason to them."

Now comfortably seated on the bed, a book from the seventies open on her lap, Rebecca looked up at him coolly. How had the man become a detective when he was so blind? Besides the fact he was a man, naturally. Whatever the politically correct crowd thought, the good-old-boy system was still alive and well. Of course, he hadn't seen the files. They were lying beneath a scrapbook beside her.

Ashdown picked up the silver framed portrait of Laura Tyler and frowned. "So that's what she looked like."

Rebecca shook her head. "No, she was a plain little thing. I can't imagine her decked out like that."

"Everybody has a fantasy life, I guess," Ashdown said with more than a little distaste and dropped the frame back onto the bed.

The penny dropped and Rebecca realized why she had had a vague sense of recognition of that picture.

"Phantasy Fotographs."

"What?" her two companions asked almost simultaneously.

"Phantasy Fotographs. See? Here's the little PF logo in the corner. It was a photography studio out on LBJ. You went and they dressed you up like your fantasy — queen, knight in shining armor, Visigoth, whatever. They were closed down about half a dozen years ago."

"Why?" Flora asked. "It seems harmless enough a pursuit." She didn't bother to add, "For those nonentities who have nothing else."

Remembering the raid and some of the props found in the carefully locked back room, Rebecca gave a cynical chuckle. "Not everyone wanted to be a monarch. And some wanted to live out their fantasies with more than a photograph. Took the Vice Squad days to get things cleaned out."

Flora blinked. "Oh," was all she said, unable to decide if such things were something a decent woman should admit to knowing about or not.

"Interesting," Ashdown said noncommittally. "Anything more in any of these?"

"I haven't been able to look through all of them, but so far most of it seems to be articles about society doings from the *Morning News* or *D Magazine* or *Texas Monthly*. And they're all about Dallas people. The Crystal Charity Ball set."

"She collected articles about socialites? That's weird."

"Not to her. And that's not all she collected." Rebecca pulled up the files and ticked them off one by one. "Isabel Orwell. Ginny Wylde. Eleanor Anthony. Miss Alicia Carruthers. Flora Melkiot."

Her color and her curiosity quickly recovered, Flora had crept in and perched at the end of the bed like an ungraceful crow. She reached out and grabbed. "A file on me? Good heavens, here's an article about the time I was chairman of ArtFest! That was a good thirty years ago or more. And here's my Morris' obituary, of all things! What . . . ?"

Ashdown took the file. "Well, now it seems we have our motive. Laura Tyler was a blackmailer."

"That little nothing? A blackmailer?" Flora was openly contemptuous.

"What did she have on you, Mrs. Melkiot?" he asked harshly. This time there was no hint of doubt in his voice. "What do you want to keep hidden so badly that you killed her?"

Beyond the dull roaring that filled her ears Flora could hear Rebecca's outraged protests. Then, for the first time in her life, Flora Melkiot fainted.

CHAPTER TEN

Life was so unfair!

Madame Norina had dragged herself to the Olympus House that morning simply because there was no place else to go. The shabby efficiency apartment she rented in Oak Cliff was too depressing to do anything but sleep in.

"Madame." Amanda Peterson's greeting was frosty, as if all the troubles of yesterday had somehow been Madame's fault.

"Mrs. Peterson," Madame returned smoothly, her head held high. It was not lost on her that the blonde from the office had been waiting for her.

"A moment, if you please." Without waiting for an answer, the blonde wheeled on her spike heels and vanished into the office, leaving Madame nothing to do but follow.

"Chust a moment," Madame said, scrabbling for any leverage or dignity she might have left. "I haf much to do."

Amanda Peterson sat down behind her desk and looked up with cold eyes. She did not ask Madame to be seated. "I don't know what. The salon is still sealed."

Salt in the wound! Madame knew the salon was still sealed. She had begged the detective to allow her to continue classes, but the heartless pig had said no, saying something about needing to maintain the integrity of a crime scene.

She had committed no crime!

Could he not understand that with every day the salon was closed, he was taking the bread from her mouth? Even worse, each day that passed made the future she dreamed of more and more unattainable?

"I must call my students," Madame said smoothly. "Ve do not vant any more comings und goings zan necessary, do ve?"

Obviously, the students had not crossed the blonde's mind. There was enough traffic now, and if a reporter should slip in undetected . . . Amanda Peterson shuddered.

"Of course not."

"Since I cannot go into my own salon," Madame said, trying to gain as much ground as possible, "perhaps zere is un office und a telephone I might use?"

The blonde's mouth tightened. The interview was not going the way she had intended. "I don't believe the caterer's office is in use today," she said with scant grace, "so you may use that. But soon we must talk about all these outside classes."

Madame's mouth tightened even more. "I know. I hope I do not lose any ov my students because ov ze untimely death of un Olympus House resident!"

Eyes flashing, Amanda Peterson started to say something, then thought better of it. Picking up an envelope from her desk, she thrust it at the older woman as if it had been an edged weapon. "Here. This was left on my desk for you. I presume you know how to reach the catering office?"

Madame waited until the door of the tiny caterer's office was safely closed behind her before letting her muscles unlock. They could have let her have a better place than this, she thought sourly. Scarcely bigger than a closet, it was wedged between the kitchen and the giant refrigerators, so there was always a constant hum of something in the background.

That woman would like to get rid of her, Madame realized. Probably had some skinny young thing like her who wanted to move in with aerobics or some other kind of strenuous exercise. An elegant salon like hers was old-fashioned, she knew, but some things didn't change. Shouldn't change.

A knife of terror ripped through Madame. Ramon had all the ancillary services — manicures, pedicures, facials, massages — sewn up in his beauty salon. Madame had only her knowledge, her wits, and her Water of Health . . .

They had called it Water of Death in the newspaper.

Her fingers had clenched so tightly around the envelope she had to release each one consciously, then smooth out the heavy paper.

It came from the Anthony Gallery, but it had not come through the mail. Trembling, Madame opened the envelope and was gratified by the size of the check, though a sticky note on the front gave her pause.

Be advised this is the only investment we will make.

CEA

The word *investment* was underlined.

Madame thought for a moment and could make nothing of it. Rich people were so strange. *The Anthonys could afford to invest ten times this and never miss it,* she thought. She was positive she could give them a good return, and they were acting as if they were giving her charity.

Nickels and dimes! Nickels and dimes; that was all this was, Madame thought in a flurry of frustration. *Damn that woman for getting herself killed in the salon!* It was going to be hard enough to get current without having to deal with the backlash of a murder on her premises. How could she approach her other ladies on the heels of such a disaster?

On the other hand, what would she do if the majors didn't pick her up quickly? This wouldn't be enough even to think about opening a second salon, and she couldn't go back to her ladies repeatedly.

Opening a second salon? This one check wouldn't bring her current with the bank, or even pay all of her other, more pressing debts.

Oh, only if she had money, real money, what she could do! In her dreams Madame couldn't decide between opening a chain of salons and having the major outlets come begging to her, or maintaining her exclusivity with just the Olympus House facility and using snob appeal to tempt the retailers. She could start her own ancillary business, with exercise clothes and cover-ups and books and videos . . .

The trouble was, the income from the salon was barely adequate for survival, let alone expansion in any direction. And if she were going to expand, it would have to be outside the Olympus House. She had time for more classes, lots of time, but the management wouldn't let her hold them. They hadn't been happy about her giving even a few classes to outsiders in the first place; they didn't want the nonresident traffic. Madame did. Now there was no chance of getting them to change their minds, none at all.

And so it all came down to money. She had a tiny breathing space to get that leech, that bean-counter, Orwell off her neck for a while. Thirty whole days. No — twenty-nine days.

And then what?

For how long? He wouldn't be likely to let things slide so long again. Not even that little tramp Ginny Wylde could distract him that much!

Madame took a deep breath and forced herself to think.

She took her battered PalmPilot from her purse and set it on the desk. She should start calling her ladies, explain what was happening, and promise to call them when the salon was open again.

And lose how many of them? It was too terrible to contemplate.

Of course, with the right information and the right contacts and just a little bit of luck, she could make more than enough to solve not only her immediate problems but give her a step up for expansion and a bit of a safety cushion, too. Just a little bit of luck! Wasn't she due some? Nothing good was ever gained without risk. Surely it was her turn at last. Otherwise, why would this financial windfall from the Anthonys have landed in her lap?

It would be foolish not to make the best use of her assets.

Her decision made, Madame reached for the telephone.

"I paid her."

Her eyes still swollen from tears, Eleanor looked up from the pillow. To her husband she had never looked so beautiful.

"How much?"

"Nothing to think of. A couple of thousand." He perched on the edge of the bed and gently pushed back an errant wisp of hair. "I also told her that this was the only 'investment' we would make."

"You know that's not true. We'll have to pay whatever she wants whenever she wants," Eleanor said with utter weariness. "Just like you're going to be caught in indentured servitude to that horrible man. At least Madame Norina only wanted money."

The sight of his wife, his beautiful, beloved wife, so beaten and haggard tore at Eddie. "No."

"What?"

C. Edward Anthony's face hardened with an expression totally out of place on his placid, unremarkable features. "I said, no. I'm not going to work with Waldo Wylde, and we're not going to pay any more money. To anyone."

Alarmed by the warlike stranger who looked so much like her mild-mannered husband, Eleanor struggled into a sitting position. "But if they tell? What about your family? The law?"

"I don't care. We can move. Go where no one knows us and no one cares. Europe. South America. The world is a big place, and we can afford to go wherever we want."

"Eddie . . ."

"I love you, darling, and I'm not going to have you going through any of this again. I'll make sure nothing is ever going to upset you again, even if I have to kill someone to do it."

"I still say I'm going to sue."

158

"You could," Rebecca said, "but it wouldn't do you much good. He didn't really do anything."

"He accused me of murder! Me!" Flora was so angry, her grammar, usually impeccable, slipped and she didn't even notice. "You're my witness. You heard!"

Inwardly Rebecca sighed. Flora Melkiot had wakened from her faint almost instantly, though it had still been enough to shake that ass of a detective considerably. Without really knowing why, Rebecca had volunteered to stay with the old lady for a while after they had hustled her back to her antique-filled condo. Ashdown's relief at her almost instant awakening had been a fair barometer of how he had been startled. Now, over painfully correct tea and cookies, Flora was back to her acerbic self, and Rebecca was regretting her charitable impulse, even if she were sitting in the midst of a king's ransom of wonderful things.

"He asked you a question. It's an interrogation tool. He didn't charge you."

"He asked if I murdered that little suburban nobody! Why would I, I ask you? If I were going to kill someone, it would be someone important, and I wouldn't get caught at it, either! I'm going to sue him and the police department, too!"

This was a frustrating situation. For once there was some real news, important news, to impart, but Flora wasn't sure she wanted to tell anyone. She had always dreamed that it would be frightfully exciting and glamorous to be involved in a murder, to solve the crime brilliantly and accept the accolades due such a marvelous feat. The actuality was something else. To be accused of a vile, totally déclassé sort of murder was simply frightening. She knew she was innocent — why should she kill a woman she barely knew by sight? — but the worst thing was that she couldn't prove it.

Rebecca shrugged. "It's up to you, but I can guarantee a suit will drag on for years. You won't get any satisfaction; it'll only tie up the courts and the only people who'll get anything out of it are the lawyers."

The older woman's face hardened. If there were anything on earth Flora Melkiot hated, it was lawyers. When she thought of how they had tried to cheat her over the settling of her poor Morris' estate, her blood pressure rose dangerously.

"I'll think about it," she conceded grumpily.

Rebecca put down her tea cup — a fine example of old Royal Doulton, she couldn't help noticing — and stood up. "Well, Mrs.

Melkiot, since you're feeling all better, I'd best be getting back to the store. Thank you for the tea. And," she added wickedly, "for a most interesting morning."

"You just aren't going to let it rest there, are you?" the older woman asked indignantly.

"What?"

"Well, if he'd accuse me of murder, it's obvious that fool detective doesn't have a brain in his head! Probably has to have help to find his shoes, let alone a murderer!"

"Stay out of it, Mrs. Melkiot."

"Someone has to —"

"Yes, and that is the police. I know all about TV shows and books where an amateur detective brilliantly solves the case, but that is fiction, Mrs. Melkiot. Fiction. Made up. Real-life murder is nothing to mess with. It's dangerous."

Flora's mouth snapped shut. So was potentially being the murderer's target, but she wasn't going to beg this woman. Once some big-time police detective, huh? Hardly. Once they lost their nerve, they weren't worth anything.

"Thank you for taking tea with me," Flora said in a sweet voice that would have alarmed anyone who knew her. "I appreciate your time, but I mustn't keep you.

Remember to call me if you get in any jewelry you think I'd like."

Seconds later Rebecca was standing in the hallway as the door was ostentatiously locked behind her. It took a moment for her to catch her breath. She had never been given the bum's rush with quite so much style — or so much speed — before.

Surely the old lady wouldn't . . . Not after the fright Ashdown had given her today.

No. She was just sulking because Rebecca wouldn't play.

Carrying her cane, Rebecca walked toward the elevator. Despite what Mrs. Melkiot had said, unless C & L managed to come up with something that was truly spectacular they'd probably lost the old lady as a customer. At the moment, though, that prospect seemed almost relaxing.

Now Rebecca could get back to the shop, finish the linen inventory that had been hanging over her head for days, and life could get back to normal.

Flora locked the door and, being alone in the apartment, gave in to the childish explosion of stamping her foot. Drat! This day hadn't gone at all the way she wanted. Why were people so blind and so dull? Was she the only person who could see the potentialities here? Of course, having to deal with idiots and slackers was a penalty that persons of superior abilities had to deal with.

She always had, and she would again.

Flora poured herself another cup of tea and sipped it slowly, working over her plan of action and what she should do next.

CHAPTER ELEVEN

Conference Room A on the mezzanine had been commandeered the afternoon before as a temporary command post. It was the nicest place Ashdown had ever held a murder investigation. Two glass walls looked out over the self-consciously rustic expanse of Turtle Creek. The table was mahogany, the chairs leather. A couple of police computers had been brought in. The management had even put in a coffee bar.

The whole thing could probably have been handled from headquarters, but Ashdown realized the psychological advantage of having a police presence on-site. Methodically he and Gus were working their way through everyone at the Olympus House, from the support staff, who were interviewed here in the command post, to every tenant, who were visited most properly in their homes.

So far they had learned nothing of interest.

Gossip, yes. Who was sleeping with whom, who was going bankrupt, who was in trouble for drugs . . . the residents of the Olympus House put soap operas to shame, but didn't get them one step closer to finding out who would want to murder Laura Tyler. Most of the people they had spoken to didn't even know her, or that her unit had been purchased.

It was as if the lady had been invisible, and that made Ashdown very nervous. When people were that invisible, there was usually a reason. Maybe they would have more luck running her past to earth in Garland, once they finished here.

He had just spent an unprofitable half hour with Eleanor and C. Edward Anthony. Mrs. Anthony looked like death warmed over, and her husband was almost melodramatically overprotective of her. Ashdown had almost expected them to lawyer up and not say a word without a battery of expensive legal counsel present, but they had answered his questions candidly.

Of course, why shouldn't they have? They hadn't told him one blinking thing. He had never seen or even heard of Laura Tyler. She had only seen her that fatal morning in class. She hadn't seen anyone near the water or the glasses except when they had all gotten their drinks. Everyone had been milling about in class looking at Flora Melkiot's new earrings, so Mrs. Anthony couldn't even say who had been near the glasses. The whole interview had been a total washout.

The entire case was becoming a total washout. Hopefully Gus was having some success with the Olympus House staff. Ashdown sighed; probably not. One of the criteria for working in a posh place like this was an ability to keep both your eyes and your mouth shut.

Now he wanted to talk to Miss Alicia Carruthers, to Ginny Wylde, and to Flora Melkiot again, this time without the presence of Rebecca Cloudwebb. Something funny there, too.

Just there? This whole case was funny. This morning, though, he had to concentrate on Isabel Orwell.

He rang the doorbell to number 904.

For a long time there was no response. He was almost ready to leave when the door opened a crack, showing a ravaged face, puffy from sleep or weeping or both. It was Isabel Orwell, all right, though it took a second glance to be sure.

"Mrs. Orwell, I'm Detective Ashdown. We spoke yesterday. I was wondering if I might ask a few more questions?"

Looking a decade older than the woman he had interrogated yesterday, the woman blinked, then shrugged and opened the door.

"Sure. Why not?" She left it for him to close the door, all but stumbling over the thick carpet to sprawl on one of the angular couches.

It was not a room Ashdown liked. Cleanly modern in style, it was done in varying tones of gray with an occasional blob of stark white or sooty black for accent. He almost felt as if he had stumbled into an old black and white movie. By contrast, Mrs. Orwell was garishly attired in a ratty pair of red shorts and a neon pink t-shirt. Against the cool gray, she looked almost like an open wound.

"Sit down anywhere. It's not like there's a crowd or anything. Want something to drink?"

A suspiciously full glass sat next to her. So she was a lush. He hadn't noticed any odor of alcohol yesterday, but it had been even earlier than this.

And, he thought with rare charity, *considering what she had seen yesterday, perhaps some drinks could be excused.*

"Thank you, but no," he said, sitting on the gray couch opposite her. "Now, you said you had never met Laura Tyler before yesterday morning."

She shook her head slowly, as if it were full of some heavy liquid. "No. I didn't know her. She was outside the doors when Miss Alicia and I got off the elevator. They talked about her condo. Miss Alicia always talks about real estate. Or the modern lack of morals." Her mouth, not pretty to begin with, twisted into an ugly knot.

"Then you went into the salon."

"Yes."

"Who was there?"

"Madame Norina, of course, and Eleanor Anthony. And Ginny Wylde." The line of her mouth got even uglier.

"Did you see anyone go near the glasses or the water cooler?"

Isabel shook her head again. "No. Not until Madame told us it was time to drink. Then we all went over at the same time."

"And that was after Miss Cloudwebb brought Mrs. Melkiot's earrings."

"Yes."

"Was this a normal thing? Do Madame's pupils make a habit of having things delivered during class?"

Isabel shook her head again, this time faster, as if she had mastered a new skill. "No. Flora Melkiot's just an attention hog.

Madame didn't like it. Madame doesn't like anything that directs attention away from her salon."

"Could you explain that, please?"

"Flora — Mrs. Melkiot — was showing off her earrings. She loves gaudy old things like that. Then everyone started talking to the woman who brought them, telling her what they collected, and Madame suddenly said it was time for our water, that we didn't want to cool down after our stretches."

"So it was Madame Norina who decided that it was time to drink the water."

"It always is. She wants to go national, you know, sell that god-awful water and her exercise program all over the country."

This was a wrinkle Ashdown hadn't heard before. If Laura Tyler had been blackmailing her, that could put a crimp in Madame Norina's plans.

But there hadn't been a file on Madame Norina. Or any articles.

That they had found. Could the mysterious Madame have removed them from Laura Tyler's hidey-hole before Flora Melkiot led them to it?

"Do you think she'll make it?"

Isabel shrugged loosely. "I dunno. Don't really care, if you want to know the truth. Nothing to care about any more."

169

"And what color was your glass, Mrs. Or-well?"

"Color?" Isabel blinked. "It was tor-toiseshell. Only pretty glass in the bunch."

"Has your husband had any financial deal-ings with Madame?" There was more Ash-down wanted to ask, but suddenly Isabel Orwell came alive. Her bleary eyes shot fire and her lips, messily colored an unattractive cocoa shade, drew back in a snarl.

"Oh, Roland has dealings with everyone! He's all over the place, he is. The son of a bitch!"

"Is it true he's been seeing — ?"

"He's been sleeping with that gray-haired bitch Ginny Wylde! He says they're in love! He wants to leave me, after all I've done for him!" Great raw sobs, primal as thunder, erupted from Isabel's throat.

So the gossip was true. Just like a cheap soap opera. Ashdown felt uncomfortable, as if he had unintentionally seen someone na-ked.

"I need to talk to your husband, Mrs. Or-well. Is he at his office?"

"I don't know!" she screamed, lobbing a light gray pillow at a dark gray vase, send-ing it bouncing over the thick carpet. "I'm just his wife! Why should I know anything?"

There was nothing more to be gained

from this interview; not now. "Is there someone I can call for you? Would you like me to have your husband come home?"

Isabel Orwell looked up with bleak and empty eyes, then down into the drink she cradled in both hands. "This isn't his home anymore. He won't come here again."

Ashdown left the Orwell apartment with a feeling of escape and the nagging sense that there should be something he could do. There wasn't, of course; Mrs. Orwell had refused all his offers of help and dully, doggedly, shown him out of the apartment.

His cell phone rang just as he punched the up elevator button.

"Ashdown."

"Johnny?" Gus's voice was thick and hesitant. "We got a problem. I think that Miss Alicia character has done a runner."

"What?"

"There wasn't anyone at her apartment, so I called her office, and they told me that she never works on Tuesday or Wednesday. Never has, and they have no idea of where she is. I checked with the garage, and she took out her car at seven this morning, just like always. She was carrying a small suitcase."

Miss Alicia Carruthers. One of the most

dignified and powerful old ladies Ashdown
had ever seen. She and the fabled Ebby Halliday and Artha Garza had dominated the
real-estate market in Dallas for several
generations. Miss Alicia and Ebby were still
powers to be reckoned with, in spite of the
incursions by the big-box chains like Cen-
tury 21 and RE/MAX. What on earth was
she doing mixed up in the murder of a possible blackmailer?

More importantly, why had she run?

Ashdown chewed abstractedly on a
thumbnail. Carruthers and the victim were
approximately the same age, he thought,
unconsciously erring at least a decade
against Laura Tyler. What connection was
there between them? Did they have a history?

"Find her. Put out a watch on her car. I
want to know where she is."

"Shall we pick her up?"

"No. Not unless she tries to get away. I
just want to keep an eye on her now. Also
call down to Rizzo at headquarters and see
if he can find any connection between Miss
Alicia Carruthers and Laura Tyler."

Arresting a business icon like Miss Alicia
Carruthers would be a dicey business, Ashdown realized. He had better have damned
good reasons before he did so, or his career

would be toast.

And since this case was probably sheer suicide anyway, he might as well go out with a bang.

"You keep talking with the staff. I'm going to talk to Mrs. Wylde."

"I still don't see why I have to," Ginny said sulkily.

"Because I said so." As far as Waldo Wylde was concerned, that was the only viable reason for anything.

"I didn't even know the stupid woman. I saw everything, and it was horrible." Ginny drew a shuddering breath. "I don't see why I should have to go through it again."

Waldo held back the sheet in an unspoken command, then laid it attractively over Ginny after she lay down.

"Because it was a crime," he said slowly, as if talking to a small child. "Because you were a witness. Because it is the right thing to do. Because, if handled properly, this unfortunate incident can bring in thousands of new listeners."

"You really are a pig, aren't you?" Ginny sat forward while Waldo arranged the pillows behind her to his satisfaction.

"A wise man takes advantage of the opportunities that come his way. We did not

173

cause the situation, and while we quite naturally regret such an incident, it would be a waste not to use it."

Ginny ran hooked fingers through her hair. "I really need a wash and set."

"Later, my dear, later. Let us deal with the constabulary first. Now lie back and let me do the talking."

Ginny lay back and allowed Waldo to place her where he wanted her. Finicky old man! He didn't know; he hadn't seen . . . Ginny had never seen anything so horrible in her life. All she wanted to do was forget it. Surely everyone else had already told the police what had happened. Why should she have to think about it again when all she wanted to do was forget it?

Waldo waddled to the door and opened it quietly. "Please come in," he said in soft tones suited to a sickroom. "My wife has agreed to talk to you, but please remember she has had a terrible shock. She is still under a doctor's care."

"I'll try not to upset her."

For a moment forgetting her assigned role of fragile flower, Ginny snapped to full attention. The policeman had a lovely voice. She had always been a sucker for a good man's voice. It had been Waldo's voice that had first caught her attention — that, and his wallet.

The policeman came to the foot of the bed, and Ginny's eyes opened in a most un-invalidish way as she took inventory. Nice, in a medium sort of way — medium height, medium brown hair, medium looks, but all put together in a most attractive package. She had never had an affair with a policeman before.

"This is Detective Ashdown, my dear," Waldo said, placing his bulk on the chair next to the bed and taking his wife's hand in his own. He had not offered Ashdown a chair.

"I won't take much of your time, Mrs. Wylde. There are just a few questions I need to ask."

Ginny nodded, not trusting herself to speak. Waldo was squeezing her hand inside his big paw.

"How well did you know Laura Tyler?"

"Who? Oh, her. I didn't."

"My wife had never seen the woman before going to class yesterday," Waldo said smoothly. "I, however, had met her before."

"Oh?" Ashdown's attention switched over like a laser beam.

"Yes. I do not remember exactly what day it was, except that Mrs. Tyler was most excited about just having purchased her condominium here. She was with Mrs. Peterson, who manages the building office. Perhaps she can remember the exact day."

"What did you talk about?"

"We did not talk. She did. A most pushy, gushing female, I must say. I had the definite feeling that she was trying to scrape up an acquaintance. That sort of encounter is all too common for those of us in the public eye, I'm afraid," Waldo said with a becoming modesty.

"And did you ever see her again?"

"No."

"What was she like in class, Mrs. Wylde?"

Ginny seemed lost in thought for a moment, wondering just how Detective Ashdown would look out of his suit. He had a trim physique. "I didn't really notice, not much. After all, she was only there for a few minutes, wasn't she? She seemed to be talking all the time, but I didn't listen."

"You didn't hear any of what she said?"

"I didn't pay much attention. Silly stuff, about how happy she was to be in the jewel class and how she looked forward to getting to know us. Dumb."

"And what did you see?"

He would strip down well, Ginny decided. Not overly muscular, but lean and tight. She wondered if he was married. He didn't wear

a ring, but that didn't have to mean anything. Pity she wasn't wearing one of her
sexy lace nightgowns instead of this granny-
ish cotton thing that Waldo had made her
put on.

Waldo's hand tightened just enough to
cause Ginny to draw a quick breath in pain.

"I'm sorry to bring up bad memories,"
Ashdown said gently, "but I need to know."

"Tell the detective everything, my dear.
We have nothing to hide."

"We were doing our stretches. Then someone knocked at the door, and Flora Melkiot
insisted that Madame Norina answer. She
doesn't like to have the class interrupted
once it's started, but that old harpy —"

"Flora Melkiot?"

"Yes. Anyway, she insisted, so Madame
did. It was that woman with the cane, the
one from the antique shop, bringing Flora's
earrings. I know Flora arranged the whole
scene, just so she could show off those
hideous earrings. She's always wearing that
ugly old stuff."

"What happened then?"

"Since class had been upset anyway,
Madame said we had to have our water."

"Her Water of Health."

"Yes. The stuff tastes like shit, but we have
to drink it. It's supposed to be good for us."

177

"Do you drink it every session?"

Ginny nodded. "Yes. Twice. Once after warm-up stretches, once during cool-down. I usually try to dump mine into one of the plants."

"Then?"

"We all grabbed our glasses and got water from the cooler. Then that old woman started . . ." Ginny began to cry and not only from Waldo's grip.

"There, there, my dear. You're all right," he said in rolling tones. "Detective?"

"Just a few more questions, Mr. Wylde. Did you notice anyone near the glasses or the cooler, Mrs. Wylde?"

"No."

"And which was your glass?"

"Red."

"And everyone always used the same glass?"

"Yes. Always. I don't know how it got started."

"We have information," Ashdown said slowly, carefully watching both of them as he changed direction without warning, "that Laura Tyler might have been involved in blackmail. Have either of you been approached or . . . ?" He left the question hanging. People who were being blackmailed didn't like to talk about it.

"Blackmail?" Ginny asked. "That little nothing?"

Waldo nodded sagely, his mind whirling with the possibilities. "A person's outward appearance doesn't always reflect their character, my dear. Detective, I'm afraid my wife is tiring, and she has been ordered to rest. This whole thing has been a dreadful shock to her, you know."

Ashdown nodded.

"If I might speak to you outside?" Waldo lurched to his feet and bent over to kiss Ginny's forehead. "Rest well, my dear. I'll be back in a few minutes."

"I hope you feel better, Mrs. Wylde," Ashdown said as Waldo led him out of the room. He had wanted to ask Ginny about her relationship with Roland Orwell, but he could see that today there was no way he'd see her alone.

"Thank you, Detective," she replied in a voice just a little too strong for the fragile invalid she was supposed to appear.

Massaging her abused hand, Ginny watched the door close. She intended to feel better, just as soon as she got Detective Ashdown into her bed. Now, what could she "remember" so she could call him sometime when old blubber-butt wasn't around? Sometime soon.

"I felt I should speak to you alone, Detective," Waldo said in a conspiratorial tone after the door was closed. "I don't want to upset my wife."

Ashdown was silent.

"There are pressures — risks that haunt a man in public life."

Having an idea of Waldo Wylde's stand on most everything, Ashdown could agree with that. "You think that Laura Tyler's death is somehow connected with you?"

"It is a possibility that I cannot ignore, Detective. What better way to distract a man from his struggle for the good of all than to threaten or . . . or —" The mellifluous voice throbbed dramatically. "— harm the love of his life?"

"So you think your wife was the target of the attack?"

"I do not know. I most sincerely hope not, as her safety is of paramount importance to me, but it is a distinct possibility. That poor woman did try her utmost to scrape an acquaintance with me that first day."

Ashdown couldn't help himself. "And then she took poison when she couldn't?"

Affronted, Waldo drew himself to his full height and looked down at the policeman with a glare that could squash a bug. "That was uncalled for, Detective."

Ashdown looked up. It wasn't often he had to look up to anyone. The man was so fat, it was easy to forget how tall he was. "I'm sorry."

Waldo ignored him. "I do not pretend to have the answers to this sordid crime, having little or no experience with the criminal mind, but I can see that you are unwilling to look in any but your preconceived direction. Obviously the woman picked up the wrong glass, but that is too manifestly simple a concept for the official mind to grasp. As always, I shall be forced to look after my own. Do not let me detain you further."

Waldo opened the front door. Ashdown knew he should be the one to end the interview, but could not think of a thing to say. As many others had learned, coming up against Waldo Wylde was like arm-wrestling a steamroller. *In more ways than one,* he thought, eying the other man's enormous hands.

"Thank you," Ashdown said with unaccustomed meekness and stamped into the penthouse foyer. The door closed silently behind him.

It was not a good morning.

Contrarily, Waldo Wylde was having a wonderful morning. He closed the door behind the detective and smiled. In spite of Ginny's predictable intemperance around an attractive new male — and he would have to oversee her very carefully during the next few days — things had gone just as he had planned.

What a pity that the law should be dependent on such unimaginative creatures of rote as Detective Ashdown, but how handy it was for him!

Waldo strolled to the escritoire and pulled out the leather folder bearing his half-finished essay. Today's show had been recorded the day before; he had just finished the tape when the call came to go home to his wife. As long as he could get this finished and recorded and get it to the station by two, he could ensure that it got on the air at the regular time this afternoon, while the story was still fresh.

Timing was everything, he thought, unconsciously echoing the late and unlamented Laura Tyler.

"Life is always difficult when a tragedy strikes close to home," he wrote. "Many of you know of the tragic death of an old woman in my beloved wife's exercise class yesterday morning. And why, we ask, should anyone choose to murder a harmless old woman, one innocently excited about her new condominium in a beautiful building? I postulate that this unfortunate creature's death was a mistake, that the actual target was my own beloved wife, Ginny. What better method to assault a seeker of freedom —"

He struck that last sentence out, chewed the end of the pen a moment, then began to write again. "What better way to wound and distract a purveyor of truth than to attack that which is dear to him? But I swear to you these dastardly, woman-killing cowards will not stop me from bringing you the truth, in spite of the police department's reluctance to look beyond the obvious."

That was good. Something for the antiauthority conspiracy theorists. Waldo smiled and continued to write.

CHAPTER TWELVE

Roland Orwell couldn't keep his mind on business. Normally the spectacular view from his fifty-fourth-story office didn't tempt him; today he couldn't stop staring at it. It seemed as if the city of Dallas just kept going until it met the horizon, as if it would go on forever.

An entire world full of people, and he was trapped between the monstrous ego of Waldo Wylde and the virago that was Isabel.

How could things have gone so wrong?

He knew they were talking about him in the office. Isabel had called so many times yesterday and this morning, he had been forced to tell his secretary not to accept any of her calls. Of course, now he knew about that woman's death in Isabel's exercise class — strange to think that while he had been firing Lina and packing some clothes, an unknown woman had been dying several floors down — but that wasn't his fault! He wasn't a cruel man; if he had known, he would have delayed things a day or two, given Isabel a chance to calm down. Naturally Isabel was upset, but he hadn't planned it that way, and he couldn't go back and comfort her.

Instead he should be comforting Ginny. Ginny had seen that atrocity too, and he was sure Waldo Wylde was as warm and comforting as a stuffed walrus. Ginny needed him to protect her, to be there for her. Isabel would manage; she was strong. Ginny, his delicate, beautiful Ginny — he sighed.

They could go away together.

The thought warmed Roland like a summer breeze. He had some money stashed away, even some Isabel knew nothing about. He could cash out everything possible, take Ginny, and the two of them could head for someplace tropical where living was easy and cheap . . .

"Mr. Orwell?"

Roland glared up at his secretary; he knew they were now called administrative assistants, but for all that she was nothing but a secretary, and not a particularly bright one. "I told you I wasn't to be disturbed! If my wife comes —"

"It isn't your wife, Mr. Orwell. This

gentleman is most insistent on talking to you."

Badge conspicuously displayed, Ashdown walked into the office uninvited. "Detective Ashdown, Mr. Orwell. I'd like to ask you a few questions."

Roland blinked. "Of course."

Uninvited, Ashdown sat in one of the cushy leather guest chairs. This pudgy, unprepossessing-looking man was the lover of the beauteous Ginny Wylde? Strange bedfellows indeed. *On the other hand, maybe not so much,* Ashdown thought. Orwell was expensively dressed in a black suit and a burgundy shirt and a tie that probably cost more than every garment Ashdown was wearing. Orwell possessed power and money, aphrodisiacs far more powerful than mere appearance for a woman like Ginny Wylde.

"Did you know a woman named Laura Tyler?"

"Hey. Where are you?" Esther asked. "Come back, come back . . ."

Rebecca put down the little china shepherdess she realized she had been holding for several minutes. It wasn't Meissen, more's the pity, even though it looked like it, and there was a thin but distinct crack on one side.

"Looks like we'll have to put this one on the bargain table."

"I know. We talked about it when we unpacked the lot, remember?"

Rebecca's brow furrowed with the effort of thinking. "Yeah . . . I guess we did."

"And it's not Meissen, either."

"I know that. Good fake, though."

Esther couldn't hold back a chuckle. "Yes, it's a good fake. Yes, it's a shame we'll have to put it on the bargain table. Yes, we discussed and discarded the idea of having it restored. Yes, it's sometimes boring arranging and pricing the stock, and, yes, the weather has been lovely." The chuckle became a laugh at Rebecca's blank expression.

"What?"

"You've been so far away you haven't even heard our conversation. What's the matter? Trouble on the case?"

"I'm not on a case. I'm a civilian, remember?"

Esther took a few ineffectual swipes with the cloth duster, then dropped it and put her hands on her hips. "You're just like Jesse was, Rebecca Cloudwebb! Once he got a hold of a problem, he couldn't stop worrying at it until he'd solved it, no matter whether it was his case or not. I've seen that same look on his face when he was mulling over something."

"I can't help it. I was there. I keep trying to see if I can remember anything."

"See?"

"But I am not on the case," Rebecca said with unnecessary fervor. "I am not anything. Just an antique dealer who isn't going to get this stock put out if she doesn't get her act in gear!"

As Rebecca pulled small decorative items from the stock basket with the speed and grace of a terrier at a fresh rat hole, Esther laughed. "For heaven's sake, girl, be careful! We don't want to add any cracks to the stuff that doesn't have any."

"It has been on my mind." Rebecca put down the gaudy Capodimonte candlesticks she was holding. "The case, I mean. I keep wondering how I would have handled it."

Esther began dusting again. "So, how would you have handled it?"

"I don't know. Unless he's got some information he's holding back, Ashdown is heading off in the wrong direction."

"He's not holding back anything," Esther said with a gentle brutality. "If he has information you don't know, he doesn't have to tell you. You're a civilian, aren't you?"

"Yes. So why are you pushing me to think about the case?"

Esther put down the dust cloth and faced her friend and partner over a table covered with artfully arranged bits of porcelain bric-a-brac. "Because," she said carefully, "as horrible as it is, with that woman's death you seem to have come alive again."

"What?"

"Ever since the day of the shootings you've been — I don't know. Different. Closed in. I'm talking about after you recovered — after you left the hospital. You haven't shown any interest in anything. Yes, you learned what you had to learn so we could make a go of this place, and you go with me whenever JJ and I drag you out to something, but it's like you aren't really there."

Rebecca's eyes began to glow with a dark anger. "Do you find that so surprising? I nearly died!"

"Yes, you did nearly die. But you didn't! Giving up on your own life won't bring Jesse back, and it won't undo what Frank Titus did!" Esther snapped vehemently, her dark brown eyes snapping with anger.

"I don't . . ." Rebecca began then stopped.

Had she? Had she so muffled herself against remembering, against pain, that she had blocked out everything else? One look at Esther's furious face gave her the answer, and suddenly the ordinary day, the ordinary china they were putting in their ordinary shop, was changed and nothing looked the same. How could she not have known, have recognized?

No. Rebecca's brain rebelled. It was too simple. She wasn't that uncomplicated or unconscious of what was going on. There were other things, other circumstances, other factors. She'd just humor Esther.

"What do you think?"

The beautiful dark face grew even more angry. "Don't give me that psychologist shit! It doesn't matter what I think. What matters is what you are."

"And what am I?"

Abruptly Esther's anger died, replaced by a mixture of emotions Rebecca couldn't name. "What are you? I don't know. Sleeping Beauty, maybe? Rip Van Winkle? I just know you aren't the same Rebecca who used to be Jesse's partner and my friend, and it isn't just because you limp now." Esther brushed back her hair and picked up the duster again, but didn't reach for any of the china, instead just running the cloth through her fingers over and over. "You changed. Fundamentally. Your body healed, but the rest of you hasn't. Chip said —"

"Chip? You and my brother have talked about me?" Rebecca was outraged. She felt naked, exposed. What else had been going on that she didn't know about?

"Of course we have, you stupid woman! We both love you. Of course we've talked about you. What makes you think we wouldn't?"

Rebecca had to grasp the edge of the table to keep from staggering. Her shattered, weakened, scarred leg — her *limp,* as Esther had so dismissively called it, suddenly seemed to have no strength. "I don't like —"

The shop bell, an old-fashioned combination of genuine antique temple bells, chimed to announce a small herd of what Rebecca and Esther called "the ladies who lunch." They came in at any time, but always in multiples, never alone, looked at everything, usually making stupid or nonsensical or slanderous comments, and seldom if ever bought anything of value.

"Good morning, ladies," Esther said with a smile, stuffing the dust cloth into the drawer of a small drum table. "What can we help you with today?"

Though there seemed to be more, there were only three of them, all about forty and admitting to thirty, dressed in designer clothes and wearing the big, bleached hair for which Dallas was famous.

"We're just looking," said the alpha. Her nose all but quivered as she glanced over the shop. She wouldn't buy anything unless it was a grossly underpriced bargain.

"Do you have any hatpins?" asked the second.

"Yes," Esther replied, heading toward the counter. "Right this way."

Esther was better with difficult customers. Esther was better with all customers; Rebecca had realized that long ago. She calmly went back to arranging the porcelain, vaguely aware that the third member of the trio was riffling through the linen display.

Great! Rebecca thought with no little rancor. *Half an hour this morning getting it straight, and now I'll have to do it all over again. Good thing we haven't put out that new shipment.*

Maybe there was a reason she had been so dilatory about getting the inventory loaded onto the computer.

The alpha shopper sidled up and began picking through the porcelain. Seen up close, she wasn't pretty at all, though clothes and make-up and hair contrived to make her seem so. She was scrawny-thin except for strategically implanted lumps of silicone and collagen, and there was a hard quality about her mouth that made Rebecca wonder if she bit.

"Lovely," she murmured with an air of surprised condescension.

"Thank you." Politely.

Her fingers closed around the non-pedigreed shepherdess and a flash of pure greed arced over the lifted, made-up eyes. "An interesting piece. It isn't marked."

"No."

"There's no price tag, either."

"We haven't priced this lot yet."

"Well, how much are you going to charge for it when you do get around to pricing it?"

"I don't know. We haven't quite agreed on its provenance yet."

"Oh . . . it's French?" She sounded disappointed.

It wasn't the first time a customer had mistaken "provenance" — the history/origin of an object no matter from where it came — with "Provence" — a currently trendy and desirable area in France. While normally happy to educate a customer, today Rebecca was grumpy and disinclined to like this creature, who probably claimed to know antiques after watching a season or two of *Antiques Roadshow.*

This woman, Rebecca realized, *wouldn't recognize a Meissen mark if she tripped over it!*

"I doubt it," she said abruptly, then in a spirit of pure mischief added, "but the glaze makes me think it might be German."

"It's lovely." The customer turned it over and scrutinized every inch of it while Rebecca wrestled with her conscience. Obviously the woman thought it was a Meissen, somehow miraculously unmarked. Should Rebecca tell her point blank that it wasn't, or wait until she asked? So far Rebecca had told the exact truth. It wasn't her responsibility what the customer thought. If she were thinking that at all. If she were even capable of thinking.

"You were at Madame Norina's yesterday, weren't you?"

The question came from so far out in left field that Rebecca could only gape. "What?"

"The exercise salon. In the Olympus House." The woman spoke slowly, enunciating each word as if trying to communicate with an idiot. "You were the one who was there, weren't you?"

"Yes."

"Tell me — what was it like?"

"Watching a woman die horribly?" Rebecca snapped, then bit her tongue. Now was not the time to lose her temper.

"The media doesn't tell us anything, and we are all students of Madame Norina's. Not the jewel class." Her voice showed her bitterness at that. "But we have all been going to her for a long time. Who was there?"

Rebecca didn't like lying, but she disliked this fashionable ghoul even less. She pasted a thin smile on her face, a very superior, snotty type of smile she hadn't used since the elementary school playground. "The police have asked me to keep all details quiet. Perhaps if you call Detective Ashdown, who is in charge of the case, he will release the particulars to you. As for that figurine, I could not possibly let it go for less than —" and she named a figure approximately that of a genuine Meissen. "It's a bargain at the price. I'll wrap it for you."

The woman's face hardened into a make-up mask. "I'm not sure . . ."

Rebecca's voice slid up a notch or two in volume even as the tone reached a new low of condescension. "Oh, well, then, I'm sure we can find something in your price range. I'm sorry if I assumed . . ."

Scenting metaphoric blood in the air, the

other two ladies turned to look. Beneath the mask, the woman's face turned a fiery crimson.

"It's fine," she snapped. "You take checks, of course?"

"Of course. With proper identification," Rebecca said over her shoulder on the way to the cash register. She hardly limped at all.

C & L Antiques did take checks as a regular practice, but never with such fine documentation. A tight-jawed Rebecca scrutinized the woman's face and driver's license picture as if screening for terrorists, then copied down all her information, including her birth date (written very large), which placed her closer to fifty than forty, and the numbers on two charge cards. The whole process took almost seven minutes and, ten seconds later, purchases in hand — one of the women had bought a half a dozen potentially lethal Edwardian hatpins — the three left the shop without a glance back.

"Rebecca," Esther asked in awe not a little tinged with apprehension, "what did you do?"

"I sold that little shepherdess. The one with the crack."

"I know! And I know for how much. You didn't tell her it was Meissen, did you?"

Rebecca frowned. "Of course not. I just told her it wasn't French, and that we thought it might be German. And it could be."

Esther made an inarticulate sound and hid her face in her hands. "I never thought I'd see the day. She'll bring it back, you know. Or stop the check."

"She'd better not. I wrote on the sales slip that it was cracked and the sale was as is and final. If she stops the check, we'll sue her."

"She'll never shop here again."

"I hope not."

The vehemence in her partner's tone made Esther drop her hands and look at her closely. "Because?"

"The world is full of bottom feeders, Esther. She claimed she and her friends were clients of Madame Norina's."

"Maybe they were."

"Then they should ask her for all the gory details that the media won't tell them. I'll bet they all park and watch when they see a traffic accident, just to count the number of body parts carried out."

"Oh, sweet Jesus! What did you tell her?"

"Nothing. I said the police had asked me to keep the details quiet. Then I suggested that she call Detective Ashdown if she wanted more information."

A giggle bubbled up through Esther. "You didn't! What if she does?"

"Then I feel sorry for her. And I feel sorry for us, because until there's some other local big news tragedy, we'll probably get more of her ilk in here." Devils danced in Rebecca's eyes as she waved the check. "And maybe we can turn a profit from it."

Esther drew a shaky breath. She had never thought that vulgar curiosity-seekers would invade their shop. She had never thought that Rebecca would act in such a way, even though the resultant check made this a very tidy month indeed. She had prayed for Rebecca to come back to life, to take an interest in things, to crawl out of her self-imposed cage. Now . . .

Be careful what you ask for, Esther thought with more than a little trepidation. *What next?*

CHAPTER THIRTEEN

By the time Detective Ashdown left, Roland Orwell was feeling less shaky. He had answered every question to the best of his ability. Yes, he'd had business dealings with Madame Norina on the morning of the murder, but was not at liberty to discuss them other than to tell him they had nothing to do with the murder at all. They were strictly financial. No, he had never met or even heard of Laura Tyler. Yes, he and Ginny Wylde were in love. He hoped that before long they would be married. Yes, he had moved out of the apartment he shared with his wife. His soon to be ex-wife.

In a way, he should be grateful to the detective, because with his intrusive questions he had cleared Roland's mind. All the indecision, all the what-ifs, all the fear was gone. He and Ginny were in love, and they deserved to be together. He would be like a knight-errant, rescuing his lady-love from the foul dragon to whom she was chained. He would avoid the servitude Wylde had in mind for him, too. Once he and Ginny were gone, he would have nothing to lose, nothing that fat slug could hold over him.

He would be free, too, free of Isabel and her annoying perfectionism, her neuroses, her problems. She had even tried to hold that unfortunate business with SunTime-Land over him. Of course, he was grateful to her for helping him straighten things out, but where did gratitude end? He shouldn't have to sacrifice his life and his happiness over that. He had supported her well over the years; that counted for something, didn't it? The fact that Isabel had threatened him with the law proved that she had never really loved him, had just regarded him as a source of support. How could he ever have thought he loved her? He would have Ginny and money and a world for them to choose from . . . And just to be on the safe side, several of those lovely beach countries had lovely non-extradition laws. What could be better?

So he had better start things happening quickly. The sooner Ginny and he were away, the better; the furor over that old woman's murder would make the ideal smokescreen for their quick getaway. If he could get things together fast enough, they might be able to leave tomorrow, or the day after . . .

Roland's heart pounded with anticipation as he reached for the telephone.

He couldn't wait to tell Ginny. Wylde should be at his office by now; Ginny should be — had to be — at home. He couldn't wait any longer.

Waldo Wylde watched with ophidian eyes as his wife stretched lazily in bed. He had seen the attraction to the policeman flare in her eyes. So it was going to be over with Roland Orwell. He'd never understood what she had seen in that middle-aged milquetoast anyway, handy though her infatuation had been. Even if Ginny was moving on, it made no difference. He had enough documentation — photos, affidavits, witnesses — to keep Orwell in line.

A policeman. Waldo sighed heavily. Well, Ginny had always had a tendency to degraded taste, but it might be handy having a police detective in the fold. One never knew what might be useful.

"If you are quite strong enough, my dear, I must get to my office."

Ginny sat up in bed and wrapped her arms around her knees. "I'm fine, Waldo."

"What are your plans for today?"

A sly smile tugging at the ends of her mouth gave him the answer. Poor policeman! He was as good as a dead duck. Still he listened attentively.

"The salon probably won't be open today, so I can't go exercise. I thought I'd have my hair done down at Ramon's. It's so scraggy."

"You're always beautiful, my dear," Waldo said with a breathtaking lack of emotion.

"Then I thought I might meet Mavis Gilbreath for drinks. It's been so long since I've seen her." Ginny regarded him cautiously through her eyelashes.

"Ah, dear Mavis. Please give her my regards." Waldo had long ago accepted that there was no such person as Mavis Gilbreath. She was just a name concocted by Ginny in a childish attempt to deceive him. Any time she wished to do something without Waldo's knowledge — such as seduce a new man — she had to see her dear old friend Mavis Gilbreath. As if she could outwit him! The Gilbreath fiction was a harmless enough conceit, though, and he allowed her to think that she had bested him.

He did not, however, believe in letting her off scot-free. "Someday," he said with a hearty grin that was so rare it was alarming,

"I hope to meet this lady who is such a dear friend of yours. She sounds delightful."

Waldo dropped an avuncular kiss on Ginny's forehead and waddled out in his oddly dignified gait. Ginny watched him go with a mix of emotions.

Yesterday she had seen a side of Waldo she would never have dreamed existed. She had been frightened, truly frightened, and revolted, and upset, and he had comforted her. Waldo! Probably it was just an act, but it had been what she had needed.

As for meeting Mavis Gilbreath, she knew that he knew there was no such person. Really, who would have the name Mavis Gilbreath? It made him happy to think that he had outsmarted her, though, and she let him go on thinking it. He didn't have to know everything.

"Hello?" Startled by the sudden tinkle, Ginny answered the phone without thinking, remembering too late that Waldo had said something about screening all calls through the answering machine.

"Good morning, darling. How are you this morning?"

Roland. Ginny made a face.

"What are you doing calling me here? You know you aren't supposed to."

"I don't care. I just had to talk to you, to

203

find out how you are."

"I'm fine," she said brightly. "How are you?"

"I'll be better once I see you. Was yesterday terribly dreadful for you?"

"Of course it was."

"That police detective was just here asking a lot of questions. He knows about us." Roland's voice throbbed with import.

That police detective? Ashdown? She would have to learn his first name. If she went to bed with someone, she really did like to know his first name. She pictured Detective Ashdown in Roland's glass-walled office, sitting across from the desk on which she and Roland had made love so many times. She'd like to make love to Detective Ashdown on that desk, the glass walls almost making it seem as if they were flying . . .

The thought of the detective next to Roland didn't raise Roland's stock. Middle-aged, pudgy, unremarkable looking; what had she ever seen in him? The detective, now! She bet he had the best looking buns. How long would it have to be before she found out?

"Roland, everyone knows about us. You know you can't keep a secret in this place. How is Isabel?"

"I haven't seen her. I don't live there anymore. I've moved into the bank's corporate apartment for now."

Good, Ginny thought. *Now I won't be stumbling over him every time I leave the apartment.*

Aloud she said, "You should check on her, Roland. She was very upset yesterday. She is your wife, you know."

"Not for long. You are the love of my life, Ginny darling, and we deserve to be together. That's why I'm calling."

"Oh, Roland . . ."

"No, listen. I've worked it out. I've a pretty good amount in liquid assets that I can cash out today. Why don't you pack a bag, and by tomorrow morning or maybe even tonight we can be on our way to paradise."

"A vacation? This is a rather funny time to be taking one."

"No, darling." Roland's voice intensified. "Not a vacation, the beginning of our new life."

"You're asking me to run away with you?"

"Yes, my dearest! Let's go someplace with beaches and sunshine and palm trees where we can be together always! Can't you just picture it?"

Unfortunately, Ginny could. Waldo was

far from perfect, but at least he gave her all the freedom she wanted. Roland would hang around her 24/7, all mushy and cloying. The idea gave her the horrors. Besides, she didn't like beaches much at all.

"Go? Leave Waldo?"

"Yes, my darling! We can be together like we've always wanted to be." Even through the telephone line Roland's voice shimmered with joy.

"Roland, I think you've carried this a little far." Ginny assumed her "great-lady" voice, designed to ward off social climbers, political liberals, and other distasteful creatures. "I never said I would run away with you."

"But we love each other."

"We had a good time together. We're both married, you know."

"That can be handled." Roland's voice was still confident, but the joy was gone.

"I don't want to 'handle' it. I have no intention of leaving Waldo. I didn't know you had any idea of leaving Isabel. It was just an affair, for God's sake!"

Suspicion rolled over the wire. "He's there, isn't he? He's making you say these things."

"Waldo? No, he's gone. I'm saying them all by myself. Look, we had a good time, but it's time to move on. I don't think we had better see each other again."

"Not see each other!" Roland's world shifted and dissolved beneath his feet. "I know he's there! You wouldn't be saying things like that if he weren't making you, I know that. It's going to be all right, my darling. I'll see to that."

"Goodbye, Roland. I don't want to see you again," Ginny said flatly before she hung up the phone.

It rang again, again, and again incessantly, but she ignored it as she went through her closet. Now, how was the best way to catch the eye of a policeman?

Once she made up her mind, Flora Melkiot was unstoppable. She wanted information, and she knew where to get information. Even though she normally made sure her appointments at Ramon's salon were scheduled for days when the fewest number of people were there, right now she wanted to find as many as she could. Ramon would always find a way to fit her in.

That afternoon she hit the jackpot.

Ramon's was full, with all three chairs occupied and a woman patiently seated in the waiting area. Flora recognized everyone by face if not by name. All but one lived in the Olympus House itself, and that exception was a woman who had been coming to the salon for years.

Good! No gawking strangers to contend with.

Even better, Ramon's personal chair was occupied by Ginny Wylde.

Flora dashed into the changing room and pulled on one of the pink cover-ups, then came out and sat demurely in the waiting area. Divided only by a small half-wall between the styling stations and the waiting area, the salon was small and intimate, allowing a free flow of gossip between those waiting and those being worked on.

Ramon must have realized and prepared for his unique position as a listening post. Both of his relief stylists were there, an impossibly pretty pair of young men who had eyes only for each other. They were gifted haircutters, though, almost as good as Ramon himself. Never bothering to remember their names, Flora had simply mentally tagged them Frick and Frack.

Of course, no one was talking about the murder. *Everyone,* Flora thought, *wanted to, but no one wanted to be so crass as to bring it up.*

The closest they came was when Mrs. Fratelli, a washed-out blonde who some said was a former Hollywood actress, mentioned that the management had allowed Madame Norina to hold her classes in the ballroom for as long as her salon was locked up. Everyone agreed that it was a wonderful idea; keeping up with a personal improvement program was so important.

So, thought Flora cynically, *was the chance of getting some good gossip.*

Every head swung as Eleanor Anthony let herself into the salon. For a moment her mouth tightened, but that might have been from the aroma of the chemicals.

"Oh, my dear," gushed old Mrs. Wayborne, a fat artificial redhead who had lived at the Olympus House ever since it had opened its doors, "have you heard? Madame Norina is going to be allowed to continue her classes."

"Really? How nice for her."

"You really need to keep an exercise program going, don't you?" said Mrs. Fratelli to no one in particular. "I know I can't wait to get back, can you?"

"I just wish I had the time for exercise," said the woman who didn't live at the Olympus House. Flora had seen her in Ramon's for years, but still couldn't call her name to memory. Hill? Hall? Something like that. The unknown tilted her head forward as Frack — or was it Frick? — brushed the curler-tight back of her hair into soft waves. "I barely get time to come get my hair done."

"Your business must be doing wonderfully," said Mrs. Fratelli as Frick — or was it Frack? — gave her completed coiffure a final bath of spray. Puffed and teased and curled, it looked as if it had been intended for a much larger woman. Mrs. Fratelli loved it.

"It sure is," the woman said. "Come by any time and I'll give you a free make-up consultation personally."

As Mrs. Fratelli enthused about the offer, Flora turned to Eleanor. "Are you going to come back to Madame Norina's class?"

"I'm thinking about it," Eleanor replied vaguely, slipping into the changing room.

"I'll be back," Flora said definitely.

Mrs. Wayborne laughed. "We know you will be, Flora dear. We know you don't like to miss a thing."

For a moment Flora's temper flared at the double entendre, then she regained her composure. She had bigger things to think about.

If you're going to make an omelet, Flora thought with truth but still no originality, *you're going to have to break some eggs!*

"So what do you think?" she asked.

"About what?" Mrs. Wayborne asked.

Flora snorted. "About the murder, of course. That Laura Tyler. I know she was a stupid creature, but one can't be allowed to murder even stupid people indiscriminately."

"Why not?" Ginny tossed her curls, disarraying a great deal of Ramon's careful handiwork, trying to decide if she really liked this new cut. She wasn't sure.

Of all people to ask that question! Flora thought with amazement. On the other hand, part of being stupid was not realizing you were stupid.

"Because," Flora replied with a poisonous pointedness, "the world would be perilously close to being depopulated if we were to rid it of stupid people."

Realizing they had stumbled into the middle of a battlefield, the other ladies kept their silence, waiting happily for the next bomb to fall.

Ginny stared at the mirror. Maybe it wasn't the cut; maybe she was just tired of being a redhead. Maybe she really should go blonde now. It had been a long time since she had been a blonde. Ramon had said he couldn't do color on her today, but if she gave him a big enough tip . . . ?

Didn't policemen like blondes?

211

"Well, what's bad about that? Isn't over-population one of the things everyone keeps yelling about?"

"As usual, you have a unique grasp of the situation," Flora said with a heavy irony that was entirely wasted.

Perhaps not completely; her expression studiedly blank, Eleanor Anthony came out of the changing room, still tying the strings of the pink wrapper. Flora stifled a flicker of jealousy that the woman could look so elegant even in one of Ramon's tacky little cover-ups.

"Waldo says that one of the hallmarks of a civilized society is the emphasis of quality over quantity." It was clear on which side of the question Ginny Wylde thought she belonged.

Something touched Eleanor's expression. "Even at the table?"

"Waldo has a glandular problem!" Ginny snapped.

As interesting as a catfight might be, Flora decided her duty to gather information came first. It seemed that detective needed all the help he could get, and for all her experience it didn't appear that crippled woman was going to be of much assistance.

"Have any of you heard the latest?"

"About what?" Ginny asked impatiently,

her eyes still on Eleanor as if on a predator. She had never liked the snotty, superior bitch.

"I assume about the murder," that maligned lady said mildly, pouring herself a cup of Ramon's excellent coffee.

"What have you heard, Flora?" Mrs. Wayborne asked, sliding into the chair Mrs. Fratelli had so reluctantly vacated.

"You know, Flora, you've become thoroughly fascinated with that murder," Eleanor said with a shadow of distaste. "Are you sure such concentration is all that healthy?"

"I am assisting the police," Flora replied with a lofty disdain for the finer nuances of truth. Ginny had risen, to Ramon's private disgust, still running questioning fingers through her curls.

"Oh, God, they must be desperate," Ginny muttered.

Ramon seated Flora quickly, as if to prevent Ginny Wylde from changing her mind and sitting back down. "A shampoo today, Madame?"

Flora shook her head. "No, just brush it and put it up for me, if you would, Ramon. Some days my fingers just won't manage the pins," Flora added mendaciously.

Mrs. Fratelli, once again wearing her own clothes, emerged from the changing room but made no effort to leave. Frick — or Frack — swooped down, got her signature on the bill, pocketed his tip, and, with much hand-kissing and compliments, escorted her to the door with such panache that she was gone before she realized she hadn't really wanted to go.

"Well done," Flora murmured so that no one but Ramon could hear.

"There is a certain element that comes in here solely for gossip," Ramon replied smoothly, taking out a handful of pins that had been put in just as precisely as he ever could. "We must do what we can."

"Gossip or not, it is a question why anyone would want to kill a stranger. That Tyler woman seemed to be such a nonentity," Eleanor murmured.

"She was a blackmailer," Flora said baldly, avidly watching their reactions in the mirror, then screeching as Ramon's fingers tightened convulsively in her hair.

The coffee cup slipped from Eleanor's nerveless fingers and shattered, spraying coffee and bringing the shampoo girl running.

Ramon swore in his native tongue, then, apologizing profusely, untangled his fingers from Flora's hair.

"My goodness, sugar," cried Mrs. Wayborne, "are you hurt?"

"I'm so sorry," Eleanor said, repeating herself several times as the shampoo girl — who was actually a middle-aged woman with a ready smile and a marginal command of English — wielded a sponge and a dustpan with practiced skill. "The cup . . ."

Ginny Wylde watched with a curious, catlike expression.

"It is nothing, Mrs. Anthony," Ramon said airily. "The important thing is that you are not hurt."

Eleanor dabbed at her legs with a handful of paper towels. The coffee had been hot and it stung her legs, but it was nothing compared to what Flora Melkiot had said. A blackmailer! Another blackmailer! No wonder the old woman had tried so hard to chat her up. She would have to leave; that was all there was to do. Three people knowing, three people draining Eddie, corrupting his life because of what she had done — it was insupportable.

To say nothing of the fact that if the police found out about her, she would become their prime suspect. If she were allowed to stay in Dallas.

She had disappeared once before. She would have to do it again.

But this time without Eddie. She could

not endanger him.

Two huge tears rose in her eyes.

"You are hurt," Ramon cried, rushing to her side. Unexpectedly released, Flora's hair fell like a jetty cloud around her shoulders.

Eleanor shook her head. "No. The coffee just stung my legs. It's nothing."

"But why would a blackmailer come to the Olympus House? It's awful to think of living so close to someone like that," Ginny said, giving a theatrical shudder.

"I shouldn't think it would bother you," Eleanor spat in an unwise fit of honesty.

"What do you mean by that?"

Ramon backed out of the field of fire. Sensing fireworks, the shampoo girl disappeared entirely, while the woman from away and Mrs. Wayborne watched wide-eyed. Flora held her breath and for once in her life hoped that everyone would forget she was there.

"I mean," Eleanor articulated with vicious clarity, "your husband."

"Waldo?" Ginny asked unnecessarily, genuinely startled. "What about him?"

"Don't tell me he doesn't use what he knows to force people to do what he wants."

This was news to Ginny, who was sublimely indifferent to her husband's activities as long as the money kept coming in, but

216

she wasn't surprised. Or dismayed. "Waldo is a great man," she said in a condescendingly superior tone. "I'm sure whatever he does is for the good of all."

Eleanor swore with a string of words that surprised all her listeners and, fists clenched, stalked out of the salon, forgetting that she was wearing one of Ramon's pink smocks and her own blouse hung in the dressing room.

CHAPTER FOURTEEN

"Hey . . . lucky you!" Esther peered around the corner of the tiny office at C & L Antiques.

Startled, Rebecca looked up. Even though the computer screen faced away from the door, she gave a surreptitious mouse click that shut off the Internet and left, showing only the innocent inventory of linens on which she should have been working.

"Huh?"

"Phone for you. Your favorite customer." Esther smiled nastily.

"Oh, no . . . not Flora Melkiot."

"The Queen of Meddle herself. Have fun!" Esther smiled again, this time with genuine amusement, and vanished into the front of the shop.

Rebecca regarded the telephone with its one blinking red eye as she would have a snake coiled on her desk. If she didn't answer, the dratted woman would just call back. Might as well get it over with.

"Hello."

"You must be doing a land office business if it takes you this long to get to the telephone," Flora said testily. "I hope you're not selling anything I would be interested in."

"You know I call you the moment we get in any pre-nineteen-thirty jewelry."

"You'd better, and you haven't done much of that recently."

Rebecca listened carefully. Flora Melkiot usually raised the art of complaining to a new level, and now she was only going through the motions. Somehow that seemed ominous.

"I hope your detecting is going better than your antique hunting," Flora said pettishly.

"I'm not detecting, Mrs. Melkiot. I am no longer a police officer. I am leaving the murder in the hands of the law." Rebecca pulled a clutch of linen napkins over the stack of papers she had printed off the Internet as if their being hidden somehow negated her half-truth. Being nosy wasn't the same as really detecting. And it wasn't as if her searches about the various occupants of the Olympus House had told her what she didn't already know.

"Didn't think so. It's a good thing I'm on

the case."

"You haven't been snooping around again! Mrs. Melkiot . . ." Rebecca began, but was not surprised when the old lady brushed her words aside.

"Well, someone has to! The police haven't been around and you aren't being any help."

"It's not my job, Mrs. Melkiot. And it's not yours," Rebecca added wearily. She hit the "save" key and then put the computer into hibernation. Onloading inventory wasn't as exciting as some of the research she had found on the net, but she sure would have preferred it to Flora Melkiot's flights of fancy. She would have preferred almost anything to dealing with that crazy woman. "The police are doing their best."

"Which isn't good enough, I can tell you that. They haven't even discovered that Waldo Wylde is a blackmailer!"

"What?"

Flora triumphantly related the scene at Ramon's, then waited with a pleasurable sense of superiority as Rebecca gasped and sputtered.

"You've got no proof," she said at last.

"I have all the proof I need. I know these women. Eleanor Anthony is a prissy creature who acts as if butter wouldn't melt in her mouth. No one has ever heard her say anything worse than 'poo' and 'piffle.' She let loose like a sailor!"

"That isn't proof, Mrs. Melkiot."

"It is," Flora returned grandly, "to me."

Rebecca started to think in spite of all her good intentions. "And you say Ramon reacted, too?"

"Reacted? Humph! He almost ripped my hair out by the roots. It's only because of my usual good luck that I wasn't snatched bald!"

While the concept of such an eventuality was surprisingly pleasing, Rebecca thought on. "So I wonder if Ramon is being blackmailed, too."

"There wasn't anything in the hidey-hole about him, was there?"

"I don't remember anything."

"That doesn't mean there wasn't, so you'd better call that idiot policeman and ask," Flora said tartly.

"Why don't you call him? You know he's going to want to ask you some questions."

"Because I don't want people to know I'm assisting the police," she declared, conveniently forgetting she had announced that very fact to everyone in Ramon's. There was a moment of silence before Flora added, "Besides, I tried, and he won't take my call."

Rebecca had been speechless at the idea

of Flora Melkiot in any official police capacity, but still she had to keep herself from laughing at Flora's last statement.

"Mrs. Melkiot —"

"And be sure to call me when you find out!" Flora ordered before hanging up precipitately.

It was ridiculous, of course. Rebecca knew she had no business getting involved in the investigation, had no real interest in getting involved, but still . . . Her father and grandfather had been proud members of the Dallas Police Department. Her brother still was. She had been. A lifetime spent in intimate involvement with law enforcement made it almost impossible for her to have any knowledge that might help the case and say nothing about it.

Would Ashdown take her call? Doubtless he would resent what he saw as her interference, especially since he had told her in no uncertain terms to stay out of the investigation. That's how she would have felt.

She could call Chip, of course, but that might be worse. As Deputy Chief he could pass on the information to Ashdown, but it would still be the same situation, with the added irritant of her having gone over his head. In Ashdown's eyes the fact that Chip was her brother would in no way alter the fact that he was also his superior.

"Want some coffee?" Esther hovered over the desk, already putting a steaming mug in front of Rebecca.

"Thanks."

"Something wrong?"

Rebecca looked up into Esther's eyes. Esther was concerned about her, she knew. The dream coming back, the murder at the Olympus House, Rebecca's involvement, Rebecca's non-involvement; all of it concerned Esther. Sometimes she was just too much of a mother hen for Rebecca's comfort. But she was also like Jesse — there was no keeping a secret from her.

"Flora Melkiot's been detecting again."

"Oh, law, that woman's a menace." Then Esther gave an impish grin. "Did she find out anything good?"

"Depends on what you call good. Would you believe blackmail?"

"I thought that was accepted, after what they found in the victim's apartment."

Rebecca shook her head. "Not like this."

"I thought they couldn't find any connection between the victim and the residents."

"Not her. Not so far, at least. I'm talking about Waldo Wylde."

Esther's eyes widened. "Waldo Wylde? *The*

Waldo Wylde? A blackmailer?"

Rebecca nodded. "Apparently."

"I thought he was making a bundle from his little neo-fascist empire. Or dare I hope that people are too smart to buy into his imperialist rantings and he's getting his money from plain old-fashioned extortion?"

"I think his blackmail is more for power — making other people do what he wants. At least, that's the impression I got from what Flora Melkiot said."

"I thought that was too good to be true. That man scares me."

"I didn't know you knew him."

"I don't. JJ had a social studies assignment to assess and compare political philosophies. He listened to a bunch of political commentators and analysts. I listened in a couple of times. They're all biased and some of them are flat weird, but Waldo Wylde is scary. Wants to remake the whole world according to his ideas."

"Liberal or conservative?"

"Neither. He's a law unto himself. He's so far out there, he makes Rush Limbaugh look like a Massachusetts Democrat."

"You're kidding."

"I wish. Last week he was telling how the Senate should be realigned and the House all but abolished. Apparently he thinks the people have too much power and they don't know how to use it correctly."

Rebecca could understand Esther's shudder. She felt a little like shuddering herself. "King Waldo, in other words."

"Exactly. Another tin-pot megalomaniac who wants to rule the world." Esther shook her head. "And some people listen to him! Who's he supposed to be blackmailing?"

"Just about everybody in the Olympus House, according to the Marvelous Mrs. Melkiot."

"Do you think she's right?"

Rebecca shrugged. "I don't know."

"Professional snoops like Flora Melkiot have a habit of being at least partially right, you know. What are you going to do about it?"

"I don't know," Rebecca said slowly. "Right now I'm going to finish loading this inventory."

Rebecca normally didn't object too much to loading inventory, if the items were interesting. Even if they weren't it was an easy job, one that gave her a chance to rest her leg and hopefully keep it from aching. Normally the lists of linens would have enthralled her; embroidered, drawn-work, cutwork, lace trimmed . . . all relics of a more formal age, when people appreciated beauty for the sake of beauty. When women had the time to create things like this. These linens must have been someone's very best, because none of them appeared to have been used.

Her mind wandered from the days of formal teas and cutwork napkins. What if Waldo Wylde were blackmailing some of the residents of Olympus House? Not all activities people wanted hidden were criminal, though the blackmail itself was. Catching a blackmailer was notoriously difficult; most people, especially those with power and money, would rather pay than have their secrets exposed.

How many people was he blackmailing? And for what?

And how did that tie in to Laura Tyler's murder?

Was it any of her business?

Ashdown certainly wouldn't think so.

Well, her conscience wouldn't let her just sit on the information. Ignoring the stack of linens, she reached for the phone.

Ashdown wasn't only not interested, he wasn't even very polite.

"Flora Melkiot is a pest," he said bluntly after hearing what Rebecca had to say. "Tell her to stay out of it."

"Since when did I become her keeper?"

Rebecca asked, her voice dripping with indignation. "You tell her."

"I wouldn't dare," he said frankly. "She scares me."

Rebecca couldn't tell if he was kidding or not. "Did you get an official COD yet?"

"Why do you want to know?"

"I'm curious."

"It's none of your business, Miss Cloudwebb."

"Pretend I'm a reporter."

"You don't want that. I'm not as nice to them as I am to you."

"Poor sods."

That brought a surprisingly nice-sounding chuckle from Ashdown. "Stay out of it, Miss Cloudwebb."

"I am out of it. It's just that the woman died in front of my eyes. Died very unpleasantly, if you want to know, and I can't help but have an interest in the investigation. Wouldn't you want to know?"

"Actually," Ashdown said after a long moment of silence, "the official cause of death was a massive heart attack. It was probably triggered by the corrosive she ingested, and if she hadn't had the heart attack she would have died of suffocation in a matter of minutes. Her throat and airway were almost completely dissolved. Some of the stuff had even eaten down into her lungs. She didn't have a chance. There wasn't anything you or anyone else could have done."

So he did understand. A haze of guilt she hadn't consciously realized existed fell away. "Thank you," Rebecca said. Then, more briskly, "It was in her water, of course."

"Yeah. It had to have been at the bottom of the glass, since the water came from the common cooler and everyone had some."

"And she wouldn't have noticed anything was wrong, since the water tasted so foul. What is in that water, anyway? You had it analyzed, of course."

Ashdown chuckled again. "Of course. A bunch of stuff — sulphur and some other minerals. Nasty, but not harmful. Not helpful either, I would think, but it's the madame's shtick. She's hoping to market it over television and the Internet."

"Might sell. Isn't there supposed to be one born every minute? I'll bet those women pay a pretty penny for her classes."

"Yeah, especially that one. That's called —" There was a rattling of papers. "— the jewel class."

"The jewel class? Because they're all so rich?"

"Should be. It's restricted both in size and to residents of the Olympus House. There are other classes to which both residents and nonresidents belong, but the early morning class is a special one. Those women actually pay a premium for that class. Don't know why."

"Some people pay a premium just to have a designer's name on their clothes or purses or whatever," Rebecca murmured. "I don't understand it."

"Too much money and too little sense," Ashdown said with brutal honesty. "Apparently this class is the only one that has the colored glasses. They all have their own personal one in their own personal color."

"But Laura Tyler had just joined the class."

"Something weird there. The manager says that the victim was very excited about joining the class. Said that she got the idea Tyler bought the condo just so she could join that particular class. Apparently she had tried to join before and was turned down."

"She had her own glass?"

"Yes. Madame said she expected some sort of ceremony." The policeman's voice was thick with contempt. "Said the victim seemed disappointed when all she had to do was pick one out of the cabinet."

"What kind of corrosive was it?"

"Sure you're not a reporter, Miss Cloud-webb?"

"Positive, but I'm beginning to sympathize with them. What was it?"

"Lye, mostly. Drain cleaning crystals, available under half a dozen names in the cleaning aisle of grocery stores all over town. Guaranteed to eat right through any clog that gets in its way."

Rebecca shuddered. "Any idea how it got in the glass? Could it have been in it when it was in the cabinet?"

Ashdown translated Rebecca's barrage of pronouns easily. "Nope. All the glasses go down to the kitchen every night for washing. They had just been put on the shelf a couple of hours before. As to how it got in there, someone put it in there. Deliberately. We found a wadded-up piece of plastic wrap at the base of one of those fake trees. Still had a grain or two of drain cleaner on it And before you ask, there weren't any fingerprints. Only smudges."

"Someone wanted to make very sure she was dead. And quickly."

"And couldn't talk, not even for a moment." Ashdown made a sound that in anyone else might have been a sigh. "If she was blackmailing someone, that some-one wanted to make sure the secret died with her."

"If someone were being blackmailed and so very desperate to hide whatever it was, why would Laura Taylor take the risk of going to such lengths to be close to her victim?"

"Does sound sort of stupid."

"Could Laura Tyler have been watching over her blackmail victims?" Rebecca wondered. She could barely remember Laura Tyler the way she was in life. She doubted she'd ever forget her in death. There was the impression of a childish, eager face, a corona of ruthlessly styled gray hair, an unfortunate exercise suit. Hardly the image of a blackmailer. Or, for that matter, a murder victim, even though Rebecca knew that appearances had nothing to do with either.

"Dunno."

Something in the studied neutrality of Ashdown's voice alerted Rebecca. "What?"

"It's none —"

"It's none of my business, I know," an exasperated Rebecca snapped, "but I'm curious. You can't just tell me part of the story. Or do I have to go to Chip?"

"Is that a threat?" Ashdown asked in a tone that left no question Rebecca had made a mistake.

"No. I didn't mean it the way it sounded." Rebecca sighed. "I just want to know. My God, I watched her die. I'd like to know why. If you were in my shoes, you'd want to know too."

"You're right," Ashdown said at last. "I would. Okay, I'm not sure she was a blackmailer."

"I had wondered about that."

"Now don't tell me you had deduced that! Or was it Madam Melkiot the Meddler?" There was a distinct tone of annoyance in the policeman's voice.

"As far as Flora Melkiot is concerned, there are blackmailers all over the Olympus House. It's not a difficult jump, though. From the little I could see of Laura Tyler's papers before you snatched them away —"

"They were evidence."

"Evidence that Flora and I found," Rebecca answered with ostentatiously sweet reasonableness. "Anyway, from the little I could see, everything she had was from public sources, mostly magazines and newspapers, and blackmailers don't generally practice their trade with what's in the public media."

"And what do you make of that?"

Rebecca ignored the sarcasm. "She was a

232

groupie. Like a high school girl with a crush."

"On other women?" Ashdown sounded disgusted. Rebecca ignored that, too.

"On society women. On their position. Women who live in the Olympus House. Women who attend the Crystal Charity Ball. Women who have the life she wanted."

"Could be. So if she didn't have something that someone wanted to keep quiet, why was she killed?"

"I don't know. As an object lesson? Could she have been blackmailed?"

"If she was, I don't know what for. Laura Holman Tyler had about as blameless and boring a life as you could imagine. Married her high school sweetheart, had four kids, six grandkids, worked in her church — Methodist, by the way — was a past Worthy Matron in the Eastern Star Lodge, played bridge with the same bunch of women for over twenty years, had memberships in a couple of museums. Husband got cancer two, maybe three years ago. Everyone said she nursed him devotedly until he died a couple of months ago. Hell, for all we found out, she could be on the short list for sainthood. If the Methodists have saints."

"Then after her husband was gone, she sold everything, bought all new stuff and a condo in the Olympus House."

"Right."

"What did her husband do?"

"Plumbing. He was a contractor and had a small chain of plumbing supply stores."

"Hardly the stuff of her society dreams. Probably for the first time in her life she's able to do what she wants," Rebecca muttered. "So she moves into the Olympus House and thinks that she's going to chum up with the women she's envied all her life."

"That's dumb," Ashdown said with a sneer. "Those women don't chum up with each other, let alone a newcomer."

"In her fantasies they did. Remember the portrait from Phantasy Fotos? I'll bet she'd been fantasizing about becoming a socialite for a long time."

"You should be in psychology, not antiques." He did not mean it as a compliment.

"Antiques are psychology," Rebecca replied only half humorously. "How else do you think we get people to buy things that other people throw away?"

Ashdown laughed at that. "So what do you say the motive is?"

"I haven't the foggiest idea."

"Well, don't go looking for one. I've enjoyed talking to you, Miss Cloudwebb, but I'm telling you, stay out of this case."

"Goodbye, Detective Ashdown." Rebecca was quite proud of the control she had over her voice. She didn't even slam down the phone, though she was sorely tempted.

Supercilious bastard! So afraid of losing control. Or status. Rebecca sneered. Yeah, like detectives had status. Especially if they had a case like this, with no clues and no solid motive.

Poor sod.

How would she have handled it, Rebecca wondered, if this case had landed on her plate?

She was glad it hadn't. There weren't any leads, no reliable witnesses, including herself, Rebecca admitted with a wince. No nothing except the dead body of a potential Methodist saint.

But there was Flora Melkiot, a born bloodhound if there ever was one. She might be a terrible old woman, but she knew how to get information.

Unbidden and unwanted, Rebecca's investigative juices were all but bubbling. For the first time since That Day her life had changed, she was actually curious about something. If she and Flora couldn't solve this case . . . Rebecca's lips curved upward

CHAPTER FIFTEEN

Of all the people in the world to come into the shop the first thing on a fine Wednesday morning, Flora Melkiot was the last one Rebecca wanted to see. Well, there was nothing she could do about that; even if Esther had been there, Mrs. Melkiot would have waited for Rebecca.

A good night's sleep had restored Rebecca's sanity. She was no longer a detective. She had no business working on the murder case, as interesting as it might be. She was not going to let Flora Melkiot bulldoze her into it, as much as she might be tempted in her weaker moments. She had a business to run.

"Good morning, Mrs. Melkiot. How can I help you today?"

"Well?"

Rebecca looked at the older woman with ill-concealed dislike. "Well, what?"

"Haven't you figured out who killed that

woman yet?"

"No." Rebecca had finally decided it was useless to say that it was not her job to do so.

"Humph! If all the police detectives are as slow as you, small wonder that the crime rate is as high as it is."

"You're just angry because Detective Ashdown won't talk to you."

"More fool he. I could tell him a lot of things. And I try to tell you, but you won't listen!"

"It's not my job." It just slipped out; Rebecca couldn't help herself.

"Well, it should be! That woman was murdered in front of you!" Flora snapped, but in an unusual burst of tact stopped at the expression on Rebecca's face. "But then, it's not the first time that's happened, is it?"

Rebecca looked up sharply. Of course, this horrible old woman had admitted to researching her.

"No."

"I'm sorry. Being injured, losing your partner. And that awful man. He got away, didn't he? It all must have been very difficult for you."

"It was, and I really don't want to talk about it." Rebecca was just being cautious. There hadn't been anything about Frank and her in the papers, though there had been a great deal about Frank and his criminal dealings. Dirty cops were always good copy. There wasn't any real way Flora Melkiot could know anything, but she wouldn't put it past the old witch to read her mind.

"Then let's talk about the case."

Rebecca submitted to the inevitable. "Let's go back to the office and get some coffee."

Surprisingly, Flora Melkiot disliked flavored coffees as much as Rebecca did, which raised the older woman slightly in Rebecca's estimation. Taking their cups, they settled into the tiny office. If Flora was disappointed in the less than lavish accommodation, so different from the lush variety of the shop, she didn't show it. She simply settled into the straight wooden visitor's chair and, ignoring the dust on the floor, dropped her purse at her feet.

"So how far have they gotten?"

Rebecca shrugged. "Not very far, from what I can gather. Now they don't believe Laura Tyler was a blackmailer."

"Then what was she doing with all those clippings?"

"Being a groupie."

"A what? Like a fan?"

"Of society women." Rebecca nodded and was startled by a rusty braying that sounded like nothing so much as thick material being shredded.

Flora Melkiot was laughing. Contemptuously.

"Society women? A fan? Of that bunch of Johnnie-come-latelies at the Olympus House? Not a drop of old society blood among them. When they came here, they probably thought Dallas was just a support system for Neiman Marcus! Well, what can you expect from a plumbing contractor's widow from Garland?"

"How do you think the poison got into her glass?"

"Someone put it there, of course."

Rebecca frowned. "Who?"

"I don't know."

"When?"

Now it was Flora's turn to frown. "I don't know."

"Why?"

"I don't know that, either. Since she wasn't a blackmailer, she didn't seem enough of a person for anyone to want to poison."

Rebecca began to toy aimlessly with a pencil. "Could it have been an accident?"

"Impossible. Those garish glasses are

distinctive, and we've all had the same ones forever."

"Except for Laura Tyler. Hers was new."

"And that made it distinctive. There'd never been a green glass out before."

"And all the glasses are different? No duplications?" Rebecca grabbed a pad and began to write. "Laura's was green."

"Isabel's is tortoiseshell, Miss Alicia's is yellow, Ginny's is red."

"And yours?"

"Blue. I adore blue. It's such a primal color. I picked it the first day we had those glasses. Did you know that Tyler woman asked to change glasses with me? Said she'd bought a blue exercise suit and so she should have a blue glass!"

"Could she have been trying to poison you?" Rebecca asked. She realized from Flora Melkiot's calm acceptance of the theory that the older woman had already thought of it.

"I doubt it. If she knew what was in the green glass, she never would have drunk it herself."

"True. So if the green glass had never been out before, and Laura Tyler had never been in the class before, it stands to reason that the murderer wanted to kill Laura Tyler," Rebecca said. "But why?"

Flora Melkiot gave a small smile of triumph. She had hooked her.

There was no crime scene tape over the
door to 406.

"Mrs. Melkiot?"

"I didn't do it," Flora replied in great
indignation. "The police took it down about
an hour ago."

"Lucky for them," Rebecca murmured.
She wondered if the old witch had put some
sort of spell on her. She hadn't had any
intention of getting involved again, but here
she stood, ready to enter the dead woman's
apartment. Again. Mrs. Melkiot said she
had permission, that everything was all
right, but Rebecca didn't know.

She would never admit that she was curious to see the place again. There was
something about it that teased at her, grated
at her, wouldn't let her go. All right, she
was nosy. If Ashdown didn't like that, tough!

Flora reached into her bosom and pro-
duced a single key on a ring that advertised
a car dealership twenty years closed, a key
that turned sweetly in the lock.

"Ashdown gave you back the key?" Rebecca asked in astonishment.

"That hard-nosed, bat-blind pathetic
excuse for a detective? That thief? Hardly."

Flora opened the door, then closed and locked it behind them. Although still gleamingly clean, the apartment smelled musty, dead.

"You had another copy?"

Flora gave a smug smile. "An intelligent woman is ready for any contingency."

"But it's a master key. That's illegal."

"Are you going to tattle?" Flora asked. There was more than a little contempt in her voice. "If you did, perhaps you might solve that mysterious series of burglaries that has plagued us over the last few years."

Rebecca frowned at her. Part of her Internet research had been on the Olympus House, which — aside from some ornamental plants snatched from the driveway two years before — had not had a robbery in over a decade.

"You should be careful to whom you say things like that, Mrs. Melkiot. Someday someone is going to take you seriously, and then you'll be in a lot of trouble."

"Oh, pooh! No one ever takes old people seriously. Not that I'm old, of course."

"Of course."

"Now what are we going to do?"

"Wait, of course." Pushing aside a herd of aggressive pillows, Flora sat on the living room couch. She ran appraising fingers over the material, then shook them as if she had touched something nasty. "Cheap stuff. Too thin for upholstery. Won't stand up. I'd be surprised if it lasts two years."

"Laura Tyler won't care." Favoring her aching leg, Rebecca eased herself down into the armchair, if one could call those over-stuffed excrescences arms. Once again she had decided against using valet parking and her leg was protesting. At least she knew better than to ask for whom or for what they were waiting. Flora Melkiot enjoyed a nicely developed sense of drama.

"Her family might. Might? Definitely." Flora gave a delicate sniff. "That bunch would argue over a quarter in the street."

"I didn't know you knew her family."

"I don't yet."

There was the smooth sound of a key in the lock and then the door opened. Rebecca's heart sank under a flood of dèja vu. Not Ashdown. Not again. She hadn't let herself be conned by this dreadful old woman — who had probably removed the police tape herself — again. Lord, what would Chip say when he had to come bail her out?

"Mrs. Melkiot?"

It wasn't Ashdown. Rebecca let out a panicked breath she didn't know she had been holding.

This man wasn't anyone she had ever seen. Medium height, chunky, balding, he was about as unmemorable as a person could get. He was wearing a simple outfit of sport shirt and slacks, but somehow they looked as if they did not belong on him.

"Mr. Tyler?" Flora rose and extended her hand to be shaken, then tried not to wince as he did. "I am so sorry about your mother."

So this was one of Laura Tyler's children. Stifling a small thrill of alarm, Rebecca struggled to her feet. What was this mad old woman planning now? *And what,* Rebecca wondered, *am I doing here with her?*

"Thank you. It's so nice to know that Mom had made a friend here. We were all so worried that she wouldn't fit in."

Flora made a dismissive gesture. "Oh, Laura would have fit in anywhere. This is my friend Rebecca."

"Larry Tyler, ma'am. Proud to meet you." He gave Rebecca a bone-crushing handshake. "Were you a friend of my mom's too?"

"No, I had just met her." Rebecca reclaimed her hand and wondered when the circulation would come back. "She seemed charming, though."

It was a lie, of course. Rebecca barely remembered the living Laura Tyler, but there was no way she could do less for the grieving hunger in the man's plain face.

"My brothers and I are real grateful for all you're doing for us, Mrs. Melkiot."

"It's the least I could do," Flora said modestly, ignoring Rebecca's blistering look of inquiry. "And Rebecca volunteered to help."

"We thank you too, ma'am. It's always hard going through someone's things —" For a moment there was a suspicious moisture in his eyes before he blinked it away.

"That's what friends are for." Flora gave a soothing smile.

"What about — Laura's — daughters-in-law?" Rebecca stumbled over the name and avoided Flora's poisonously warning glance. "Didn't they want to help?"

Larry looked embarrassed. "Mom didn't get along real well with the girls."

Rebecca waited for him to say more and when he didn't, finally said, "Oh."

"Troubles in a family can be such a problem." Flora patted Larry's arm. "Did you bring any boxes?"

"Yeah. They're in the hall. I'll get them."

As soon as he stepped through the door, Rebecca grabbed the older woman's arm.

"Flora Melkiot, what do you think you're doing?" she whispered.

"Looking for clues. With the permission of the family. If there's anything here, we'll find it."

"But the police have been through everything."

"And found nothing. That does not mean there is nothing to find."

There weren't many boxes, but then there wasn't much in the small flat. Apparently Laura Tyler had intended getting all new things as she found them.

Larry suggested that Rebecca might make them some coffee. She went into the kitchen against her better judgment, loath to leave that poor bereaved man alone with Flora Melkiot. Who knew what that terrible old woman would do next? And what, Rebecca thought wryly, would she be able to do about it anyway?

The coffeemaker was new and very red. While the coffee dripped, Rebecca opened cabinets. The contents were sparse. Some staples — flour, sugar, pasta, coffee, tea — and a few cans of soup and vegetables. A service for four in high-end earthenware, with matching glasses, the pretty, trendy kind of stuff sold by Fitz & Floyd and Horchow. A drawer of silverplate flatware so

247

shiny it had to be new.

In a cabinet beside the small stove were a couple of dazzlingly enameled pots and pans, obviously part of a brand-new starter set. A drawer held a small assortment of knives and spatulas and things, the basic tools of cooking, all of them looking as if they had never been used. Another drawer held four elaborate lace placemats with matching napkins. They had never been used either; the store tags were still attached.

Rebecca looked around her with wonder and just a little revulsion. She had never seen a room so devoid of personality or personal touch. Everything was new, probably purchased the day Laura Tyler purchased the apartment. There was nothing from her old life here, nothing — not a spatula, not a clock, not a hot pad made by her grandchildren.

But Laura Tyler had come from a large suburban home, and large suburban homes were usually full of lots and lots of things. Surely her children hadn't stripped her of everything; if that were true, how could she have afforded this condo and her new furnishings?

Short of having to start over because of losing every possession in a catastrophe, Rebecca couldn't imagine such a completely fresh start. It didn't make sense, and Rebecca didn't like things that didn't make sense.

The coffeemaker gurgled to a stop, bringing Rebecca back to the present. There were a sugar bowl (full) and a creamer in the cabinet; they matched the china. The milk in the nearly bare refrigerator was still fresh. That tugged at Rebecca's heart. The milk was still good, but the woman who had bought it now lay dead and disfigured in the morgue.

There was a pretty painted metal tray with the price sticker still on the back; Rebecca put the coffee carafe, three coffee cups and saucers, the creamer and sugar bowl, and a handful of spoons on the tray. For napkins she took paper towels, somehow not wanting to use the pretty cloth ones Laura Tyler had never had time to use.

"— but Pop thought she was a fool. He had no use for society people."

Flora and Larry sat in front of the sizeable entertainment center. Flora was in an armchair, a stack of papers in her lap. Larry sat on the floor; obviously he had been digging in the cavernous space beneath the television. It had yielded only a meager handful of commercial movie DVDs.

The Women.
My Man Godfrey.
High Society.
The Philadelphia Story.
There were a few more and all of them were society-oriented, though to a society of several generations past, Rebecca noticed. There was one old VHS tape crudely labeled *Family,* though no videotape player.

"Here's coffee."

"Thank you, dear," Flora said, her fingers still busy in the paper-filled drawer. "I don't see anything in here but legal papers about her buying this condo and some receipts for the furniture and such. I haven't found anything more than two months old."

Larry looked up and gave a singularly sweet smile that all but transformed his face. "That's great. Thanks. Ed kept all the papers from when she sold the home place. Made him mad as fire."

"Oh? Did he want it?"

He grabbed a cup and poured for himself. "No, he and Donna Rae have a big new home out in Allen. No, we were all pretty upset because Mom didn't tell us what she was going to do. We would have tried to talk her out of it."

"Why?" Beneath the sweetness in Flora's voice, there was a definite edge.

Larry looked startled. "Because that was her home. Pop built it special for her, for her to have forever. Put everything in it a woman could want. It was even paid for." He plopped great amounts of sugar and cream into his coffee, but still made a face at his first sip.

"Damn."

Rebecca looked up from pouring cups for Flora and herself. "Is something wrong?"

Again that nice smile. "No, it's just this fancy coffee Mom was always drinking."

"Starbucks French Roast," Rebecca said with a smile. She loved it herself, but very seldom indulged.

"Yeah. She tried it a long time ago, but Pop said it tasted like mud and made her go back to plain old Folgers. She switched back to this stuff when Pop got too sick to have coffee, but she used to keep some Folgers around for us."

Flora's expression was getting darker. "Sounds like you boys were very much like your father."

"Thank you, Mrs. Melkiot!" Larry all but glowed. "We sure tried to be. And we all wanted Mom to be happy. That's why we couldn't understand why she'd move away from everything she'd known her entire life to this place."

"I gather your father wouldn't have liked it," Rebecca said quickly, before Flora could make the probably unwise comment that was obviously dancing on the end of her tongue.

"No, ma'am. Pop never did hold with Mom's interest in society things. Thought she was cracked for keeping up with things like that." Larry slurped at his coffee. Rebecca thought the expression on his face showed that he pretty much agreed with his father on that. "We were all worried that she'd get her feelings hurt trying to make friends with a bunch of stuck-up snobs."

The coffee did not go down well when Larry belatedly realized what he had said. While he didn't quite spew it out, choking it down was a complicated exercise, which Rebecca and Flora watched with varying expressions.

"I mean, that's what we thought when she first moved here. I didn't know she'd make friends with such nice ladies like you." He wasn't very good at backpedaling, either. "We didn't know any of the people who lived here, so we thought — I mean, y'all are so nice —"

Rebecca didn't see fit to enlighten him. "But your mother went ahead without consulting you, I gather. Didn't that make you angry?"

Larry nodded, his ruddy complexion now an uncomfortable scarlet. "Yeah. Al and Ed and me talked a lot about it after we found out she'd sold the house. Even talked to the company lawyer to see if we could get the sale reversed."

"But you couldn't, could you?"

"Nope. Mom was a smart woman in most things, and she'd been around Pop and his business sense for years."

Rebecca could all but see the steam rising from Flora's ears. There was probably some coming from her own.

"And Mom wanted it so bad that we let her do what she wanted. I mean, Pop was gone and it was a big house for one lone woman."

Because you couldn't do anything to stop her, Rebecca thought.

"So your mother didn't inherit from your father?"

"Oh, no, Mrs. Melkiot. Pop took care of Mom just fine. She got the house and the cars and everything, except a few keepsakes for us boys. Of course, we got the company, but she was to get an income from it for as long as she lived."

"Oh. That's very generous. I just thought that since you 'let' her, she didn't have any money of her own." Flora's tone was almost too innocent, but there was a dangerous gleam in her eye and Rebecca could almost read her thoughts. *Imagine one's children "letting" you do anything if you had your own money.*

Rebecca threw herself into the breach before the look in Flora's eye could become an actuality. "Do all of you boys work in the business?"

"No, ma'am." Larry dumped the DVDs into a box and pulled open another cabinet door, revealing a stack of photographs in worn dimestore frames. At least Laura Tyler had saved something of her old life. He held up a fading five-by-seven — four young men from mid-teens to early twenties in fashions thirty years past — and pointed. "That's me, that's Al, that's Jeff, but we always called him Skeeter, and that's Ed. Ed's the oldest. He became a CPA. Does the books for the company, too. Al and I run the company — I handle the residential plumbing part of it and Al runs the stores."

"And what about Skeeter? Doesn't he work with you?"

It had been a casual question, but Rebecca was astonished when Larry flushed and looked away, his face tight.

"Skeeter's the youngest. Mom always

spoiled him so much Pop said he'd never amount to anything."

"Go on," Flora prompted somewhat tactlessly.

The floodgates opened. "That's one reason we — Al and Ed and me — weren't very happy about Mom moving in here. Of course, by the time we found out it was too late. Skeeter has a gambling problem, you see. That's why Pop put his part of the company in a trust and he only gets an allowance."

"No," Flora said. The papers in her lap were forgotten. "I don't see."

"Skeeter always hung around with a bunch of lowlifes. Anybody who'd gamble with him or help him gamble. We all tried to help him. Pop even put him in some sort of rehab place once. It didn't help. As soon as he got out he was running around looking for a game."

"Mr. Tyler," Flora asked in a terrible voice, "are you telling me that there is a gambling operation here in the Olympus House?"

Larry was both startled and defensive. "No! At least not here in the building. At least I don't think so. It's that doorman, that Chuck Jernigan. He and Skeeter go way back. There's no kind of gambling in Dallas he doesn't know about."

CHAPTER SIXTEEN

"Und von und two . . . Stretch, my lovelies, stretch . . . Reach for ze beauty zat can be yours."

Madame Norina should have been grateful. This morning the management — meaning that sour bitch Amanda Peterson — had decided to allow her to continue her classes in the ballroom, probably because of the many calls from her students. Madame knew they had been motivated more by vulgar curiosity than any desire for self-improvement, but she knew not to look a gift horse in the mouth. The announcement had come too late for her to contact her jewel class, but the other classes were astonishingly full, and attendance at even one session meant payment for an entire month. She was seeing pupils she hadn't seen in months, and some she had never seen before, no matter how they protested they were old students.

There really was, apparently, no such thing as bad publicity.

Even better, there had been enough interest that she had had to schedule two completely new classes. Mrs. Peterson had raged at that, but Madame had held firm and only hinted at how much she could tell the press about the goings on at the Olympus House. Nothing so crass as overtly stated blackmail, but that twiggy blonde had gotten the message. Mrs. Peterson obviously did not agree that there was no such thing as bad publicity, for she caved quickly, though Madame knew there would be a price to be paid soon.

There was always a price to be paid.

Worst of all, no matter how much money her classes brought in, it would neither be enough nor in time to rescue her from her obligations. The class money might buy her some time from the bank, if she could work her way around that small-minded stick Orwell, but the holders of her other debts were hardly so obliging. They would be satisfied with nothing less than every penny.

If only her plan would work . . .

It had to. She had checked every reference, called in every bit of knowledge she could, used whatever leverage was in her power. It just had to work.

If only she could have just a little luck.

For once.

"Again, my dears. Stretch . . . Remember, you are striving for something zat is chust beyond your reach . . ."

Detective Ashdown was not happy. Neither was his partner Gus Spencer.

"Do you mean we don't have any idea where she is? The old lady has just vanished?"

Gus shrugged. "Guess so. Guess we should have put out an APB to pick up. Most road guys don't have time to mess with 'person of interest' bulletins."

The fact that Ashdown knew this was true did not improve his temper. "She could be in Uzbekistan by now."

"Why there?"

Ashdown shook his head. "No reason. It was just the farthest point I could think of."

"Oh."

"Find anything out about her?"

"Nothing concrete that couldn't be printed on the front page of the *Dallas Morning News,*" Gus said, his face glum. "Lots and lots of information, but it all boils down to a very rich, very hardworking old woman who has no family and no social life that isn't business related. Finances are sounder than a lot of small countries, no debts to speak of, no real enemies, though none of her employees are exactly what you would call fond of her."

"Any problems there that she might have been running away from?"

Gus snorted. "From what I've heard she wouldn't run away from a charging tiger. No, she's just a real tough boss, but even the ones who don't like her say she's fair."

"And her offices haven't heard from her?"

"Nope. Her secretary says she is always off on Tuesday and Wednesday. Always, no exceptions. No contact while she's gone, no idea of where she goes."

"Any history with Laura Tyler?"

Gus shook his head lugubriously. "Nothing that we could find. Other than they live in Dallas, we can't match up anything where they might have connected."

"And yet no one knows where she goes on Tuesday and Wednesday."

"Nope. What kind of secret life could an eighty-year-old broad have?"

"I don't know," Ashdown said grimly, "but I'm sure going to ask her when we find her. If we find her."

"I knew he looked familiar," Rebecca said.

Flora lifted her glass, making the ice cubes rattle. "And you didn't do anything? Didn't say anything?"

Despite all their work, it was early to be drinking, but Rebecca had been unable to resist Flora's offer. Now she was doubly glad; Mrs. Melkiot's Scotch was excellent — a single malt of the age and quality Rebecca had seldom tasted. They sat in Flora's antique-filled living room. Somehow in here — with the unquestionably real antiques that made Rebecca's mouth water — it was almost possible to believe that time had stopped and they were in an older, gentler age. Flora had even set out tiny hemstitched cocktail napkins of real linen.

"After so long on the force, just about everyone looks familiar. And even if I had recognized him, that wouldn't mean anything. He could have gone straight and now be an upstanding citizen."

"Humph!" Flora left no doubt as to her feelings about that. "Leopards don't change their spots. To think of a creature like that working in the Olympus House! I'm going to have a firm talk with that brainless blonde in the office."

They hadn't found out anything in Laura Tyler's condo, except that she had bought several new outfits and — to her son's blushing embarrassment — all new frilly, lacy, somewhat risqué underwear. Aside

261

from the cache of framed photos and the single *Family* tape, there was nothing that was not new, expensive, and impersonal. Rebecca had finally realized what had been nagging her about that apartment. Other than the weighty business and residence telephone books, there were no books. No Bible, no dictionary, no books at all. Rebecca, a dedicated reader, found that lack not only heartbreaking but downright spooky.

Flora had been as good as her word, though, and they had labored through the afternoon to help Larry Tyler pack up the new, pathetically few remains of his mother's life. Finally, when every small item of Laura Tyler's had been put neatly in boxes, he had taken them and left, full of gratitude and promises of perpetual family rates on any plumbing needs for the both of them. The furniture, he said, would be picked up by a moving company tomorrow, though — Larry said in all innocence — he didn't know exactly where it would go. Ed's wife thought it might do for their lake house, but Al's wife had mentioned it might look good in their rec room and Larry's own spouse had already decided it should go to their oldest daughter's apartment.

At that Flora had given Rebecca a significant look, which Rebecca refused to acknowledge. Flora thought it was because the younger woman did not like admitting she was right; actually, Rebecca was much too close to giggling than was seemly in a staid antique dealer.

An uncomfortable antique dealer. "You can't do that, Mrs. Melkiot! We only have Larry Tyler's word about this."

"And who should know better about his brother's problems?"

"I'm going to call Ashdown."

"Larry Tyler said he would do that. Why should we give him leads we've found? He's not helping us."

"This is not a game, Mrs. Melkiot."

Flora's face tightened. "No, it's not. It's murder, and I can't see that anyone is doing anything to solve it except me. And maybe you. A little. Maybe."

"The police —"

"Aren't doing diddly-squat. That dumb detective is in such a swivet about Miss Alicia disappearing, as if she hasn't left town every Tuesday and Wednesday since Moses was a babe."

"Miss Alicia left town after being cautioned not to?" Rebecca stared in astonishment. "But that's stupid. That's almost an admission of guilt!"

Flora frowned. "As if Miss Alicia would commit a murder! Ridiculous! No one knows for sure what she does when she goes away, but surely she has a right to her privacy."

"She could be charged with obstruction of an investigation, at the very least. Running like that after being cautioned to stay in town —"

Miss Alicia Carruthers was a force, an icon, in the Dallas business scene, but that didn't automatically put her above suspicion. In fact, Rebecca could appreciate that a single woman making the mark on the business world Miss Alicia did, when she did, had to have a very strong and forceful if not ruthless character.

Strong enough to murder a little old lady with drain cleaner? she wondered.

"Oh, pooh! A person has a right to continue her life. It's not like she was arrested or anything. She'll be back tonight, just like always."

"But where does she go? What does she do?"

Flora shrugged. "I don't know. Nobody does. She's just done it for donkeys' years, and that stupid detective is making a big thing about it and forgetting about the rest of the case while he does it!"

"Oh, I doubt —"

"Well, I don't, and I for one don't intend to give up. Maybe you're used to seeing people get killed in front of your very eyes, but I'm not. I don't like it. I find it very frightening."

Rebecca was silent for a moment, any thoughts of Miss Alicia's mysterious behavior blotted out by memories of a rain-slick street and spitting death, of pain and Jesse falling bonelessly, dead before he hit the ground. No, you never got used to seeing anyone get killed in front of you. Never.

"Do you see any connection between Skeeter's gambling and his mother's death?" Rebecca asked after a minute, her voice carefully controlled.

"Aren't mobsters supposed to teach losers a lesson when they welsh on a bet?" Flora asked. She was always a gracious winner. "What better way to get a man's attention than to kill his mother?"

"Or to make him so disgusted — or scared — he goes underground. Besides, if he didn't have money to pay, why would . . . ? Oh. They thought he would have an inheritance. But that doesn't work. If they gambled big enough with him for him to lose the kind of money that would call for such a drastic step, don't you think they

265

would have investigated him first and found out about his financial situation?"

"He could have lied to them," Flora said, but she didn't sound convinced.

"Nice theory, but not logical enough. Too many holes. You might write it as a TV movie, though."

For one moment Flora actively considered it. Considering the quality of television today, writing a decent movie should be child's play. She knew she could do it easily if she just put her mind to it, but she really didn't have the time.

"No," she said at last, killing Rebecca's almost-born hopes of deflecting this juggernaut. "There's too much real-life stuff going on to be worrying about fiction. What we need to do is talk to Skeeter."

"What makes you think he'll talk to us? We're not official. And how do we find him?"

"But we are dear friends of his late mother." Flora gave a synthetic smile. "What should be more natural than we should go to her funeral and convey our sympathies to her sons?"

Rebecca's mouth fell open.

Ashdown looked dispiritedly at the piles of paper in front of him. Notes. Interview

266

results. Anonymous tips — God, what a morass it was! Somewhere there were people truly convinced that the Olympus House was the door to the Devil's Kingdom through which Satan was sending his dark armies, that it was the hub of a totalitarian group dedicated to taking over the world, that it harbored a kinky sex organization —

Well, considering some of the things he had discovered, Ashdown decided that last part wasn't too outrageous. If half the things were going on that people said were, this was one supremely kinky place in spite of its mantle of respectability. He wondered how much of that was truth and how much was fantasy.

His phone rang.

"Detective? This is Ginny Wylde."

One thing, he decided as soon as he answered: at least half of what he had heard about Ginny Wylde had to be true. The details were too identical, the stories too widespread.

"Yes, Mrs. Wylde. How can I help you?"

"I'd like to talk to you, Detective. Alone. There are things I need to tell you . . . without my husband present."

Come into my parlor, said the spider to the fly . . .

"Certainly, Mrs. Wylde. Come right down

to Conference Room A. That's where we're set up."

There was a slight intake of breath over the phone. "Oh, no, please. That's too public. What I have to tell you is . . . private. Could you come up here?"

"It's nearly four, Mrs. Wylde. Won't your husband be home in a little while?" Ashdown knew the offices for *Wylde Times* were on Oak Lawn, only half a dozen blocks away, half a dozen blocks that Waldo insisted on being chauffeured morning and evening.

"Not tonight. The magazine goes to press tomorrow. He always works late the night before printing. Can you please come up here? Please?"

Ashdown was silent a moment. He was a modest man, but an honest one, and knew he was not considered bad looking. He had also seen the acquisitive flicker in the merry Mrs. Wylde's eyes that morning. Hers was a well-known type, the sort who liked to have lots of scalps hanging from her belt. For some reason, some women found policemen particularly attractive.

He was a big boy. He could defend himself.

"I'll be there, Mrs. Wylde. Say in twenty minutes?"

Ginny Wylde hung up the phone and literally licked her lips. The hunt was on again and every atom in her body tingled. This time it would be different; policemen were big and strong and rough. There wouldn't be any of that stupid romantic crap she'd had to go through with Roland — no love notes, no secret signals, no sappy calls every twenty minutes.

A policeman would be a real man, a strong man. She wondered if he might hit her. The thought gave her a delicious thrill.

The phone rang again and she grabbed it automatically, holding her breath. What if something had happened and he couldn't come? What if they solved the stupid case before she got what she wanted? How could she make sure she would see him then?

"Hello?"

"Ginny? Darling, are you alone?"

Inwardly, Ginny swore. "Hello, Roland."

"I know Waldo's at work, so I can come over. We've got to talk, darling. I've been making plans."

She found the abjection in his voice disgusting. "We agreed we wouldn't see each other anymore, Roland."

There was the sound of an indrawn breath on the other end of the line. "I know you had to say that because Waldo was listening in this morning, darling, but you don't have to worry anymore. I've got everything taken care of. All you have to do is bring your passport and a few things for overnight."

"Why?"

"I've made reservations for us tonight. We can be in Rio by morning."

"Are you still talking about us running away together?" Ginny tried to keep the disgust out of her voice. The idea of Rio was interesting — Carnival, the jewelry stores — but only for a few days, and never with Roland Orwell. God, how had Isabel stood twenty years with the man?

"Yes, darling. It can be done. All I have to do is pick up the money downstairs and then we can leave and be together always."

Ginny was fidgeting. Time was passing, and she had to get ready for Detective Ashdown.

"Roland, I don't want to," she said with surprising brutality. "It's over. We had a fling. We're both married to other people. That's it. Go back to Isabel if she'll still have you. I don't want to see you again, and I don't want you to call me again. Is that clear?"

She didn't wait for an answer, but slammed the receiver down into the cradle. The phone rang again almost instantly and kept ringing, but she paid no attention. If she had to, she'd unplug the stupid thing before the detective got here. Why couldn't the man understand simple English? Their affair was over!

What had she ever seen in him, anyway? Probably just because there hadn't been anyone else of interest when she was interested. Plus, he was rich. She fingered the diamond tennis bracelet he had given her, one so big it looked like those cheap CZs. They were diamonds, though, and good ones; she had checked. There was something so attractive about money, even when it came attached to a big doofus like Roland Orwell.

When the bell rang exactly twenty minutes later, Ginny was ready, as carefully prepared as a leading lady on opening night. She had chosen a simple caftan woven of a dark blue silk so fine that it seemed to float around her while it gave tantalizing hints of the body beneath. Very elegant, very classy. Ginny knew instinctively the cheap blatant seduction she had used with Roland wouldn't work with Detective John Ashdown. He mightn't be rich, but he had a class Roland Orwell would never obtain.

She had brushed her hair until it had fluffed around her head in a flattering corona, loosening up some of the rigidity

Ramon had put into her new cut. Pity she hadn't been able to persuade him to make her blonde today; pale, sunlight colored hair would go very well with this caftan. She applied very little lipstick, but paid careful attention to her eyes, smudging the liner and applying a dark blue mascara.

She had also unplugged all the telephones.

"How kind of you to come up, Detective Ashdown," she purred, closing and locking the door behind him.

He was as good-looking as she remembered — not in a flashy, movie star way, but solid and well put together and very attractive. She licked her lips.

"Good evening, Mrs. Wylde." Ashdown walked into the living room. This morning he had barely noticed its opulence; now it seemed to leap out at him. Everything seemed oversized, from the yards of Oriental carpet to the deep leather sofas. "I hope you're feeling better."

Ginny gave a tremulous smile. He was probably a protective type. "I am, but I don't think I'll ever get over it. Seeing that poor woman . . . Won't you have a seat?"

She had gestured toward the smaller of the two sofas. A fully outfitted drinks tray sat on the coffee table in front of it. Ashdown thanked her and sat in the lone freestanding chair.

"Can I offer you something to drink?"

Ashdown shook his head. "Sorry, not while I'm on duty. You said there was something you wanted to tell me?"

Ginny fixed herself a vodka tonic, taking her time to do so. "Can't I even interest you in a soft drink? Or something to eat?"

Ashdown shook his head again. "No, thank you. Now what were you going to tell me?" He whipped out his notebook and pen and sat, ready.

Inwardly Ginny sighed. Okay, he was going to be difficult. Going after easy conquests like the parking attendants and Roland Orwell had spoiled her. She was going to have to work for this one, but that would make her triumph sweeter than ever.

"I don't know if you know this or not, but Roland and I were having a . . . fling." Ginny fluttered her eyelashes downward, the very picture of maidenly modesty confessing.

"I had heard that, yes."

"It's not what you think. I thought he was a lonely man who needed a friend." One look at Ashdown's face convinced Ginny that line wasn't going anywhere. "He wasn't. He — he was obsessed with me. Is obsessed with me."

"He says the two of you are in love."

"He is. I'm not. Like I said, it was just a fling."

"He said you two were going to be married."

"In his dreams! He seems to forget that we are both married to other people."

"And you have no intention of leaving Mr. Wylde?"

"Waldo and I have a very comfortable marriage, Detective Ashdown." She raised her eyes shyly, peering through her lashes. "We each have our dreams to follow, and we don't get into each other's way. Waldo is very understanding about my activities."

Ashdown was silent for a moment. "He knew about Orwell?"

Ginny nodded.

"Very liberal indeed. What does your husband say about him?"

Ginny shrugged. "Nothing. I'm through with Roland, though. He's becoming much too possessive. He keeps calling here even though I've told him we shouldn't see each other anymore. He just can't understand that it's over."

"You've told him it's over?"

"Several times. He just keeps talking about how he's going to carry me away to some foreign land. I'm frightened, Detective Ashdown. He's getting more and more irrational every time he calls." Ginny blinked convincingly and hid her face in her hands.

"Have you told your husband about this?"

"No. Waldo has so many cares, I don't want to add to them."

"He would protect you, though."

Ginny gave a helpless little sob. "I guess so. Oh, Detective, I'm so afraid! Can't you help me?" She reached out beseechingly and took his hand. "I need someone strong, like you. Can't you help me?"

"I would suggest that if you are that afraid, you should swear out a restraining order against Orwell. That way if he bothers you again, he can be arrested."

"That won't do any good! Roland doesn't obey the law, he thinks he's above it. Please . . ." Without letting go of his hand, Ginny stood and moved next to the over-stuffed arm of the chair. She had thought about balancing there, but believed he would regard it as too forward too soon. Even standing, she was perfectly positioned for Ashdown to pull her down into his arms.

Gently but remorselessly, the detective detached his hand from her stranglehold. "If you are afraid that you are in danger, I can post a uniformed officer outside your door tonight."

"Can't you stay? I'd feel so much safer with you . . ." Ginny purred, even as she seethed inwardly. Not a response at all; was the guy gay? She hadn't expected him to jump into bed with her this minute — though that would have been nice — but there had been no answering flash, no hint of response. He was acting as if he didn't even know she was female!

"I'm afraid not," Ashdown replied politely. "Shall I send for the officer?"

Ginny released his hand and hopped up, flouncing across the room. She wasn't going to get anywhere today. Landing Detective Ashdown was going to take some work. The challenge was irresistible.

"No, Waldo will be home before long, and I can ask Security to send someone up. Thank you for coming, Detective. Don't let me keep you."

Ashdown put away his notebook and stood up. Mrs. Wylde was already at the door, tapping her foot. She had sounded snippy and looked very unhappy. As he said the proper thanks and gave the proper cautions, Ashdown didn't care that she slammed the door behind him, cutting off his final words.

Talk about swimming with the sharks! Or maybe the piranhas would be a better analogy. Either way, Ashdown felt as if he had escaped a tightening snare. Ashdown pushed the elevator down button. Now he could go home, relax a little, then go out for a good meal. He deserved it. Nothing could change his plans.

The elevator doors whooshed open to reveal the travel-weary form of Miss Alicia Carruthers.

CHAPTER SEVENTEEN

"I believe we need to talk, Miss Carruthers."

Carrying a small, battered overnight case, Miss Alicia walked wearily around him to her front door. "Must it be now, Detective? I am very tired."

"I'm afraid so, Miss Carruthers."

She had her key in her hand. Ashdown watched carefully, half expecting her to jump inside and slam the door. He thought she seemed a little old for such shenanigans, but he wouldn't have thought she would leave town when requested to stay, either.

"Very well. Come in." She stepped into the darkened apartment and left the door open. In a moment the room blossomed with faint light and Ashdown, half-amused at his instinctual reluctance to go into a darkened room, followed her.

The room was nice, nicer than anything he'd ever owned, but it didn't feel right.

Ashdown sat in the chair Miss Alicia indicated even as she went toward the kitchen, claiming she needed a drink and would be just a moment. Somehow Ashdown had expected a gazillionaire like Miss Alicia, who owned a penthouse in the Olympus House and had real-estate offices all over, to have a fancier home.

That was it. This place was plain. Common. He'd seen the condos of most of the other people in the Olympus House, and they ranged from modern showy to museum. This place was nice, sort of untouched, as if no one really lived here, and commonplace.

Sort of like Laura Tyler's apartment.

Were there any other connections between the two women? He'd have to start digging deeper.

He could hear rattlings and an ominous hiss in the kitchen, then Miss Alicia appeared bearing a tray. He jumped to help her with it, but she refused, putting it on the coffee table, then sat heavily with a sigh. She looked, Ashdown thought, every minute of her age and then some.

"I hope you will join me in some tea, Detective. It is a pleasurable restorative."

At least he wasn't going to have to fend her off like he had Ginny Wylde; at least, he hoped not!

"I would appreciate a cup of tea."

Miss Alicia poured with more efficiency than grace. "A sentiment shared by few of your generation. Or your profession. How can I help you, Detective?"

Straight to the point; Ashdown appreciated that, too.

"Why did you leave town?"

"I am always gone on Tuesday and Wednesday," she replied unapologetically. "There are any number of people who can tell you that."

"And they did. What I want to know is why you left when you were cautioned to stay in town."

Miss Alicia sipped at her tea and savored it. "I have obligations," she said at last. "I did not commit that horrible crime, I know nothing about it that I haven't already told you, and I assure you that where I went and what I did have nothing to do with it."

Ashdown believed her. If she had really wanted to run, she could have been in Uzbekistan or anyplace else by now. That didn't negate the fact that she had gone against a direct order in an active investigation.

"I could charge you, you know."

Her composed expression didn't flicker —

innocence, fatigue, or iron will? Ashdown would have bet on a combination of all three.

"With what?"

"Obstructing a criminal investigation."

"You could. It would make you look like an idiot, but you most certainly could. I am not in any way involved in your crime except as an unwilling witness, and I have a great number of friends in this town who will be more than happy to vouch for me."

Vouch and any number of other things. Ashdown could just imagine the circus that would ensue if he brought in Miss Alicia Carruthers. He'd be lucky to get out of it with a whole skin, let alone any kind of career.

"Where did you go, Miss Carruthers?"

"That is none of your business, Detective. As I have told you, I have followed the same routine for years, and none of my actions have anything to do with your investigation. Now if you are finished with your tea, I am very tired and tomorrow is a workday. Please either arrest me or go away." The old lady stood, commanding in spite of her years.

Ashdown waited a moment, then drained his cup and put it on the tray. "Don't leave town, will you, Miss Carruthers?"

"Not until next Tuesday," she replied.

Gus was still in the conference room, doggedly writing up the last of his notes.

"Everyone gone?" Ashdown asked. Silly question; they were alone, and even the coffee bar was unplugged.

"Yeah, I sent them on. Start up again tomorrow morning. If there's anything to start up on. We're spinning our wheels here."

"Anything?"

"Nope, unless you count the fact that some of the kitchen help peddle a little grass on the side, or that a woman on the eleventh floor has a brother who's a sex offender against little old ladies, but he's safely locked up in Kentucky. I spoke to his warden myself."

"That's all?"

"I've talked to all the employees, the service people, even the pool company. Nobody knows nothing. I've uncovered enough motive, means, and opportunity for half of this damned building to do away with the other half, but I have not found one single person — not one! — who had anything against Laura Tyler. I even had the devil of a time finding anyone who had ever even heard of her, let alone met her."

Ashdown groaned and stretched. "So the answers aren't here. They've got to be in her past."

"Sounds logical, but . . ."

Ashdown groaned again. With Gus, there was always a "but." Worse, he was usually right.

"If it was someone from her past, how did they get into the salon?"

"I don't know. We know the glasses were washed at night; we know that unless Madame Norina was there, the place was locked; we know that no one admits to seeing anyone going near the glasses during the jewel class. So that means it has to be one of the staff. Who has keys?"

Gus grunted. "Who doesn't? They all but leave them hanging on a nail down in the kitchen."

"Is there only one master key?" Ashdown asked with a foul taste in his mouth. "Does the key that opens the public rooms also open the individual condos?"

"Nope. The Olympus House rooms — this room, the kitchens, and everything has one key. There are individual keys for the salon, for the hairdresser's and the gym. There's another master key for the residences; the mechanical chief has it. There's

283

only one, and he guards it with his life —
keeps it on him at all times."

"So he thinks," Ashdown muttered. How
had Flora Melkiot gotten a copy of that key?
She was about as unlikely a murderer as he
could imagine, but he had seen stranger
things.

But at the moment she was the best
suspect he had.

"Well," Gus said, heaving his bulk up out
of the chair. "If it's all right with you, I'm
heading out."

"Yeah, fine. See you in the morning," Ashdown answered abstractedly.

Flora Melkiot was definitely in the spot-
light. She had a master key. She was meddling in the case, saying she wanted it
solved, but was she really just muddying the
waters? And she had dragged that Cloudwebb woman into it. Neat strategy; the
Cloudwebb woman had to be innocent —
he would bet his life on that — but by putting the two of them together, Melkiot the
Meddler had given herself a shield. Any
policeman would have to be very, very sure
of himself before accusing the Deputy
Chief's sister.

The telephone rang, slicing through his
melancholy thoughts.

"Ashdown."

"Detective Ashdown, you're the one I was looking for. This is Larry Tyler."

The dead woman's son. What else could happen?

"Yes, Mr. Tyler. What can I do for you?"

"I talked to my mother's friend Flora Melkiot today, and she said I should talk to you. There's something about my little brother and the Olympus House I think you should know."

Esther had locked up and gone by the time Rebecca got back to the shop. She parked her car in the shed behind the old house, then — after checking the area — walked across the roughly paved parking area and climbed the back steps to the second floor. After locking the door behind her, she shut off the insistent beep of the alarm, then reset it for *Stay.*

Silly precautions, perhaps, but there were lots of people she had arrested who might like to even a long-standing personal score, to say nothing of those who might want to rob the shop. In spite of a burst of urban renewal, this neighborhood was quiet and lonely at night.

And Frank Titus was still alive somewhere.

As a cripple, she would be an easy target.

Rebecca stopped for a moment, her hand

still on the light switch, and stared at the cane in her hand.

Cripple?

Was that what she was?

Suddenly the hateful, totally non-PC word that had been rooted so deeply in her psyche since That Day felt alien and uncomfortable. She limped, yes; she would probably limp some for the rest of her life. Did that make her a cripple?

Her leg was scarred; there was nothing she could do about that. It was also weaker than her good leg, but was that totally because of her injury or because she had stopped doing her therapy when she had gotten far enough along to walk as well as she thought she should?

Was that what Esther had been trying to tell her all those months they had battled about the benefits of therapy?

I was interested in walking, Rebecca thought with wonder. *Esther was talking about living.*

Bemused by the revelation, Rebecca realized she was holding both the light switch and the cane as if they had been lifelines. The cane was a tool, nothing more, not a symbol of what she was. If she could learn to do without it — no, more than that. If she could learn not to need it at all . . .

She wondered if it were too late for her to go back to physical therapy. This time she would actually do the exercises like she was supposed to.

It would probably cost the earth and a half, but if it worked . . .

If it worked, it would be worth it. Any improvement would be worth it.

And I won't tell Esther, she decided. *At least not until I know I can do something with this.*

But I am going to try.

I am.

I can do it.

I can't do it.

Isabel Orwell took another drink, but the glass was empty. She frowned. Hadn't she just refilled it? Owlishly she looked around the floor. It must have spilled, but she didn't know where. She'd get another one in a minute, and this time she'd put it in a decent-sized glass. The old-fashioned glass — one of the pretty, green and gold trimmed set that Roland liked so much — was just too small.

Isabel took another look at the glass. Roland had given her the set for some occasion, as usual giving her something that he really wanted for a gift.

She flung the glass against the far wall and

listened to it shatter with satisfaction. Then she giggled. That made two glasses she had thrown in her whole life, both in less than a week. First the crystal goblet at that whore Ginny Wylde, and now one of Roland's favorites. Pity he hadn't been here.

With difficulty Isabel turned her attention back to the closet. Roland's closet. The mirrored fronts of their two closets covered one entire wall of the master bedroom. It was one of the reasons Roland had decided to buy the place, so he could watch them bouncing around in bed.

Isabel wished she had smashed the glass against the mirrors. Maybe one of them would have broken.

And she would have to clean up the mess, since that bastard had fired Lina, and there was no way he would spring for a cleaning woman. Isabel snarled at the memory.

She could do it.

She would do it.

Staggering forward on unsteady feet, she slammed his side of the closet open with a force that almost knocked the mirrored panel off its tracks.

Roland might not live here anymore, but he certainly had left a lot of clothes behind. The enormous walk-in closet was almost full. *He sure was a clotheshorse, with nothing very impressive to hang the expensive gar- ments he liked on,* Isabel thought, then giggled again.

She opened one of the built-in drawers. He hadn't taken any pajamas with him. Every silky, monogrammed pair was still there. Of course, he probably wouldn't be wearing any pajamas, not with Miss Hot Pants Bitch writhing around in his bed. He'd make sure there were lots of mirrors around there, too.

Isabel grabbed every pair and threw them on the floor, then stomped on them for pure childish pleasure. Then she started ripping every garment out of his closet and throwing them on the pile. That horrible Hawaiian shirt with all the big leaves and flowers that he never wore. All his shirts, each in a subtly different tone of gray, each starched to perfection. His suits. His slacks and sport coats.

From there she went back to the drawers, flinging out socks and undershorts and handkerchiefs and t-shirts. The pile was now almost up to her hips.

What was she going to do with all this stuff? Pity the living room fireplace was just gas; she would love to burn them all. Maybe she could just throw them off the bal- cony . . .

No, because then Roland would make a fuss. And probably get his stuff back. She wanted to make sure he never got anything. He wanted that slut Ginny Wylde, so let him have her . . . and not one other thing. She was his wife, and she had to look out for their two daughters.

God, when the girls found out! Isabel gave a cry of pain. They loved their father, looked up to him. This would shatter them.

Maybe she should kill Roland and Ginny. That would make her a widow. People respected widows. Somehow being a widow sounded so much nicer than being a cast-off wife.

She needed to think. She needed another drink so she could think. This time she'd just bring in the bottle and not bother with any of those dinky glasses.

Yawning, Isabel sank down on the bed. She'd just rest a minute before getting her drink. Clearing out more than half of her life was exhausting work.

Less than a minute later she was asleep.

Eleanor Anthony lay still in the dark, listening to the suddenly sweet music of her husband's snores.

What was she going to do? Eddie had rescued her once, but she would not allow him to put himself in danger because of her again. His entire family would come down on him if they even suspected and cart him off like a package. They had never liked her. They would love to have something to hold over Eddie to bring him back into their stifling family fold.

Tomorrow she had to do something.

First she would go to the bank. Her private account, the one not even Eddie knew about, was of good size. She could clear that out and no one would be the wiser. That would give her safety and mobility.

Then she would have to vanish, but to where? And as whom? She didn't know anyone in Dallas who could create a good fake identity, so that meant traveling without a paper trail until she found someone she could trust. And how much did things like that cost nowadays? Suddenly the amount she had so painstakingly squirreled away against such an eventuality seemed frighteningly puny.

Well, whatever it was, it had to be done. She could treat herself to one, maybe two more days. Then she would have to go.

Dying couldn't hurt any less.

Eleanor swallowed. It was an option.

CHAPTER EIGHTEEN

Rebecca's good intentions lasted through the night, and she awoke with the desire to test herself still strong. She rolled out of bed before the alarm rang and took a deep breath, then stretched like a cat. The exercises — like most things one hates — were still fresh in her mind. Stretch . . . stretch . . . foot just so . . . stretch . . .

Pain washed over her, even if she moved gently. After several more tries, her face dripping with sweat, her teeth clenched, Rebecca stopped, and fell on the bed, trying to rub the pain away.

What a fool she had been, calling the physical therapist last night! She'd been gone, of course, but Rebecca had left a message. Now she'd have to deal with embarrassment as well as a throbbing leg when the girl called. She'd urge Rebecca to come back to therapy and give painstakingly detailed images of what she could achieve if she'd just try.

Rebecca knew now she had lost whatever chance she'd had, if she'd ever had a chance to be normal again, thrown it away after leaving the hospital. She was going to be a cripple with a cane for the rest of her life, useless, an object of pity.

The picture of her future fate was so black it pulled Rebecca around. She had done okay so far, hadn't she? Or maybe Esther had made her what she was now. Rebecca had no illusions that she would even have survived without Esther's constant attention.

She just wasn't sure that Esther had done her a favor.

Rebecca pulled herself to her feet, shuddering at how her leg felt when she put weight on it, and — reaching for her cane — went in search of coffee.

Ever since her husband had died, Larraine Clark had been terrified. Of course, before his death she was a timid, shy, apprehensive woman, convinced that every shadow held numberless villains intent on ravishing her money or her person. Her late husband, Bill, had been less than sympathetic, and his crushing sarcasm had helped hold her terrors in check.

Now that Bill was gone, though, Larraine just knew that Someone Was Out to Get Her. Over time she drove less and less (carjackers), refused to allow any serviceperson into her apartment unless she had several friends with her (rapists), ordered more and more of her groceries over the telephone instead of going to the store (robbers), and refused categorically to travel (terrorists). In spite of anything her friends or children could do, her world shrank pretty much to the confines of the Olympus House. There she felt safe.

Or she had, until that woman had been murdered just last Monday. If "they" could get to that woman in the theoretical sanctuary of the Olympus House, "they" could get to her. She barely had left her apartment since hearing of the incident. When her insensitive daughter had refused to drive down from Plano to bring her mail up from the basement mailroom and all her friends were suddenly busy, Larraine had finally convinced herself that it was perfectly safe for her to go down alone. It looked like she would have to if she were ever to get her accumulated mail. If she were raped or murdered on the way, it would serve her selfish child right! It would also be an object lesson to those unsympathetic biddies she had once counted as friends who had told her flatly to quit being such an idiot and go on by herself.

Her door was not too far from the elevator, and she waited until the hallway was deserted before venturing out. She wasn't too sure about getting into an empty elevator — no telling who could get in on another floor — but at this early hour there were very few people about.

By the time the elevator reached the first basement where the mailroom was located, Larraine was feeling quite proud of herself. She wasn't a scaredy-cat. There was nothing to be afraid of.

Halfway down the hall there was a large gray lump on the floor. Carpet? Padding? Just abandoned there? Larraine's lip curled with righteous distaste. Really! The standards at the Olympus House were decreasing every day!

Then the lump moaned and reached for her and Larraine began to scream.

C. Edward Anthony was a gentle soul, respectful of his fellow man and kindly to a fault. It was that much more surprising, then, when he practically giggled with glee at the news.

Already startled by his sudden and unexpected return so soon after breakfast, Eleanor looked blankly at her husband. She was still at the table, nursing a last cup of coffee before exercise class and going over her plans again. "Waldo Wylde? He was attacked here, in this building?"

"Down in the hallway to the mailroom."

Eleanor took a deep breath and put down her coffee cup so it wouldn't shake. "How did you find out?"

"The doorman. Some woman from the eighth floor found him. Poor thing! She was so upset they had to call a doctor for her. Went into complete hysterics. According to the doorman, she kept raving about the carpet trying to rape her."

"What?"

Eddie brought in a fresh cup and handed it to his wife. It took all of Eleanor's self-control to pour without sending coffee splashing everywhere.

"That's what he said. Apparently the woman was completely off her rocker." Eddie grinned. "Something of a recluse, from what I hear."

"So what happened to Wylde?"

"According to the doorman, who got it from the paramedics, someone coshed him on the head, then apparently kicked the shit out of him."

Eleanor's eyes widened. Her husband never swore, and she had never seen him delight in the misfortunes of another, even a human slug like Waldo Wylde. It alarmed her no end.

"Do they have any idea of who did it?"

Eddie's grin died. "No. And I hope they never do."

"Eddie!"

"I'm not going to be hypocritical, Eleanor. That disgusting excuse for a man deserves whatever he gets for all the misery he's caused. You don't think we're the only people he's leaning on, do you?"

"We aren't?"

"No. From what I've learned, there's half a dozen people in this building alone who are being squashed under his thumb. The man's a menace."

"Is he going to die?"

"Probably not." C. Edward Anthony scowled. "Dammit."

It couldn't be happening.

"What?"

The man on the telephone repeated himself, speaking very slowly so there would be no chance of her misunderstanding.

As if she could misunderstand.

Madame hung up the phone while he was

still talking. She felt as if she had been struck by something large and heavy — a car, or maybe a truck.

Noon.

They were coming for payment at noon.

Dear God, what was she going to do?

It had been such a sure thing! Every statistic, every scrap of gossip said that Nile Naiad would win in a walk. She should have made more than enough to settle all her debts and have a nice chunk of seed money to start her expansion.

Who could have thought the stupid horse would stumble and fall only yards from the finish line?

Dammit, why couldn't she have just one little bit of good luck for a change?

Now not only was every penny she possessed gone, she was in debt for ten, maybe twenty times that amount. And now no one in town would grant her any credit. She probably couldn't even put down a two-dollar bet without handing over the cash.

Madame took a deep breath and tried to force down the terror clawing its way up her throat. If she ever let it loose, she'd start screaming and not be able to stop. She had been on the edge of panic ever since the night before, when she had heard of Nile Naiad's fate.

Panic was not the way. She had to think. She had to get money, and quickly. Vegas Charlie's bunch wouldn't wait. Noon. She just had until noon to get together a small fortune.

Where could she get that much money? God, it made what she owed the bank look like chump change.

Rising, she walked through the salon. The police had told her only late the previous evening that she could start using it again. Only the water cooler and the jewel glasses were missing. She had spent most of the night scrubbing and cleaning, making sure everything was fresh and clean and every mark of chalk or fingerprint dust was gone, scrubbing as if she could wash away the threat of Vegas Charlie.

This salon was a dream, her dream, the dream she had cherished for many long, stark years. It was just as she had wanted it — her life's work. And she was going to lose it. One way or another. There was no way she could come up with the kind of money Vegas Charlie was going to demand.

It was over. The only hope she had was to disappear.

The idea of leaving the salon grieved her more than any of the husbands with whom she had parted ways.

Oh, why couldn't she have had just a little bit of good luck, just once in her life? Would it have upset the world just to have that one horse win that one race? Just that one race . . .

Someone rattled the door, which she had so carefully locked, and Madame's heart jumped within her ample bosom. Surely it couldn't be Vegas Charlie's boys yet.

More viscerally, panic began to rise. The door wouldn't hold them out, and there was no other exit. She was trapped.

"Madame? Are you in there?"

Madame gave a gusty sigh of relief. Ginny Wylde. There was no mistaking that shrill, whiny voice.

Perhaps . . .

Just perhaps . . .

"Coming, my angels! Coming!"

Pasting a smile on her face, she threw the door open.

John Ashdown had not slept well. He'd had nightmares of Ginny Wylde chasing him while Miss Alicia kept moving the solution to Laura Tyler's murder from room to room. He had waked unrested and more than a little cranky.

His mood had not been improved by a request to see Deputy Chief Charles Cloudwebb first thing in the morning.

He had met the Deputy Chief a couple of times before, primarily at official functions, and been vaguely impressed with him. Now, sitting across his large, clean desk (so different from his own) Ashdown could see the striking resemblance to his sister.

"I hear," Cloudwebb said in an eerie echo to Ashdown's thoughts, "that you have met my sister."

"Yes. A most memorable lady."

"That's one of the things you could call Becky, I guess. Has she given you any trouble?"

After digesting the incongruity of anyone calling Rebecca Cloudwebb "Becky," Ashdown thought a moment. Being a sort of nosy pest wasn't truly trouble; were the circumstances reversed, he would be curious too. "Not really. Did she complain to you about how I treated her?"

Cloudwebb chuckled. What were strong facial features in his sister were merely pleasing in him. "No, I haven't heard a word from her on the subject and, believe me, if she were really unhappy, I would have."

Ashdown gave an inward sigh of relief. You could never tell with ex-officers. Or women. Or anybody, for that matter.

"No, someone noticed her name in the

301

report and mentioned it to me. When you have a name like ours, it's hard to mistake. And for the record, she should be treated like any other witness, as should I or anyone else. No favoritism."

Ashdown waited.

"I don't want to horn in on your case," Cloudwebb said after a pause that was a heartbeat too long, "but I'm just curious as to how it's going."

Yeah, Ashdown thought, *and I'm going to take up tatting.* But he would play the game. "At the moment it isn't. We're still talking to people in Garland and business associates of Laura Tyler's late husband. I've got enough motive and opportunity for half the residents of the Olympus House to wipe out the other half, but the only real thing I've learned is that no one had any reason to harm Laura Tyler. She was an older suburban widow who had always dreamed of moving in society circles, so she bought a condo, and a couple of days later she's dead. Before that she led a simple and blameless life as the wife of a plumbing contractor."

Cloudwebb did not look happy. He made a sort of gurgling noise deep in his throat.

Deciding he had made the man wait long enough, Ashdown went on. "We have uncovered one lead that looks interesting. Her

302

youngest son is a chronic gambler and he stays in deep. We also believe that the doorman at the Olympus House — Chuck Jernigan — is deeply involved in organized gambling and might be using the place as a cover."

"He is," Cloudwebb said simply.

"You knew about this?"

"We suspected."

"And you didn't tell us?"

Cloudwebb shrugged. "This is part of a longtime ongoing investigation by Vice. The FBI is interested, too."

Ashdown gave a low whistle. "The Feebs? Why weren't we informed?"

"Need to know. And we didn't think it linked with your case."

"But you've been reading the file."

"Right now we're interested in anything to do with the Olympus House. There's a lot going on there."

Ashdown shifted in his chair. "Any time there's that much money in that small a space, you know there's going to be a lot going on."

Deputy Chief Cloudwebb laughed.

"Anything," Ashdown went on, "that I should know about besides some of the kitchen boys supplying a little grass?"

Cloudwebb half-smiled at that. "You have

been digging."

"It's my job."

"Well, then, I might as well tell you that the hairdresser has a side scam going too."

"Ramon?" Ashdown was not really surprised. He hadn't like the man. Too flamboyant and oily for his taste. "What?"

"He's running a sort of escort service on the side, for some of the lonely ladies in the Olympus House."

"Escort? Or stud?" Ashdown could not help asking, and both men laughed. Ashdown felt a small sense of triumph; not even the nosy Flora Melkiot had sniffed this out. Or, he added scrupulously, if she had, she hadn't mentioned anything about it. Was she a customer? The idea made him shudder.

"We've left the grass and toy-boy scams alone. They're small potatoes and basically consensual and we can get them any time we want. What we don't want is anyone upset at the Olympus House until we get this gambling thing wrapped up. It's big and it's mean and it's widespread. The Olympus House is only a small part of it."

"You're talking about out-of-state influences?"

Cloudwebb nodded. "That's why we're holding off. We could have picked up Jernigan weeks ago, but we want to backtrack from him to the big boys."

"Any progress?"

"Yes, but you don't need to know that."

"What about the Tyler murder? Is it connected?"

"Not that we can tell."

"So what are you telling me?"

"Be careful. Solve your case, but don't upset our applecart doing so."

Ashdown was tempted to ask which case held priority, but he knew. One obscure woman's death against the incursion of a major out-of-state gambling family that could cause no end of havoc . . . the answer was obvious, as much as he hated it.

His cell shrilled, breaking the thickening silence. He answered, listened, then snapped the little phone shut with more force than necessary.

"Then you're going to be interested in this," he told his superior. "Looks like Waldo Wylde could have been right when he said that the killer might have been targeting his wife instead of Laura Tyler. Someone has just beaten him half to death in the Olympus House."

Drat! She had overslept!

Disregarding the thunder in her head and

the foul-tasting cottony stuff that filled her mouth, Isabel flung herself from bed. Not bothering to shower, she yanked on a leotard and tights from the drawer, only to swear as her carefully manicured nail poked through the leotard. This would happen to her on the day she was late! No way could she go to class in something with a hole in it! Cursing her luck, Roland, and life in general, she grabbed another leotard at random and slithered into it.

She hoped her head wouldn't fall off.

Madame would be angry. She didn't like anyone to come in after a class had begun.

Well, tough! It was bad enough her life was falling apart and she felt as if ten thousand devils were dancing in her head; she wasn't going to become a fat pig. There hadn't been any classes on Tuesday and she had missed Wednesday's session. No way was she going to miss today. She brushed her hair back and clipped on a headband. There wasn't time for anything else. Grabbing her cover-up, Isabel ran, every step jarring her fragile head. Somehow that was Roland's fault, too.

Even so, she was late, but Madame Norina had not yet locked the door. Apparently everyone was still shaken.

"You are late," Madame said needlessly.

"We have already begun our stretches."

"I'm sorry, Madame."

No matter what happened, one always had to apologize to Madame. Never the other way around.

Isabel tossed her cover-up into a chair — another infraction; it should have been neatly hung on the corner rack, but somehow such niceties didn't seem all that important anymore — and stepped into place. She began to stretch, but no one else did. A titter of genteelly subdued laughter skittered around the room.

"What?"

"A most unusual outfit, I must say." Ginny Wylde didn't quite meow, but she might as well have.

A flush of embarrassment turned Isabel's face an ugly red. She looked down at the shiny Lycra leotard and tights that clung to her slim body, a body that was in pretty good shape for a woman well past thirty-six who had borne two children.

Oh, Lord, did this one have a hole, too?

"It is a far cry from your usual good taste," Miss Alicia said with a touch of acid.

"What's wrong with it?" Isabel snapped.

"Nothing, if you're trying to start a new fashion trend, or if you just emigrated up from one of the projects in South Dallas,"

Ginny said in an amused drawl.

"Cranberry and chartreuse are an unusual combination," Eleanor said.

One could always depend on Eleanor to act like a lady, even if she did seem distracted.

Isabel looked down at her outfit in spite of the pain it caused her throbbing head. It didn't look bad to her, but she never paid attention to things like that. She paid Lina — had paid Lina — to worry about such things. Another black mark against Roland.

But not just against Roland. He never would have thought of firing her maid if that little bitch Ginny Wylde hadn't put him up to it.

She raised cold eyes to stare at Ginny's amused ones. "Some of us have better things to think about. Not all of us are so shallow." Isabel turned her head to Madame, effectively eliminating the others from her consciousness. "Isn't it time to begin, Madame?"

Madame Norina had been watching the exchange with well-concealed dismay. Nothing had gone right lately, nothing. Not since that suburban simpleton had gotten herself murdered in class, and this was what Madame had feared. The personalities in her jewel class had always been uncongenial, but there had been a civility among them. Now that civility was gone. How could she approach them for money — lots of money — when there was this discord and it was getting closer and closer to noon?

The door opened and closed again, making Madame jump.

"Are you ill, Madame?"

Madame looked into Flora Melkiot's ugly, avid face. Was everyone late this morning?

"I am fine. Lock ze door, please, Eleanor, und in a moment ve vill begin vith our stretches. But first, I must talk vith all ov you . . ."

CHAPTER NINETEEN

At least the crash was a quietish one, which meant that it was most likely books or linens instead of china or glass.

"JJ!" Esther roared.

"I'm okay, Mom."

Esther and, more slowly, Rebecca sped out of the main room into the hallway. When they had converted the old mansion into their shop, they had made the twin front parlors, dining room, and entry hall into the sales area. The kitchen had become the workroom and the tiny butler's pantry the office; both were closed off from customer view. The hallway was used as a specialty show area, and the stairs that led up to the storage attic and Rebecca's second floor flat were unobtrusively blocked by various clever sales displays.

At least, until JJ Longfellow decided to help by bringing down some stock. Now he lay at the bottom of the stairs like a discarded doll, but a funny, loose-limbed doll festooned in lace and linen.

"JJ! Oh, honey, are you all right?"

Waiting to give them the full enjoyment of his ridiculous situation — but before his mother could smother him with anxious embraces — JJ struggled to a more upright position and began to pluck off bits of fabric.

"Have you broken anything?" an anxious Esther asked, but Rebecca merely smiled.

"Leave it. You look good in crochet."

JJ grinned. "Is that what this is? Not my style."

"Oh, honey, you've just got to be more careful. Are you hurt anywhere?"

"Chill out, Mom. I'm fine. I just forgot how little those stairs are."

"Or how big your feet are getting." Bracing herself against the thick newel post, Rebecca extended a hand for JJ to pull himself upright. "I swear, you get six inches taller every time I see you."

"That's why we're keeping the jeans companies in business," Esther said, pride and ruefulness equally mixed in her voice.

JJ was a handsome boy who looked older than a middle-school student. Or perhaps that was because when Rebecca looked at him, she was seeing his dad all over again.

JJ had been a little boy when Jesse had been murdered; now he was just on the edge of young manhood. Jesse would have been proud of him. How many boys his age would have voluntarily given up a day with their buddies to help their mom at the shop?

"Stop feeding him, or you'll end up with a giant." Rebecca was accounted to be a tall woman, but she was almost eye to eye with JJ. "On the other hand, think of the basketball scholarships."

JJ laughed. "What a stereotype! I'm tall and black, so I've got to play basketball. I've decided I'm going to become a psychiatrist. Five hundred dollars an hour and no work on Wednesdays."

"Career days at the Y," Esther said in response to Rebecca's stunned expression. Last week JJ had announced that he was definitely going into Computer Science. The week before that it had been Forestry and Land Management.

"Still?"

"All summer long. It's a good thing, though — exposes the kids to all kinds of careers they might not consider otherwise." Esther was picking up the old linen by the handful and stuffing them back in the box, but she stopped to shake a stern finger at her son. "And I'll tell you one thing, young

man . . . don't knock basketball or scholarships, especially if you're going into one of
those expensive careers."

For a moment JJ's expression became serious, and for that instant he was his father.
"I know, Mom. I still go to basketball
practice every chance I get. The important
thing is to get through college, right?"

"Right. Now can you take this box into
the office without dropping it again?"

JJ laughed and stuffed the box under his
arm as if it weighed nothing. The two
women watched him until he turned the
corner.

"You're a lucky woman, Esther."

"And don't I know it." There was a little
catch in her voice. "His dad would have
been so proud of him."

"Yes. He would have. Sometimes life is so
damned unfair."

Esther gave a tight smile. "So we make
the best of what we've got. I'm going to re-
arrange china. You still on linen inventory?"

"I may be on linen inventory the rest of
my life. It's been moving well. Think JJ
would bring down a couple of more boxes?"

"He probably would, but I don't think so.
That attic is just too stacked up. I don't
want him anywhere near anything breakable
right now. He's just too clumsy. I know he'll

outgrow it, but right now he's all elbows and knees. In spite of that, though, I thought I'd take him with me to that estate sale preview tomorrow — if I can keep him from knocking over everything."

"Going to make an antique dealer of him?"

A genuine quicksilver smile flashed over her face. "Why not? It's cheaper than psychiatry."

"But he won't get Wednesdays off," Rebecca said with a solemnity that set them laughing. They had learned the hard way that between keeping the shop open and the never-ending need to find merchandise, antique dealers seldom got any days off.

"What do you want me to do now?" With the puppylike gait of the adolescent, JJ seemed to enter the room in only casually connected parts. "Need anything else down from the attic?"

Esther shook her head. "We've got enough now."

"You just don't want me dropping anything else, right?"

"Right!" Esther and Rebecca answered in chorus.

"You see, that's all part of my plan. I break things, then I don't have to work anymore."

"You break things and we can't afford to

feed you anymore," Esther chided only half jokingly. All three of them knew the shop operated on a terrifyingly slim margin of profit.

Sometimes, Rebecca thought, *it was good to laugh at your greatest fear.* She only wished she could do it.

Aloud she said, "You could mow the lawn."

"I just mowed it last week."

"And it's shaggy again. It grows as fast as you do."

JJ shrugged in acquiescence, not really displeased. He preferred being outside to hauling around things that inexplicably seemed to break around him. He started for the door, followed by his mother.

"And don't skip the part back by the forsythia. Mosquitoes just love the long grass under it."

"The what?"

"The bush with the golden flowers."

"Gold? They look yellow to me."

"You just see colors weird. They're gold."

Rebecca looked after them. What a pleasure JJ was. It would be a shame when in a year or two — or less — he turned into a teenager. He had already reached that in years, but not in behavior. When she had first joined the force and worked as a plain patrol officer, she had seen the story so often. Sullen, rebellious teenagers — a cliché simply because it was true — getting into trouble, acting out, being at best a pain in the behind. How many times had she heard a hurt, grieving, angry mother protest that her kid had always been a good child, that just recently . . .

Well, with a mother like Esther and an honorary aunt like Rebecca, JJ shouldn't be able to go far wrong. Rebecca hoped. She had learned never to underestimate the ability of a teen who wanted to do something.

Linens. More linens were waiting.

Rebecca limped into the office, leaning heavily on her cane. Her leg still pained her, but less now. Esther had seen her using the cane earlier and said nothing, but then she wouldn't when JJ was around. She'd give her partner the third degree later.

JJ had left the box on the desk next to the computer. Rebecca opened the correct inventory file, then dug in the box and lifted out an exquisite crocheted collar. Like all their linens, it had been washed as soon as it had been brought into the shop, but it was still a little dingy. They really should clean this properly before putting it in the store. With the right display and accessories, it could be a money-maker. She reached for a pad to make a note about it.

The telephone rang and Rebecca answered it, even though they didn't open for at least another half hour.

"C & L Antiques."

"Miss Cloudwebb? This is Flora Melkiot."

Rebecca groaned.

"Drop whatever you're doing and get over here immediately. Someone just tried to kill Waldo Wylde!"

Although she had been properly shocked, Rebecca's lack of enthusiasm to investigate irritated Flora. As usual, she would have to do all the work herself. She had always known she could be a great detective if she merely applied herself. It was merely a matter of gathering information, and, after all that had fallen in her lap this morning, it should be a piece of cake.

She showered and dressed quickly, formulating her plans as she did so.

Larry Tyler had said the doorman, Chuck whatever-his-last-name-was, was involved in gambling. The best way to prove that was to gamble. He knew who she was, and he probably knew that she had a good bit of money; after all, one could hardly own an apartment in the Olympus House without having some money.

So, she would put down a bet. It had better be on horses. She didn't know anything about poker or other games, but on occasion she and Morris had gone to the races. She'd ask for Chuck's help and advice; men like him adored thinking women were helpless little things, especially if they were helpless little things who were willing to lose money. Such a devious course rankled Flora, who had always known she was a self-assured woman of the world, but the truth was, she knew very little about horse racing, other than not to talk when the horses were running.

Flora was right. After her first, carefully tentative inquiries into how one would go about placing a bet, Chuck became very friendly. Places where bets were taken, he said, were not the kind where a lady should go. As a special favor to her, he said, he would be happy to take her money and place the bet for her — at just a small percentage.

So small a percentage that it shocked Flora; he must, she decided, be getting paid from the other end for bringing in new suckers. Or this was just an introductory offer, and he would sink his claws into her later. As there was not going to be any later, it didn't matter.

That was how she explained it to Rebecca when she showed up some half hour after the dirty deed was done.

"You did what?"

"More coffee?"

They were back in Flora's living room, but this time Rebecca was so aghast she was scarcely aware of the wealth of antiques that surrounded her.

"Of course not," Flora went on, peering at her guest's cup. "You haven't even touched it. Would you prefer tea?"

"Mrs. Melkiot! You haven't heard a word I've said."

Flora had. Ever since she had told Rebecca of her foray into gambling, the younger woman hadn't stopped telling her how wrong she was. Flora knew she was and always had been magnanimous and exquisitely mannered, but this constant denigration of her investigation was beginning to wear quite thin.

She had been surprised Rebecca had appeared at all. Had she known she was coming, Flora could have worked out a much more satisfactory plan. On the other hand, she would have missed learning a great deal about how to bet on a horse race.

"You'll probably never get your money back."

"Oh, I'm sure I won't. I bet on a horse with a dismal record. Hasn't got a chance. It's amazing it hasn't been sent to the glue factory already. Do they still send old horses to the glue factory?"

"I haven't the slightest idea," Rebecca said. "But your money —"

"It wasn't much, just fifty dollars. Just enough to whet his interest. I didn't want to appear too eager. Chuck tried to talk me out of that horse, by the way, but I was insistent, and doubtless he thinks me the silliest female on the planet. If he thinks I'm easy pickings, he'll be sure to come back."

"And I hope he gets here before the police! Do you realize there are laws about off-track betting? And consorting with known criminals for certain illegal purposes? You could be in a great deal of trouble, Mrs. Melkiot."

Really, is my generation the last to have any imagination or gumption? Flora thought with some rancor.

"I doubt it. I told him I wanted to use my middle and maiden names, Albertine Conroe, just so my children wouldn't find out what I was doing." She took the last sip of coffee from her cup and then refilled it while her guest spluttered.

"That's not going to do any good! When

320

the police take him, they'll have his records. They'll check every name, and it won't make any difference."

"My middle name is Bernice," Flora said with maddening patience. "And my maiden name was Donaghey. It will be his word against mine, and whom do you think they will believe?"

"I don't believe you." Rebecca sagged against the back of the couch. "You're incredible."

"Just so you will know, I gave him two twenties and a ten. I wrote the serial numbers down and put them in my desk. Just in case. I know I should probably have had them notarized, but I didn't want to draw any more attention to my scheme than necessary. Do you think that will be enough?"

Rebecca's mouth was moving slowly, but no sound came out. At last she managed a small, "My God! I'm glad you're on our side."

"I told you I would be useful," Flora replied. "Now how about some fresh coffee?"

"Please. Now tell me about Waldo Wylde. Or have you solved that already?"

Moving Rebecca's cold, untouched coffee aside, Flora took a clean cup from the tray

— she always brought extras, in case of company — and filled it. "I haven't even tried. I heard about it this morning in exercise class."

"The police let Madame Norina have her salon back?"

"Yes, but I don't think she's going to have it for long. Before we started she gave us a sales pitch — about how she was going to expand and go national with franchises, but to do so she would need just a little more capital. She was willing to let us in on the ground floor as her first investors."

"Hasn't she been talking about expanding for a long time?"

Flora shrugged. "Who listens? What made me suspicious is that she needed us to commit today. This morning."

"This morning?"

"And in cash, preferably, but she said she would take a check."

"Pushy. How much?"

"She said the initial subscription would be twenty-five thousand dollars each, but she would give each of us as much as we wanted if we wished to invest more."

Rebecca started in astonishment. "Twenty-five thousand dollars? Each? In cash? This morning? That's incredible. I hope none of you bit."

"Of course not. If there's anything my Morris taught me, it's that nothing good is done in a hurry." For a moment a tiny smile that had nothing to do with the situation at hand teased Flora's lips, then with a visible start she pulled back to the present. "And there was something funny about her attitude. She seemed edgy . . . almost afraid."

"I can't imagine her being afraid of anything. Do you think it's connected with the attack on Waldo Wylde?"

"I don't know." Flora frowned. "There certainly was something funny going on. When she started, Eleanor Anderson got very angry-looking and stalked out of class. Miss Alicia was extremely negative and Isabel Orwell and Ginny Wylde just laughed. Only time I've ever seen them agree on anything. Quite frankly, we were pretty much all laughing at Isabel. I've never seen her turned out so eccentrically — all red and green, just like a Christmas elf. I thought the woman had taste. Anyway, all of us would probably have left if the policemen hadn't come in just then looking for Ginny. Regular uniformed officers, not that idiot detective or his cretinous partner." Flora stopped for a moment. It was almost possible to hear her thinking. "I just remembered something. Madame had locked the door and when they pounded on it, she jumped as if it had been a shot."

"Scared?"

"I think so."

"I wonder . . ." Rebecca pondered for a moment. "You still haven't told me about Waldo Wylde."

"He was found this morning by one of the residents down in the corridor leading to the mailroom. It's in the first basement and about as dreary a place as you can imagine. Well lit and wide, but utterly blank. I don't know what they were doing when they put the mailroom down there. This idiot female from the eighth floor is a real character; afraid of everything — seldom leaves her apartment, thinks the entire world is just waiting to get her, as if anyone would want her," Flora added tones more waspish than truth usually required. "Anyway, she nerves herself to go down all by herself and get her mail. When she steps out on the first basement level, about halfway down this interminable hallway she sees a great big lump lying on the floor. It was Waldo Wylde. Someone had beaten him severely, though with all his fat, it's a wonder that they could get through enough of it to do his interior organs any real damage. The woman went hysterical and they had to call an ambulance

324

for each of them."

"Any idea who did it?"

"Other than just about anyone in a large chunk of the politically liberal population of the Western Hemisphere, no. Ginny, of course, went off into very pretty hysterics and the officers had to take her to the hospital immediately. She probably wanted to make sure she got there in time to be filmed for the early news. She does look very good in an exercise suit."

"That's pretty cold."

"And honest."

"I wonder what connection there is between Laura Tyler, Madame Norina, and Waldo Wylde. It's hard to imagine three more different people," Rebecca said at last. "There's nothing in common about them, except the Olympus House."

"There's blackmail. They could be a gang, or a coven or whatever you call them."

"Laura Tyler wasn't a blackmailer. Even Ashdown believes that now."

Flora snorted at his name. "That man blows in the wind so much he could get a second job as a weathervane. What if she weren't blackmailing, but was being blackmailed?"

"Oh, come on! From what Ashdown told me, the woman was practically a saint.

About the worst thing she could have done was not pay a parking ticket."

"You're forgetting her son. Skeeter. The gambler."

Rebecca blinked. She had forgotten. "And that ties in with Chuck Jernigan."

Somewhere in the back of her brain synapses flashed and a memory appeared. It hadn't been long before That Day — three, four months maybe. She had been part of a squad that raided a sleazy strip joint just off Harry Hines, and a nasty stew it had been — gambling, prostitution, drugs, child porn. Name your illegal pastime and it was there.

Chuck Jernigan had been there, too, trapped in one of the back cribs with a hooker who might have been fifteen, no matter how often she said she was nineteen. When she could talk, that was; she had been worked over pretty badly, even to the point of a broken jaw. They had arrested Jernigan, sure that he was either the enforcer for the girl's pimp or a customer who liked the really rough stuff, one of the customers pimps used to discipline unruly girls.

It had come to nothing. When the girl, the child, was conscious enough to talk, she had said that it was another john who had beat her up — she couldn't remember what he looked like, or whether he was short or tall, or even his race, but she was adamant that it had not been Chuck Jernigan who hurt her.

She was lying, of course. Jernigan said he had heard the girl scream and rushed in to save her. He hadn't even tried to hide his skinned knuckles and the smears of blood on his hands. Rebecca had worked with the girl, talking to her, promising her protection, but couldn't sway her in her story. Jernigan had not even been charged, and the girl had disappeared.

Rebecca felt vaguely sick.

"I wonder who else is involved?" she murmured.

"Another person?" Flora demanded, indignant. "You're making it sound like the Olympus House is a den of thieves!"

"There has to be another person. Someone killed Laura Tyler. Someone assaulted Waldo Wylde. From what you say, Madame Norina is terrified. Jernigan isn't smart enough to pull all that off by himself. There has to be someone else."

"Who could it be?"

Rebecca stood up. "I think it's time we talked to Madame Norina."

CHAPTER TWENTY

Isabel Orwell felt as if she had been run over by a truck. What was happening to her world? She needed a drink . . .

No, she didn't. Not at this hour. After the bender she had pulled last night — and the aftermath this morning — she might never drink again. She wished. Maybe just one, to help her forget . . .

She slammed the condo door behind her and began stripping off her exercise suit. This was the last time she'd ever go to Madame Norina's. It would save some money, anyway, and she had the horrible feeling money was going to matter a great deal before long. Roland would want every penny to spend on his little whore and probably wouldn't give her enough to keep an efficiency apartment in a South Dallas housing project.

Maybe Waldo would die, and then Ginny would see how it felt to have a husband taken away from her. She probably wouldn't mind. She might even have arranged for the attack herself, so there wouldn't be any impediment between her and Roland.

But there was. Roland's wife.

Isabel decided maybe she had better see a lawyer. Quickly.

Her heart jumped. There was someone else in the apartment. She could hear footsteps in the kitchen.

Maybe Lina had come back? She'd have stayed away because of Roland's anger, but she was loyal to Isabel. At least that was what she had always said.

Maybe it wasn't, Isabel thought in sudden terror. Maybe there had been arrangements made to take care of her the way Waldo had been.

Clutching her discarded leotard and tights against her naked body, Isabel backed up until the front doorknob was in her hand and unlocked for instant escape. She'd look funny running around naked, but at least she'd be alive. She hoped.

"Lina?"

"I fired her, remember?" Roland said, stepping out of the kitchen. He had a sandwich in his hand.

He looked awful. Not in his dress; he was as nattily perfect as ever — gray suit, gray

329

shirt, black and white patterned tie. It was his face, and his voice, and the horrible emptiness of his eyes. He looked like he had been through hell.

Isabel was startled that she didn't feel one shred of pity for him.

"What are you doing here?"

"I live here."

"No you don't. You moved to the bank's corporate apartment, remember?"

"I still pay the bills here." That comment was vintage Roland, but it had none of the punch it formerly did. It was almost a whine.

"What do you want, Roland?"

"Are you going to run naked down the hall?" His tone was flat, almost disinterested. Isabel wondered if he had been drinking this early in the day.

"If I have to. What do you want, Roland?"

"I'd never hurt you, Isabel. You know that."

The wronged wife snorted. "Yeah. Then what do you think you have been doing the last few weeks?"

"Making a fool of myself. You were right."

Isabel stared and so forgot herself that she loosed her grip both on the doorknob and her discarded clothes. Roland Orwell never, never admitted that he was wrong about anything. Ever.

"She threw you over."

He nodded miserably.

"She wouldn't leave Wylde."

Another nod, this time edged with a sigh.

Isabel felt an unfamiliar, corrosive surge of power go through her. "So you thought you'd just come home and I'd welcome you with open arms."

"I'm not stupid, Isabel. I know you hate me."

"If I do, it's because you made me."

"I know. I saw the bedroom. You are throwing me out."

"You left!" she spat. "I'm just cleaning up the mess you left behind, like I always have to."

With an angry dignity, she snatched up her exercise clothes and stalked across the living room into the bedroom and on to the bathroom, not even looking at him.

To her surprise, he was still there when she came out of the shower some time later, wrapped in her white cotton robe and her newly washed hair turbaned in a towel. She had thought she had given him plenty of time to get what he wanted of his things — presumably the reason for his presence — and get out.

Why hadn't he gone? Oh, Lord, how she

wanted a drink, but she wouldn't show that weakness in front of him! Roland Orwell was always quick to exploit any weakness he found.

At least, the Roland Orwell she knew had been. This new strange Roland Orwell was sitting on the bed, hands hanging limply between his knees, his head bowed, looking as miserable as it was possible for a person to look. If it had been anyone else but Roland, Isabel would have been moved to pity. The things on the floor — his clothes, toiletries, keepsakes — were untouched.

"What are you doing still here?"

"I need to talk to you, Isabel."

"I'm getting a lawyer. Talk to him."

"Isabel . . . Please. This is important."

"Our marriage was important."

Roland gave a sob — Roland, crying! — and buried his face in his hands. "I'm in trouble, Belle," he said, using the pet name that had not crossed his lips in more than a year. "I'm in so much trouble."

"My God, Roland, what have you done? You didn't steal from the bank for that whore, did you?"

He shook his head. "I thought about it, though, but I haven't. It's worse."

"Worse?" In spite of herself Isabel sat on the bed as far away from him as she could and still be on the same side. "What have you done?"

"I had everything worked out. I was going to take all the money and Ginny and I were going to go to some nice country with beaches and no extradition laws."

"You were going to leave me penniless?"

His silence was eloquent. What else had she expected? At last he said, "I was going to leave you this place, and the cars, and some of the stock."

Everything that would take time to liquidate and with no guarantee of profit. Isabel's mouth thinned to an unforgiving line. "So what stopped you?"

"I called Ginny and told her to pack a few things, that we were leaving tonight. She told me not to be ridiculous and that she'd decided it was over, that we'd best not see each other again."

Vindication felt very sweet to Isabel. She had told him Ginny would dump him, but she wouldn't remind him. There was more to come and since she was now having to look out for herself, she needed to know everything.

"I knew she was only saying that because Wylde was standing there making her." His voice turned thick with loathing. "I knew she really loved me. So I decided to kill him."

"It was you?" Isabel asked, genuinely shocked. Roland had always been a devil with words and with financial revenge; she had never ever thought of him as someone to react in a physical way. "You attacked Waldo Wylde?"

"Yes. That's why you've got to tell anyone who asks that we've reconciled and I've been with you all last night and this morning."

"You want me to lie for you. Again."

"Please, Isabel!"

She gave a snort of disgust. "I don't believe this. You aren't the type to beat up anybody, including something like Waldo Wylde. How'd you do it?"

Roland seemed glad to unburden himself. "I called and told him there was a package at the mail room he had to sign for personally. He came right down. I had disguised my voice. I really just wanted to talk to him, to convince him that Ginny and I really loved each other and that he should let her go . . ." His voice broke. "He laughed at me and told me his wife had already picked her next paramour, that I was old news. He laughed at me! So I hit him . . . and it felt good, so I kept hitting him and kicking him and hitting him and kicking him . . ."

Something in his voice made Isabel shiver. She stood up slowly and, keeping her eye on him as if there were a wild animal in the room, began to back up.

"So I killed him. And I need your help."

Isabel felt as if she just might kill him herself right then. "You mess up again and expect me to make everything all right? Don't you ever learn anything?"

"This will be the last time, I swear. I'll be good. I'll never do anything wrong again . . ." His face distorted by sheer terror, he fell to his knees and crawled after his retreating wife, grabbing at the edges of her robe like a frightened toddler does his mother's skirts.

Isabel slapped his hands away and ran to the other side of the room. "And the first minute after things are settled you'll go back to her, won't you, and leave me holding the bag again?"

Roland collapsed into a sobbing heap on the floor. "No. I called her and told her I had talked to Wylde. I didn't tell her I'd killed him. I didn't want to upset her."

Even now hearing him left a gash in Isabel's heart. He didn't want to upset that whore, but he came to her to make everything right. He didn't care if he upset her or not! Oh, she needed a drink. She needed one now. How much was she supposed to bear?

"She laughed at me, too. Said she couldn't wait to hear what I had told her precious Waldo. That she'd never leave him. That she'd met someone else for her . . . adventures." Giving a primal howl of pain, Roland curled into a fetal position and continued to scream with a sound that wasn't quite human.

Oh, great! Isabel thought. *Now the neighbors are going to call security to find out what's going on here.*

The doorbell rang.

"It's them! It's the police . . ." Roland babbled. "Save me, Isabel, save me — tell them I was with you when Wylde was killed. I'll be good, I promise . . ."

Isabel walked around him, carefully staying out of reach, and walked to the door.

"You don't have to worry on one count, Roland," she said as she crossed the living room. "Waldo Wylde didn't die."

Roland was shocked silent as Isabel opened the door.

"Mrs. Orwell . . ."

"I've been expecting you, Detective Ashdown," Isabel said with a quiet dignity. "Roland is in the bedroom."

336

■ ■ ■ ■

Madame Norina was frightened. She had locked the door to her salon, but had no illusions about how safe that made her. None of her jewels were interested in helping her. She had nothing. Vegas Charlie was going to send someone to collect in just a short time, and she had nothing to give them. Nothing.

Running was her only hope. Her new class would be here in just a few minutes. She would let them in, then make up some excuse why they should come with her to her car. Surely Vegas Charlie and his minions would be too smart to approach her when she was with a crowd of women. Once at the car, she would simply get in and drive away.

And go where? She didn't know.

On what? She didn't know. There was perhaps twenty, twenty-five dollars in her purse. All in the world she possessed.

She wouldn't even dare go back to her dreary room for clothes. She would just go.

There was a sound, and Madame's blood froze. Paralyzed, she sat as someone very quietly unlocked the doors, came in, and then relocked them again.

■ ■ ■ ■

Eleanor Anthony was swamped with emotions — anger, grief, regret. After soaking her for several thousand dollars, that horrible old woman was trying to get more money from her, and from everyone else. Oh, it was couched as investment, but she knew Madame would be contacting her directly for a special contribution.

It was time to go.

It wasn't the way she had hoped to handle the matter; she had planned one last, magical night with Eddie before she vanished, but she had to go now. It was really for his own good; she had to protect him, and this was the only way she knew how to do it. He shouldn't have to keep paying and paying for her mistakes.

She had poured out her feelings and her emotions in the letter that she now sealed, kissed, and put in the middle of the desk, where he would see it immediately. Hopefully it would convey something of her love, her hopelessness, her despair. He was free to divorce her, she said, but in her heart she didn't think he would. At least, not for a long while. She hoped he would, and that he would someday find happiness with a woman worthy of him, someone he didn't have to be ashamed of.

Finally she knew she could delay no longer; she picked up her single suitcase and put her purse over her shoulder. With tears in her eyes, she looked for one last time around the apartment that had been dearer than heaven to her, then walked out, closing the door firmly behind her.

"Drat!" Flora said as they stepped off the elevator.

A dozen or so women, all in cover-ups over exercise wear, milled about the hallway in front of Madame Norina's Temple of Health. The big double doors were closed.

"What are you all doing here?" Flora demanded, elbowing her way through the clot of women.

"Who are you?" responded the woman closest to the door, taking the spot of group spokeswoman.

"Flora Melkiot, and a resident of the Olympus House. I don't recognize any of you."

"We're Madame Norina's new class. She called us yesterday and said to be here today at noon to begin, but the doors are locked."

"Locked?" Rebecca grabbed one of the knobs and shook it. The door was flimsily locked — flimsily, but definitely.

"I've waited months to get into one of Madame's classes," one woman said, and was echoed by several others, most complaining that the Olympus House was too restrictive in who could attend Madame's salon.

"Why would she call us to come, then not open the door?" asked another.

"Are you sure someone's in there?" Rebecca asked.

Some of the women nodded. "We all arrived pretty much at the same time," one said, "and we waited until exactly noon to try the door."

"Madame makes such a fetish of punctuality," said another.

"And we heard sounds," said the self-appointed spokeswoman.

"Thuds," another added. "Like she's moving furniture in there."

"But she stopped when we knocked and called her name."

"Has anyone come out?" Rebecca asked, then when the answer was negative, asked Flora, "Is there another entrance?"

"Not that I know of."

Rebecca took a deep breath. She had long thought it dead, but her sixth sense was tingling. Most cops had it; those who didn't develop one — or those who ignored it — met with grief. She had only ignored it once, and not only she, but Jesse and Esther and JJ had paid the price.

She yanked her cell phone out of her pocket and handed it to Flora. "Call the police."

"The police? Why?"

"Because I'm about to break the law."

Flora snapped open the phone and obeyed.

The simple snap lock on Madame Norina's Temple of Health was meant to keep out only the law-abiding. One determined shove and the double doors swung back, revealing a picture from a nightmare.

The anteroom was small, hardly more than a place to hang coats and pictures; it gave almost a complete view of the exercise room. There was a mat on the floor, forming a grossly misshapen lump as it draped over something.

Something that was bleeding. A finger of red snaked out from under one edge.

Chuck Jernigan stood between it and Rebecca, as ugly and as dangerous as a cornered wolverine. If she had seen him like this, Rebecca realized, in jeans and a t-shirt instead of his comic-opera doorman's outfit, she would have recognized him at once.

"Well, if it isn't the famous cop, Detective Cloudwebb," he snarled. "Ex-cop."

"We've got you now, Jernigan. You won't get out it of this time."

"You think?" He held a cosh, drawing it lovingly through his fingers. Eight inches long, made of heavy, supple leather with a core of lead at one end, it was a vicious weapon. It was also wet and red. Probably none of the ladies clustered curiously at the door even knew what it was, but they instinctively realized how dangerous it — and he — could be. With little squealings of fear they scattered.

"Yeah. You've bought it, Jernigan. This time we've got you."

Keep him talking, Rebecca thought. Keep him here until the uniforms get here. What would be the response time? Three minutes? Five? Her heart sank. She'd do well to keep control of the situation for thirty seconds. He was too smart, too skilled at staying alive.

"Got a message for you," he said with a grin.

"You don't know anyone I'd want to hear from."

Keep him talking!

"Frank Titus says hello."

Rebecca was thunderstruck. It was just

what he was waiting for.

Chuck Jernigan rushed forward, swinging the cosh like a mace, using it more for intimidation than for its true purpose of smashing bone and skin.

Rebecca recovered just in time, banging her cane against his knee. The impact almost knocked the heavy wooden stick out of her hands, but it startled him and made him stagger, sudden pain distorting his face. Without giving him time to recoup, Rebecca feinted, first giving a hard blow to his elbow, hopefully numbing the hand that held the deadly cosh. She took a quick sideways step, then held the cane tightly with both hands, swinging it like a baseball bat against the side of his head.

There was an awful sound of impact and a jarring shock that rippled through her body like a flood, numbing her hands and fingers and making her stagger. She held onto the wood only by an act of will.

Jernigan went down like a redwood and was still. The only sound in the room was Rebecca's ragged gasps for breath.

Flora crept further into the room. "Did you kill him?"

At the moment Rebecca didn't care. He hadn't killed her, and that was enough.

Frank Titus. How did he know about

Frank Titus?

Frank Titus.

Was he back in town?

Was he watching her?

Rebecca began to shake.

Bending over, Flora peered closely at the inert form. "Drat. He's still breathing."

"Did you call the police?"

"Yes. They're on their way, with their usual speed and alacrity," she added sourly. "I've had that Ashdown underfoot for days, getting in my way and not doing a thing, but where is he when we need a cop?"

"Watch him." Steadying herself with the cane, needing it more than she had those first few days out of the hospital, Rebecca worked her way around Jernigan's prone form carefully. Thank goodness the sturdy old wood hadn't broken under the impact. She didn't think Jernigan could be faking, but she didn't want to take chances.

"What if he starts to wake up?"

"Knock him out again," Rebecca answered vaguely as she tugged the exercise mat away from what she knew it hid. The mat was heavier than it looked.

Secretly wishing that Jernigan would stir, Flora took Rebecca's instruction to heart. She picked up one of the bronze figurines, an impossibly lithe and beautiful young woman (a not-bad copy of an Erté was Rebecca's professional opinion), and held it over her shoulder, ready to bash Jernigan's skull at the first sign of life.

Once the exercise mat at last slipped away, Rebecca thought Madame Norina was dead. She lay in a pool of blood, so battered that in another place Rebecca would never have recognized her. Sharp ends of bone protruded from raw flesh. Bits of teeth lay beside her bleeding mouth. Rebecca didn't know where to touch for a pulse. Nothing seemed to be where it was supposed to be.

She was breathing, though. Her chest rose and fell, slightly but steadily. She was alive. Considering the severity of her injuries, Rebecca didn't know if this was a kindness or not. She had an idea of the horrors of recuperation that awaited Madame.

But life does go on, Rebecca thought with something like wonder. *You do get through dark tunnels.* She had been shot and left for dead. She would probably never walk easily again, but with nothing but a plain old wooden cane she had taken down a tough, vicious criminal who had probably killed several times. She had triumphed. She was alive.

"It's going to be all right, Madame Norina," she murmured, patting her ankle, the

CHAPTER TWENTY-ONE

The aftermath was anticlimactic. Even the first responding officers, thinking Flora, her bronze statuette still ready for action, was the culprit, were worth no more than a tired smile to Rebecca. It was different for Flora; she was angry and would carry a prejudice against uniformed officers for years.

"How dare they," she would say to anyone who would stand still, "think that I was a criminal? They would never have solved the case had it not been for me."

Madame was still alive when the ambulances finally arrived, though the attendants were not optimistic about her prognosis. A safely handcuffed Jernigan had just regained consciousness as he was being loaded onto his own gurney. While he was trundled out, he was muttering about filing assault charges against Rebecca, the DPD, the Olympus House, and anyone else he could think of.

Rebecca wanted to talk to him. She wanted to ask him about Frank Titus. How Jernigan knew the name. Where he was. She made no move, though, knowing that the uniforms would never let her near him.

And when she questioned him about Frank Titus she wanted them to be alone.

"It's his day off," Flora murmured later, working things about Jernigan out in her mind. "He probably knows every way to get in and out of the building without anyone seeing him. Doubtless he has a dozen 'friends' who will vouch that he was with them all day."

"But Madame had started a new class. He didn't know that there would be customers. He expected her to be alone for the rest of the afternoon," Rebecca added. "Bastard."

"To think that someone like that has been so close to all of us!" Flora shuddered dramatically. "It makes my flesh creep."

"And it still doesn't answer who killed Laura Tyler. If Jernigan had done it, he would have just coshed her over the head, like he did Madame. I can't see him being subtle enough to put drain cleaner in her glass."

"I hardly call that subtle!"

"Perhaps it was the wrong word choice,"

Rebecca admitted.

They were pacing the hallway outside the salon. The officers had not wanted them to leave, as the detectives would want to talk to them, but both ladies had been firm. They had seen too much in that salon and both needed a change of scene. Only when they had sworn to stay on the mezzanine balcony within full sight of the officers were they permitted to step outside.

Flora put the command down as another instance of the stupidity of the police. "As if we would run away," she had sniffed. "We are the good guys!"

"Where is she?" Eddie Anthony exploded out of the elevator, in more of a violent temper than anyone had ever seen him. "What's going on? Where's that bitch Madame?"

Rebecca grabbed his arm. "You can't go in there. It's a crime scene."

"You're right, it's a crime scene. Anywhere that woman is, is a crime scene! I've got to talk to her."

"Mr. Anthony, calm down!" Flora said in a voice copied from her son's second grade teacher that had always commanded instant obedience. The trick still worked. Eddie Anthony stopped dead in his tracks.

"What is your problem with Madame Norina, Mr. Anthony?" Rebecca asked.

"That blackmailing bitch made my wife run away." Impotently he shook a sheet of creamy vellum stationery closely covered with handwriting. "It's bad enough that fascist Waldo Wylde was trying to strong-arm me, but when a bloody exercise teacher tries to shake down my wife twice in one week . . . !"

"That spiel about investing in her expansion?" Flora asked after a moment's thought. "She pulled that on all of us this morning, and I assure you I have never done anything for which I could be blackmailed." Surreptitiously she crossed her fingers behind her back.

"This wasn't the first time. Eleanor — I — had just 'invested' a few days ago."

"You said Waldo Wylde. You know what has happened to him?" At his nod, Rebecca took Eddie's arm. "Mr. Anthony, Madame Norina has just been beaten nearly to death by an expert. I think we need to talk."

In mirror image, Flora took his other arm and within seconds they were through the doors into the small restaurant. Flora headed straight for her usual table and ordered three iced teas.

"Who are you?" Eddie asked, perhaps a

trifle late. "You're in Eleanor's exercise class."

"Flora Melkiot. And this is Rebecca Cloudwebb, formerly with the DPD. We're trying to help the police solve Laura Tyler's death."

It amazed Rebecca how Flora could state the exact truth and make it sound like something else entirely. Any correction she could make would only sound phony.

Eddie thought for a minute before he realized. "The woman who was killed in the jewel class? How . . . ?"

"That's what we're trying to ascertain," Rebecca said. *In for a penny, in for a pound.* "You said you and your wife were being blackmailed by Waldo Wylde and by Madame Norina. What did they want?"

"Wylde has been wanting to send me to Washington as his puppet senator. I think he was leaning on Roland Orwell, too, since Wylde told me he would be taking over the financial control of the campaign. Orwell used to dislike Wylde's politics as much as I."

"And you didn't want to."

"No. I'm not politician material. I wouldn't want to run even if I did agree with Wylde's crazy politics. I just want to stay at home, run my gallery, and be with

Eleanor. That's all."

"What about Madame?"

"I don't know how or when she found out, but the day after that woman died she asked Eleanor for money . . . for an 'investment.' " He made the word into an obscenity.

"Did she give any to her?"

"Nothing much. A couple of thousand."

Rebecca felt her sympathy, usually marginal at best for anyone weak enough to let himself be blackmailed, start to slip. A couple of thousand was anything but "nothing much."

"How did Wylde and Madame find out about whatever it is you're hiding?"

"I don't know. We tried so hard to keep it quiet. We even changed Eleanor's name."

"So it was something about your wife," Rebecca said, pushing just slightly. Her training in interrogation surfaced so quietly and naturally she was unaware of it.

Eddie looked both startled and guilty. His expression indignant, he opened his mouth as if to deny it, but could not. Although he did not move, it was as if he had collapsed inside and the slight nod of his head was the sign of an imminent cave-in.

"Mr. Anthony," Rebecca asked slowly but inexorably, "what did your wife do that you want so badly to keep hidden?"

"I can't."

"One person has been murdered and two have been beaten almost to death, Mr. Anthony. This is no time to keep secrets. Your wife may be in danger."

Eddie's face went even paler. "They wouldn't hurt her?"

"I don't know. We can't know much of anything if you are hiding the facts from us."

He swallowed heavily and stared at his tightly clasped hands as though they might vanish if he looked away. "I met Eleanor in Carson City, Nevada. I went to bid on some pieces at an estate auction. She was . . . working there." The words came slowly, hesitantly, as if each were having to be individually formed and molded. "She was in the entertainment industry. The private entertainment industry."

"She was a call girl," Rebecca said unsentimentally, pushing just a little bit harder.

"Yes. I called for company and she was sent. We hit it off and I asked for her every night I was there. I even stayed over so we could be together. We fell in love."

Rebecca kept her mouth shut and glared at Flora to do the same.

"But she had contracts. Said she had to work even though she didn't want to. One night there was a man . . . She didn't want to go, but her boss said she had to. He had asked for her specifically. He was a bad man. He liked to hurt women, beat them up. Eleanor went, intending to tell him that she wasn't going to stay. He wouldn't listen to her. She fought back, and he died. She didn't mean to kill him. It was an accident. She came to me for help." The ghost of pride in that last sentence was almost pathetic.

"Why didn't you go to the police?"

"He was a state senator and an important man. Who would take the word of a call girl?"

"It still sounds like self-defense. You could have gotten her the best lawyer in the country, couldn't you?"

Eddie was picking at a fingernail. Rebecca knew there was more to the story, so she took a long drink of the iced tea that had at some time materialized in front of her. Flora opened her mouth, so Rebecca unceremoniously kicked her under the table. The older woman glared but said nothing.

"Yes," Eddie said after a long time, "but I was afraid."

"Afraid of what?" Flora asked. Rebecca was amazed the old woman had stayed silent so long.

"That if she got off she wouldn't need me anymore. Besides, Eleanor —" His voice caressed the name. "— said it wasn't the police she was afraid of so much as the people she worked for."

"So you two got married."

He nodded. "She hadn't been using her real name with her work, so we went to Reno and got her real name changed, just to be on the safe side. Then we got married. We didn't want to leave a trail."

"Mr. Anthony . . ."

"I know what you're thinking. That she married me for convenience. For my family's money. That she didn't really love me. I know she didn't. I know she married me just to get out of there alive and safe. But she did come to love me. I know that. We have been happy for all the eight years we've been married. Then this . . ."

Eddie Anthony put his head down and wept unashamedly, not even noticing that his torn and ragged fingernail was dotting the peach-colored cloth with drops of blood.

"Did your wife gamble, Mr. Anthony?" Rebecca asked.

He looked up. "What?"

Resigned to always be the practical one, Flora dunked her napkin in his glass of tea and wrapped it around his bleeding finger.

"Did your wife gamble?"

"No. Never. Gambling and partying and things like that reminded her of her life in Nevada and she wanted to forget all that. She wouldn't even go to bingo night at our church fundraisers."

"Never?"

"Never."

Rebecca frowned. Had Madame been blackmailing Eleanor Anthony, or had the woman simply overreacted? *Or,* a nasty part of her mind asked, *had eight years been enough and the perfect Mrs. Anthony took the chance to disappear?*

But if that were true, why wait until now? She had money; she could have walked away at any time and simply vanished. Why now?

And how was Waldo Wylde tied in to the mess? Rebecca couldn't see him gambling; his ego wouldn't allow him to lose, and the outcome from gambling he could not control. Unless he was one of the big bosses and he could control it. No, that was getting into fantasy territory. *Uber-fascist* Waldo Wylde and the criminal element? It didn't fit.

But everything had to be related somehow, unless within a week the Olympus House had turned into a hotbed of criminal activity.

And who had killed Laura Tyler?

And why? Somehow Rebecca couldn't believe Flora's pat solution of the gamblers killing her to bring Skeeter Tyler into line. Professional gamblers wanted their money, not the melodrama of murder.

Madame Norina had been beaten almost to death. If they hadn't come in when they had, she probably would have died. She still might.

Madame Norina had no money. She had been frantically trying to raise it from her jewel class.

Could the gamblers be using her as an object lesson to others who wouldn't/couldn't pay their losses? Or had Chuck Jernigan gotten a little enthusiastic about enforcing?

Rebecca groaned. So many facts that didn't tie in together. There had to be something she was missing. Either that, or her deductive powers had totally rotted since she had left the force.

"Are you ready to order, Mrs. Melkiot? The kitchen is almost ready to close," said the waiter, who had been patiently hovering and waved away half a dozen times.

A shadow fell across the table.

"Don't bother ordering, Miss Cloudwebb. You and I need to talk," said a very displeased Detective Ashdown. "Now."

"Nice office," Rebecca said, settling into one of the comfortable conference room chairs. In all her investigations, she'd never had accommodations like these.

In all her investigations she'd never had a case like this, either.

"Yes, and it's a lovely view, and I doubt if very many investigations get such a fancy office. Now that we've got all the polite conversation out of the way, perhaps you can tell me why, almost every time I am called to a crime in this place, you are standing over the victim." There was no humor in his tone.

"I wasn't anywhere near Waldo Wylde."

"Two out of three are still impressive odds, Miss Cloudwebb."

"I agree. And I can't give you an answer."

Ashdown tented his fingers and looked at her as he would a criminal. "I can. You're meddling, Miss Cloudwebb. You're sticking your nose in where it doesn't belong. I've asked you to butt out. Now I'm making it an order."

Rebecca's mouth compressed into a thin line. Flora Melkiot was right. He was a glory-grabbing idiot. "First of all, I was delivering a purchase at the request of my customer when Laura Tyler died. I hardly see how even you can construe that as 'meddling.' Secondly, I was nowhere near the building or anyone concerned with the case when Waldo Wylde was attacked."

"I know."

"And I didn't have anything to do with it."

"I know that, too."

"You do? Have you caught him?"

Ashdown sighed. "The chief has called a press conference for as soon as booking is completed, so I don't guess it will matter if I tell you. Roland Orwell has confessed."

"Because Wylde was blackmailing him?"

"Blackmail? He tried to kill him because he thought Wylde was keeping Ginny from leaving. Orwell planned to take Ginny and escape to some nice beach where they don't have extradition. Only thing was, Ginny didn't want to go, and Orwell wouldn't believe Wylde wasn't coercing her."

So Ashdown didn't know about Wylde putting the pressure on Orwell! If it were true, and the way Eddie Anthony had said it, she tended to believe that it was.

Well, let Supercop Ashdown find out for himself. She was definitely not feeling very charitable toward him or doing her civic duty at the moment. Since he thought he knew it all, he could obviously figure out the problem easily without any prompting from her.

"Just for curiosity's sake," he asked in a much more friendly tone, "how did you find out about Wylde? The news only hit the media about an hour ago."

So now he was ready to play nice? Rebecca didn't think so. "A friend called and told me about it."

"Flora Melkiot, I assume. I'd be careful of that old woman. You'd better stay away from her. She's trouble."

So am I, Rebecca thought mutinously. Aloud she said in a quiet voice that portended danger to those who knew her well, "Are you daring to put limits on whom I may and may not have as a friend?"

"I will if they interfere with my investigations."

"Well, your investigations aren't doing so hot, are they? Flora Melkiot and I discovered Laura Tyler's secret stash, not you. Flora Melkiot and I discovered the gambling connection between Laura Tyler and Chuck Jernigan, not you. And if I hadn't wanted to talk to Madame Norina, you would be facing another murder investigation without a suspect. I kept Chuck Jernigan from killing Madame outright and kept him from disappearing. I, not you. Now you tell me what you've done!" Rebecca was almost whispering in her fury by then. It didn't do her temper any good to realize the madder she got, the calmer he became.

Ashdown was fully aware of what she was saying, and he didn't like it. His own face and voice tightened until the words came out like small ugly darts. "I don't have to report to you, Miss Cloudwebb. You are a civilian. Stay away from this. I don't want to see you messing around in this case again. Go back to your antique business and stop nosing around in things that don't concern you. That's an order."

She was right. Rebecca knew she was right, and he was too much of a self-righteous slob to admit it. Somehow that wasn't surprising. Deliberately Rebecca stood, picked up her cane and her purse, and started toward the door.

"I'm not finished talking to you!"

She stopped, her hand on the doorknob, and turned around. "Are you arresting me?"

"I could. Obstruction."

"But are you?"

"Not now."

"Then don't you dare tell me what to do!" she snapped and closed the door firmly after

361

CHAPTER TWENTY-TWO

"Do you think he's on the take?"

Rebecca looked up, startled. "Who? Ashdown?"

Flora rattled the knife in the mayonnaise jar, scraping out the last little bit. "Of course Ashdown. Who else have we been talking about? I hope you don't mind if the tuna salad is a little dry. I seem to have run out of mayonnaise. Isn't it dreadful they way they're putting everything in plastic jars these days? They never feel really clean."

They were in Flora's combination kitchen/ breakfast nook, tastefully decorated with a frieze of gaudy Mexican painted tiles. Here there were no valuable antiques, merely things of a certain age. Flora had a goodly collection of kitchen appliances — blender, toaster, food processor, mixer — all of which looked expensive, old, and well used, which sort of surprised Rebecca. Flora Melkiot did not seem to be the domestic-goddess type who enjoyed cooking.

Rebecca shrugged. She had honestly never paid any attention to how things were packaged. "That's fine. I'm just grateful you offered to fix lunch."

"Pity we couldn't have eaten in the restaurant, but it does close promptly at one on Thursdays. Silly policy. If that stupid detective hadn't interfered . . ."

For once Rebecca was in complete agreement, at least about Ashdown's mental ability. "He may be stupid, but I don't think Ashdown is on the take. He has that noxious sanctimonious air about him."

Of course, she had been wrong once before. She had nearly paid with her life for believing in Frank Titus's honesty. Jesse had; Frank had murdered Jesse as surely as if he had shot him himself. To take away the taste of a bad memory, she sipped at the Diet Coke Flora had provided and, once the sandwich and potato chips were placed in front of her, took an enthusiastic bite.

"Did you believe Eddie Anthony?"

"This is delicious. Thank you." Rebecca dabbed at her lips with a surprisingly mundane paper napkin. "Yes, I think he was telling the truth."

"Which does not mean the same thing as that what he said was the truth."

Rebecca looked up in surprise. "You're sharp."

"You don't get to be my age without learning the difference. Eddie Anthony told us what he believes to be the truth. It may or may not be. I could never see what Eleanor saw in him, but they seemed a more than averagely happy couple. Which is more than I can say for Isabel and Roland Orwell or Waldo and Ginny Wylde." Flora bit into her own sandwich and masticated silently, her eyes dreamy with thought.

"Do you believe what he said about Eleanor having been a hooker?"

Flora swallowed and gave a nasty little laugh. "Yes. It might be some men's fantasy to have a prostitute for a wife, but not Eddie Anthony. He and his family are starchier than a parson's knickers. As for Eleanor, yes, I can believe she was once a hooker. She was so determinedly a pattern card of a lady — always proper, never a step out of line — it was obvious she was trying too hard. Not that it would have made any difference. Nowadays it seems that a great number of our leading 'ladies' have a dark secret of some kind or another in their past, and it doesn't seem to hurt their position a bit, more's the pity. Not like it was when I was a girl, when wearing the wrong color of shoes at the wrong time of year could cloud your reputation."

"So you think the Anthonys were only trying to hide their connection to the Nevada state senator's death. If it really happened," Rebecca murmured, wondering just how much of Flora's life was a dark secret.

"I think it really happened, and I think Eddie was delighted it happened. It gave him the woman of his dreams."

"And drove her away."

Flora nibbled at a potato chip. "I don't think Madame was blackmailing Eleanor. I think she was trying to raise money and accidentally pushed Eleanor's hot spot. I do, however, think Waldo Wylde really was trying to pressure him by using her."

"How do you think he find out?"

"I have no idea. The man seems to have all kinds of contacts everywhere, though. Look at all the money he's raking in from that show of his. And going into politics to boot. He couldn't have chosen a better candidate for his pet senator. Eddie's very handsome, very personable, comes from a good family, and hasn't an original thought in his head," Flora said uncharitably. "How do you think he found out?"

"I'm not sure he did. Wylde's a bottom feeder. Probably found or figured out that there was some mystery about Eleanor Anthony. Then, if he didn't really know, he just bluffed and let Mr. Anthony believe he knew their great secret and would make it public unless he cooperated. The Anthonys' guilty consciences did the rest. I wonder why she left — surely she knew he'd protect her no matter what."

"He and I talked for a while after that idiot detective marched you away." Flora finished off the last of her potato chips. "She left to protect him. He let me see some of the letter she wrote, and I think she meant it. No one could write sappy romantic drivel like that and not mean it, I hope. The whole bit about how he was too good for her, she couldn't let him ruin his life protecting her, she'd always love him . . . Faugh!"

"You're kidding."

"No. I wish I were. It was straight out of a particularly bad romance novel. And he believes it."

"So what did you tell him to do?" Rebecca asked and took a bite of her sandwich, sublimely ignoring Flora's rising eyebrows.

"What makes you think I told him any-thing? I'm not in the habit of meddling in my neighbors' affairs!"

Rebecca was glad of the necessity of chew-ing, because it kept her from laughing out loud. Even in their short association, she had come to realize that Flora Melkiot had no qualms about arranging things and people the way she thought best.

"Because," she said, heroically swallowing, "you are a caring woman with a sense of the way the world works. Besides, he was in no fit state to tie his shoes, let alone make a life-changing decision. What did you tell him?"

Mollified, Flora relaxed. "I told him he should talk to the best lawyer he could find — one with no ties to his family or their businesses — and tell him everything. Let him investigate the murder, if there was one, back in Nevada and see about getting Eleanor in the clear. In the meantime, get a team of private detectives working on finding her."

"Just what I would have told him myself," Rebecca said. "But it was probably easier for him to take coming from a neighbor." She took another bite of sandwich, chewed, and then said, "The bad part of all this is that we still don't know who killed Laura Tyler or why."

"You really don't believe it was the gamblers, do you?"

"No. Chuck Jernigan isn't the type to put poison in a glass."

"Having seen him in action, I agree." Flora nodded sagely, then added with distaste, "What a Neanderthal. A total savage. I don't know how we put up with something like him for so long."

Rebecca shrugged. "He only showed you what he wanted you to see. And that is what's been the trouble all the time."

"Jernigan?"

"No. We've only been seeing what people wanted us to see. We've got to get to the truth, unpleasant as it might be. The glasses were brought up to the salon from being washed in the kitchen that morning, right? Now the drain cleaner had to be put in the glass after it was washed, either in the kitchen or in the salon."

Flora's eyes widened. "And if it was done in the kitchen, why was the piece of plastic wrap in the salon? If it had been done in the kitchen, there wouldn't be any."

Rebecca nodded as if at a particularly bright pupil. "A kitchen worker would have made sure not to leave any traces. At least, that seems the most obvious way. But the plastic was left in the salon, which means that it and the drain cleaner had to be put there by someone in the jewel class."

"Dear God." Flora's mouth tightened. "That means one of us is a murderer. I know every one of those women."

"I think we can discount Madame Norina. She wouldn't take the risk of such damaging publicity for her salon."

"Agreed. She needed money too badly to upset the boat. Even if the Tyler woman were blackmailing her, she wouldn't have offed her in her own salon. With her history, she'd be too smart for that."

"With her history?" Rebecca put down her sandwich and stared. "You had her investigated, didn't you?"

"That's a little formal," Flora replied with unruffled serenity. "There was nothing so grand as an investigation. I merely had some friends of mine nose around a little when she came into the building. Someone had to do it, and no one in their right mind would trust that brainless blonde in the office!"

"What did you find out?"

"Her real name is Nora O'Malley, and the Middle European accent is fake. She's from New Jersey, I believe, and had a long history of various get-rich-quick schemes when she was younger. Never anything really, really illegal, but sometimes a little shady. She had been in this exercise thing for a while though, as everything from an aerobics instructor to a yoga teacher, and it all seemed to be straight. She had a small exercise studio in Kansas City for a while, then suddenly appeared in Dallas as Madame Norina." Flora bit into her sandwich, totally unconcerned that Rebecca was staring at her. "Although it seems she has always had a bit of a gambling problem."

"You have some friends. They researched me, too, you said. How much?"

"As much as necessary."

Rebecca almost asked what she had found out, but then thought better of it and changed the subject. "Eleanor Anthony is a good suspect. She had something to hide, she had a shady past where she learned only heaven knows what, she believed Madame was blackmailing her and might have thought this would save her."

"But why did she leave then?"

"Good question. We don't know. Anyway, she's not here for us to talk to, so we'll have to keep her in the 'possible' category. That leaves Isabel Orwell, Ginny Wylde, Miss Alicia Carruthers . . . and you."

Flora was too astonished to be outraged. "I? You honestly think I could have done it?"

"You were there. You had means and opportunity. Maybe a motive we haven't found yet."

"But I've been working to solve the case!"

"What better way to muddy the water and misdirect suspicion away from you?" Rebecca asked, startled at the fury that leapt to life full-blown in those old eyes. She had regarded Flora Melkiot as a meddler, a basically harmless old snoop. That might have been a mistake. There was power in that thin face, and fury, and a cold intelligence. Given the right provocation, this woman could kill someone. "I don't think you did," Rebecca said in all sincerity, then threw that maddening man to the wolf with no compunction. "Ashdown regards you as a suspect, though."

"I have said from the beginning that man was an idiot," Flora said in tones that boded no good for Detective John Ashdown. She was not a woman to take insult lightly,

"And I agree. So, that leaves us with three women to talk to. We probably won't be able to get near Ginny Wylde for a while, so we have our choice of Isabel or Miss Alicia."

"It's Thursday. Miss Alicia will be at work until five at the earliest. Woman runs like a metronome." Flora did not mean it as a compliment.

"So that leaves Isabel." Rebecca stood up purposefully. "Let's go talk to her."

■ ■ ■ ■

"So what do you want to talk to me about?"

Isabel Orwell sprawled back on the sofa, her glass clutched tightly in her hand. It was a large glass, meant for a Texas-size serving of iced tea. It was close to full, but not of iced tea. The entire apartment stank of alcohol.

Rebecca never would have recognized the slovenly, drunken woman in front of her as the elegantly turned-out matron from the exercise class. Her face was tight; so was the orange and white romper suit she wore. Neither of them were overly clean and her mismatched crew socks — one red, one gray — were positively grubby. Her hair was scraped back into sweaty chunks with randomly placed bobby pins.

"We're looking into the murder of Laura Tyler," Rebecca replied. "We're talking to everyone who was in the class that day."

"Thought you were an antique dealer." Isabel took a noisy slurp of her drink. She had not offered anything to her guests.

"I am now."

"Miss Cloudwebb was formerly a detective on the police force," Flora said, calmly overriding her. "Her brother is currently a

373

deputy chief. Detective Ashdown spoke to us about working on the case."

Rebecca shot Flora a startled glance. Ashdown certainly had spoken to them most strongly about working on the case, but not in the sense she managed to convey. Again every word was true, but none of them reflected the way things were. The old woman was amazing. Rebecca promised herself never to believe anything Flora Melkiot said.

Isabel shrugged. "It should have been Ginny Wylde who died. The bitch. That cheap, husband-stealing bitch. She deserved it." She downed another hefty swig from her glass.

"But it was Laura Tyler who died," Rebecca reminded her gently. If the woman had been drinking like this since this morning, it was a wonder she was even conscious, let alone reasonably coherent. How much of what she said could be trusted?

"I know." Great oily tears surfaced and left smeary tracks down Isabel's cheeks. Another drink. "It's all Ginny Wylde's fault. She should have left Roland alone. Did you know the police arrested him?"

"We had heard —" Flora began, but Isabel didn't stop.

"He's weak, you see. No one knows it, but

374

he's so weak . . . Did you know that when she turned him down he beat up Waldo Wylde? Blamed him for it. Then he asked me to cover for him. Again."

"Again?" Eyes fox-bright, Flora leaned forward, only to retreat at Rebecca's unexpectedly fierce glare.

"That will all come out at his trial probably."

Isabel shook her head. "No, hidden too well. But I know, and he knows I know. It was our secret." Another gulp of her drink, one that seemed to half empty the glass, and a deep breath seemed to steady the woman. "Everything was going so good. Now, because Ginny Wylde was bored and wanted a new man to play with, I'm going to lose everything."

"I noticed the boxes." Flora's glance flicked over to a stack of assorted cardboard cartons in the corner of the room. "Are you planning to move?"

"Have to. Can't afford this place." A great big sniff and a few more tears, but her expression was rapidly becoming more dull and glazed than grief-stricken. "I'm leaving. Roland left me, so he's just going to have to deal with it." Isabel Orwell leaned forward in a drunken burlesque of confidentiality. "I've already cleaned out all our bank accounts. Did it first thing this morning, right after they arrested him. No need to wait, is there? I even emptied the safety deposit box. Tomorrow I'm going down and try to get a quick divorce."

"Can you do all that?" Flora asked.

" 'Course I can. We're still married. Besides, it's what he was going to do to me. Told me so. Told me he was going to strip everything and take Ginny away. So he can't complain if I do it to him first. He said he was going to leave me this condo, but then he didn't have a choice. It's in my name, you see. My maiden name. Something to do with taxes. So I'm going to sell it, and keep all the money. Serves him right."

Isabel's words had been coming slower and slower, in almost direct proportion to the droop of her eyelids. Rebecca acted just in time to snatch the glass from her flaccid fingers before she slid into an ungraceful heap on the couch.

"Well!" Flora said. "Such examples of marital devotion."

"I think Roland deserves every bit of it," Rebecca snapped. "He betrayed her. He cheated. He lied to her. He turned her life upside down. He didn't play by the rules. Do you think we can just leave her like this?"

"I don't see why not. She's going to have

to sleep it off."

With a surprising delicacy Rebecca straightened Isabel's head to a less grotesque position, then lifted her legs onto the couch. Isabel began to give out little malodorous snores.

Not having a key, they couldn't lock the door, but only pulled it tightly shut. Even though the interior hallway of the Olympus House had no windows, it was like stepping from a dark and noisome cave into a place of light and rationality.

Rebecca checked her watch, then pushed the elevator up button. "It's after five-thirty. Let's see if Miss Alicia is in."

"I never thought I'd look forward to talking to that straight-laced old moralizer," Flora said, "but she'll be a breath of fresh air after that. I never would have guessed!"

"You've never seen her drunk before?"

"Oh, at one or two of the building parties I've seen her get giggly — almost like a schoolgirl — but never like this. Even when she threw the glass against the wall at the Wyldes' party she wasn't drunk, at least not like this."

"She has reason," Rebecca said, earning a covertly searching glance from Flora. "What I want to know is how she stands that apartment . . . all gray and black like an old movie. Creepy."

"I'd never seen their place, but I agree. Hardly in tune with Isabel's usual style. At least, what was her style until Roland fired her maid."

"Huh?"

"Of course, I only saw Isabel at exercise class and occasionally at functions here in the building, but every time I saw her, she looked exquisite. Hair done, nicely coordinated clothes, manicure . . . like you would expect a resident of the Olympus House to look," Flora said complacently, patting her own sleek chignon.

"Well, you must admit that she's been through a lot recently. Style doesn't become that important when your life is falling apart."

Flora's expression was eloquent about what she thought of that. "I think the maid put her together every day. Picked out her clothes and accessories."

Rebecca jabbed the elevator button again. "Well, some people have taste and some don't. And her husband fired her maid when he was planning to run away with another woman? That seems downright mean."

"I suppose so. Isabel always wanted things just so. A perfectionist if there ever was one.

Couldn't stand to have anything less. We worked together once on the building holiday party committee, and I swore I'd never do that again."

"Well, it looks like you won't have to. She's moving."

"We'll tell Miss Alicia," Flora said with a nasty little smile. "Giving her a heads up on a potential sale might make her feel more kindly toward us."

CHAPTER TWENTY-THREE

Miss Alicia was not in.

"Do you want to come back to my place and wait?" Flora asked.

"No. Let's stay here a few minutes just in case."

The sumptuously appointed landing was just what the penthouse floor of an exclusive high-rise should be — marble floors, wood paneled walls, indirect lighting, a very good fake plant, and a sculpted metal bench covered with brocade. It looked better than it sat, as Rebecca soon found out.

"What did they stuff this thing with? Doorknobs?"

Flora snorted. "Construction debris, I would guess. It's all for show. We're probably the first people who ever sat on it."

"And hopefully the last. Let's give it five minutes and then go. If all else fails, we can make an appointment with her at her office."

Flora snorted again. "Not unless we're interested in buying a house. And then we'd probably be shunted off to some underling. Miss Alicia Carruthers only makes time for making money. Except for Madame Norina's class. That's the only thing I've ever heard of her doing that wasn't directly involved with business."

"Something for her health, I suppose. If you're sick you can't do business. Wonder how much money she has socked away?"

"Millions, I would guess. However much it is, she's earned it. Has no private life at all. That anyone knows of. What she does on Tuesday and Wednesday is a complete mystery. Though there are rumors . . ."

"There would be, wouldn't there? Sounds like the stuff of a bad novel. What does the wealthy magnate do in her secret life?" Rebecca thought of the slim margin on which the shop existed and for a moment thought enviously of such riches. "Probably just goes away to meditate or read uplifting books."

The elevator doors opened and Ginny Wylde, still in her exercise costume — a rich garnet color today that should have clashed with her hair but didn't — stepped out.

"What are you doing here?"

"Waiting for Miss Alicia. She's late." Flora rose, somewhat creakingly, hands outstretched to grab a startled Ginny's. "I'm so glad we were here, though, so we could tell you how sorry we are about what happened to your husband."

"But you didn't like Waldo."

Flora wasn't fazed. "No, we disagreed on a number of things, but I am so sorry that he had to undergo such a horrible experience. It's hard to think of something so devastating happening here in the Olympus House . . . we're almost a family . . ."

Rebecca watched in wonder. During her years on the force she had had the authority of her badge to enforce her will. Flora had no such backing, yet before Rebecca could be quite sure how she had done it, she had all three of them inside the Wylde townhouse, comfortably ensconced in the living room while Ginny poured them each a gin and tonic.

Rebecca loathed gin and tonic, but she would have drunk anything to keep the mood going.

She would have drunk it just to see the inside of this penthouse. Now this looked just like a penthouse should look. The outside wall of the living room was glass, giving a spectacular view of the North Dallas sprawl. The high ceilings were deeply coffered and the walls paneled in dark wood, giving a carefully vague impression of an English manor house. There were no real antiques, but everything in the place was a carefully crafted reproduction of one. The result was incredibly rich and harmonious. Small wonder that Roland Orwell preferred a woman from this ambiance than his own wife back in that comfortless film-negative place of theirs.

The only false note in the genteel richness was Ginny herself tottering back from the bar, three tall icy drinks precariously gripped in her hands, her dark red exercise suit looking as if it had been painted on.

"How is your husband?" Rebecca asked, reaching out to help.

"Oh, Waldo's going to be all right. He's complaining loud enough that he can't be too badly hurt."

"But from what I heard, it was a pretty savage attack," Flora said.

The telephone had begun to ring almost immediately, but Ginny seated herself in a leather armchair and took a big sip of her drink.

"It was. He was just lucky that Roland was such a wimp. No muscle tone at all."

"Would you like me to bring you the phone?" Rebecca asked tentatively, unwilling to shatter the mood but annoyed by the constant *Brrrt . . . Brrrt . . .* Apparently Waldo Wylde did not believe in euphonious ringtones.

"Oh, no! Just ignore it. Probably some of the reporters downstairs who followed me from the hospital. They kept shooting pictures even though we told them not to. I don't want to talk to them."

"I can imagine you've been besieged. How annoying!" Flora said.

"It's part of living with a famous man," Ginny began, preening.

Brrrt . . . Brrrt . . .

"— and Waldo is having everything handled from his office because —"

Brrrt . . . Brrrt . . .

"— he doesn't like it when I talk to the media," she finished.

Brrrt . . . Brrrt . . .

Rebecca could believe that. This overtly sexual, self-centered, selfish creature was not the ideal wife for a man in public life.

One last, desperate *Brrrt . . .* and the phone went silent.

"What did Roland Orwell think he was doing? You had already told him you wouldn't go away with him." Flora was nothing if not blunt, but the question didn't seem to faze Ginny. Apparently it struck her as normal that the entire world should be talking about her and her affairs.

"Roland is a jerk. I don't see what I saw in him," she admitted. "It was just a fling. Who would have thought that he would take a silly fling so seriously?" She stretched out her long legs and arched her back like a cat. "God, it's tiring sitting around in the hospital. I kept telling Waldo I needed to come home, to change clothes if nothing else, but he wouldn't hear of it. Said I was perfect as I was."

The telephone began again. *Brrrt . . . Brrrt . . .* Ginny ignored it.

Rebecca's mind went off on a tangent. Since Waldo Wylde was such an unappealing specimen himself, perhaps a show-off, physically beautiful trophy wife was the proper accessory for him. The story of his attack might have faded from the top of the news, but if the media could get pictures of his beautiful, distraught wife — especially a beautiful, distraught wife who looked like a million bucks in a skin-tight exercise suit — that could keep the story going for a couple of more broadcasts.

Brrrt . . . Brrrt . . .

Rebecca, my girl, she thought, *you're getting cynical!*

Brrrt . . . Brrrt . . .

"Roland didn't really think he could force

you into going away with him, did he?" Flora leaned forward, an incongruously rapt expression on her face.

Brrrt . . . Brrrt . . .

"Who knows what old Roland thought," Ginny said contemptuously. "He wasn't even all that good in the sack. But apparently it was just like him to hurt Waldo. He was a mean man at heart. He even tried to put Madame Norina out of business."

Brrrt . . . Brrrt . . .

"What?" Rebecca and Flora said in unison, startling Ginny.

"You mean you didn't know?"

Brrrt . . . Brrrt . . .

"No, we didn't," Flora said. "When did this happen?"

"That morning . . . Monday. The morning the old lady died. He went in to talk to Madame before the class. I saw him coming out, and he was angry. Said the old lady — Madame — had to straighten up her act or he'd close her down."

Brrrt . . . Brrrt . . .

"Ginny," Rebecca asked gently, "can you think of any reason anyone would have to kill Laura Tyler?"

Brrrt . . . Brrrt . . .

"Who? Oh, the old lady who died. No. Who knew her? It was her first morning there. I must say, she didn't seem like the type to fit in, but Madame said she was a resident."

Brrrt . . . Brrrt . . .

"Did Roland know her?"

Brrrt . . . Brrrt . . .

"How should I know? He knew lots of people. Damn that phone!" Ginny said with sudden, unexpected vehemence. "I'm going to put it on silent answer. I simply have to have some sleep. I look like a hag."

She did look tired and more than a little wrung out, but there was no way on this earth that Ginny Wylde could look like a hag. She stood, and both Flora and Rebecca realized that they were being given their marching orders. That was all right; they had learned more than they had expected.

A few polite phrases, some basically insincere protestations of sympathy, and they were standing in the landing area, staring at each other.

"Did you ever?" Flora murmured. "She has the manners of a field hand."

"Did you hear what she said about Orwell? He was in the salon that morning. He could have put the drain cleaner crystals in the glass!"

"I wonder if that idiot detective knows?"

Rebecca's lips curved up into a feral smile.

"Let's go down to your place and find out."

"Good afternoon, Detective," Rebecca said in her plummiest voice. Ensconced in one of Flora's genuine antique chairs (one could always tell, no matter how good the reproduction) with a glass of white wine in one hand to wash away the nasty aftertaste of gin and her cell phone in the other, she felt quite in control.

"Good afternoon, Miss Cloudwebb," Ashdown answered. Even over the telephone his voice was thick with wary civility. "What have you been doing that I won't approve of?"

"What an attitude you have! What makes you think I'd do anything you wouldn't approve of?"

"Because you do all the time."

"What is the status of the case? Surely you can bring me up-to-date."

"And if I don't, you'll call your brother, right? All right, nothing. Laura Tyler's body was released to the family yesterday. There's going to be a memorial service tomorrow, I believe. We are pursuing several promising leads at this time. That's all. Goodbye, Miss Cloudwebb."

"Wait! You'll regret it if you hang up."

"What?"

"Was there any financial connection between Roland Orwell and Laura Tyler?"

"Not that I know of. We've glanced over his accounts — with the bank's permission and cooperation, I might add — and there was nothing for her or for the plumbing company or any of the Tylers personally. He did give a rather large, undersecured loan to Madame Norina that was badly in arrears."

"So you knew about that already." Rebecca tried not to sound too disappointed.

"Yes, we did, Miss Cloudwebb, and so will everyone else when the chief gives a press conference this afternoon. Now go sell your old stuff and stop meddling in police business!"

"I guess you already know," Rebecca said slowly, "that Roland Orwell was in the salon that morning, just before the jewel class began."

"What?" Ashdown's explosive response all but knocked the phone from her hand. "Where did you learn that?"

"From a friend who heard it from her friend."

Flora wasn't the only one who could manipulate the truth.

"Flora Melkiot, I bet. Look, Miss Rebecca Cloudwebb, you and that meddlesome old

389

witch keep out of this case!"

"You know, Detective, I am getting very bored with you telling me what I can and cannot do. I should think you'd be glad of any information I pass on, but instead you yell at me."

Rebecca's was a very good cell phone; she could hear Ashdown grinding his teeth clearly.

"Goodbye, Detective."

"Well?" Flora asked once the little phone snapped shut.

"Apparently Roland gave Madame a very large loan on very little collateral. It was also long past due. There was no sign of any connection to Laura Tyler."

Flora muttered a word not really suitable for ladies. "No one knew the woman, no one had ever really met her. She was just a silly little creature from the suburbs, so why did someone murder her?"

It should be raining. It should be gray and gloomy and cold. The bright Texas sun washing everything with brilliant yellow light — and heat enough to poach an egg — was an insult to Eddie Anthony's mood.

He pulled the drapes shut, knowing that watching the big circular drive for Eleanor's return was a waste of time. She was gone, sacrificing them, what they had been together, for him. What she didn't understand was that without her, he was nothing. He would have paid every penny he had or could beg, borrow, or steal to keep her by his side.

And she would come back. If any mere human effort could get her back, she would come back. When a big job was in the offing, people were more than willing to work odd hours. He had come back to the apartment directly from his conversation with Flora Melkiot and followed her instructions to the letter. His work on the problem had gone on most of the night.

Already private detectives were looking for Eleanor in every major city in the country. He had given them her married name, her real name, the name they had changed it to, even the name under which she had worked in Nevada. He had given them pictures and her social security number.

He had put a team of lawyers on the problem of the dead man in Carson City. They had all seemed to think the matter could be handled with little fanfare, if it had happened as Eleanor had said. Self-defense was self-defense, even if it was from a hooker against a state senator.

And if there was enough money involved, Eddie thought cynically. He was a dreamer, but not a fool.

If necessary, he would even take out ads across the country. But he would find her.

He would find her.

Unknown to Mr. C. Edward Anthony, Detective John Ashdown was doing much the same thing, only with many fewer resources and a much smaller budget. Photographs and descriptions of Eleanor Anthony had gone out all over the country as a "Person of Interest." Ashdown knew not to call her a suspect, which she was, technically, but if he had, the very wealthy and very powerful Anthony family would have him obliterated, professionally speaking. He simply didn't have enough evidence to make her a suspect.

Hell, he didn't have enough evidence to make anyone a suspect.

And that damned Rebecca Cloudwebb calling up sweet as pie and dropping the bomb on him that Roland Orwell had been in the salon the morning that Laura Tyler had died. How many people had known that? And how many had not mentioned it? And how the hell was he supposed to know to ask?

Ashdown drummed his fingers on the desk in frustration.

Who else had been there that morning?

Who had killed Laura Tyler?

And why? Why?

The penthouse landing was deserted, for which Rebecca was glad. There could have been security waiting if Ginny had regretted her little confidences. Or the police.

"What if she's not here this time?"

Rebecca shrugged. "I don't know. I just know that if we don't talk to her soon, Ashdown is going to come back and talk again to everyone that was in the salon that morning, and I want to talk to her first. No," she amended, "I want you to talk to her."

"I? Whatever for?"

"Because I've seen you in action, and either you're the greatest natural interrogator ever born or you're some kind of witch. People who should throw you out end up telling you everything but their shoe size! It's magic."

"Oh, piffle," Flora said inelegantly, but with a visible pleasure. "It's nothing but charm. Charm and empathy. Young ladies were expected to learn graces like that when I was a girl."

Rebecca swallowed as she pressed Miss

Alicia's bell with authority. It was all she could do not to choke. Charm? Empathy? She could think of a number of words to describe Flora Melkiot — and doubtless Ashdown could come up with more — but those two were not on the list.

The door opened, revealing a very tired-looking, very old-looking real-estate tycoon. "Yes?"

"We'd like to talk to you, Miss Carruthers," Rebecca said.

"Flora Melkiot! And you're the woman who was there when that woman died. What do you want to talk to me about?"

"Miss Cloudwebb was formerly a detective with the police," Flora said smoothly, "and Detective Ashdown has spoken to us about helping with the case."

Flora spoke first; the untruth sounded just as plausible to Rebecca as it had the first time, and she knew it wasn't true. Unrestrained, Flora Melkiot could be a menace.

"I don't know that I could help you, and I'm very tired. Please go away." Inexorably the old woman began to close the door.

"Please, Miss Carruthers," Rebecca began, but Flora was more direct, slapping her hand against the door.

"We know about your child," she said.

Miss Alicia Carruthers fainted.

CHAPTER TWENTY-FOUR

"How did you find out?"

Although she had recovered from her faint almost immediately, Miss Alicia still looked shrunken and shocky. Flora had sent Rebecca to make some tea with lots of sugar. Miss Alicia sipped it now, carefully, from an ancient mug with a chipped rim. No fancy glasses or expensive tea sets in the Carruthers kitchen, or much of anything else, either.

"There were some rumors years ago," Flora said in a gentle voice.

"I didn't think anyone paid any attention to them."

"Most people wouldn't. Somebody did, though, didn't they? You've been blackmailed."

Miss Alicia nodded. "Yes. I don't know how he found out. I never could find out how he knew."

Rebecca thought she had never seen such a bleak look on another human's face.

"How long?"

"Over fifty years."

"Fifty years!" Flora cried in honest astonishment. "Miss Alicia, who has been blackmailing you?"

"Clint Dashell." The words came out like small, hard pebbles that had been cemented in place so long it was almost impossible to break them free. "He was my corporate attorney. And her father. Retired now. Lives out in Scottsdale. Plays golf every day, he says."

"On your money, I'll bet!" Flora snapped.

"He wouldn't marry you?"

"He was already married," Miss Alicia said slowly. "I didn't know."

"But more than fifty years!" Rebecca was baffled. "After all this time, what does it matter? I'm sure your child wouldn't want you to suffer like this."

Miss Alicia stabbed her with a hard glance. "You didn't know, did you? You were guessing."

"I knew some of it," Flora said, her voice still uncharacteristically gentle. "Why don't you tell us the whole story?"

"Why should I?"

"Why shouldn't you? Fifty years of blackmail, of anger, of hate. What does it matter now? It can't be good for you to keep it bottled up."

Miss Alicia sighed and for a moment looked older than her age. "You're right. Someone should know the story. I was a brand-new schoolteacher. My family had nothing during the Depression, and they all sacrificed a lot to help me get an education. I was then supposed to help the others because I had a job and made good money. Back then any money looked good."

"Then you met this Clint Dashell?" Rebecca asked and the old lady nodded.

"We met at school — the University of Texas. There was only the one in Austin back then. I was an undergraduate and he was in law school. He said he loved me. And I was a fool. Then I found out I was pregnant and he was married." Her gaze, now calm and steady, locked on Flora's face. "You remember what it was like back then, during the war and just after. Just being alone with a man after dark could ruin any girl's reputation, and schoolteachers had to be so much more careful than most. Once you were fired on moral grounds, you never got another job teaching.

"I went to an old aunt whom I knew could keep a secret. I intended to give the baby up for adoption and then get my life back on track. But my daughter was born . . .

damaged. She would never be normal, even to the extent of looking after herself. The doctor told me she might never be able even to dress or feed herself." The old chin lifted with an unmistakable flourish of pride. "She has learned to do both over the years."

Rebecca was aghast. The "child" was at least fifty, probably older, and still the mother was proud that she could feed and dress herself. Esther might understand, but Rebecca, childless and cynical, was appalled.

"I knew if I kept her, my life would be destroyed. I knew no one would ever adopt her and she would probably end up warehoused in some horrible place. I could never do that, nor could I ruin what future I had by admitting she existed. My aunt kept her and I went back to work, but I felt I had to warn other young women to stay out of the trap that was consuming me."

"So you became a tireless crusader for morality," Flora murmured.

"I did. And I hope I saved a few women from the hell in which I lived. At first it wasn't too bad. I was used to being poor, but I always needed more money. My family wanted to be repaid for what they had done for me, and there was never enough money."

"You never told your family?" Rebecca asked. "Why? Wouldn't they help you?"

"You don't know my family," was all Miss Alicia would say. She put down her empty cup and Rebecca refilled it almost immediately from the ancient, stained teapot. "My aunt was the best of the lot. She arranged everything, up to and including my false name and excuses to my family about why I had to go away for a while. The authorities weren't so picky then about identities and birth certificates. Then she took care of the baby when I went back to work. After she died, I had to hire people to look after my daughter. That's when I started in real estate. I had to make money."

"Then Dashell showed up."

Miss Alicia nodded. "He demanded money or he would tell about the child."

"But she was his daughter!"

"He was revolted by her and said so. Said I should have killed her at birth. I didn't have a choice. So much of a real-estate agent's reputation is based on personal integrity and I had just started to make some real money. I paid him. And paid. And paid. Then he decided he wanted to be my corporate attorney."

"You didn't hire him!" Flora was scandalized.

"I did, and it was a good move, believe it or not. The more money I made, the more he got. And I still had to pay him. He also made sure I wasn't hiding anything from him in the corporate accounts. Oh, he left us enough to live on, but . . ."

"And you've just let him soak you all these years." Rebecca was indignant.

"I didn't dare rock the boat. I had a child to look after, a child who would need looking after all her life, even after I'm gone. I go to see her every Tuesday and Wednesday; even change cars on the way so I can't be followed. She's so sweet and loving, it breaks my heart. I wish I could hold her and protect her for every day of her life. I've managed to sock away a trust for her for after I die, a trust he doesn't know about and can't touch, but I always wonder if it's enough." She licked her lips. "I had to think of her."

Flora called the unfatherly attorney a name that sent Rebecca's eyebrows rising. She wouldn't have thought Flora knew such language.

"But you're sitting on a gold mine," Flora said slowly. It was almost possible to see the wheels turning in her head. "You can get revenge and cash at the same time."

"What?"

Flora's smile broadened into an expression that sent chills down Rebecca's back. "It's time," Flora said, "to end this charade. Go public. Go to the police. File charges. File a civil lawsuit. Write a book. Write several books. Go on TV and make them pay for the privilege of interviewing you. Make the biggest, most profitable stink in the world. If he denies fatherhood, sue him for a DNA test. That way you can help yourself and show the world what can happen to a naïve young girl."

Miss Alicia and Rebecca both stared at her in open-mouthed awe.

"You've fought for your vision of morality for your entire adult life," Flora went on. "Use your experience to help others. And let's face it, at your age, what do you have to lose?"

Miss Alicia was silent. Rebecca could almost see Flora's ideas sinking into her brain like a drought-breaking rain into the earth.

After a long silence, Rebecca finally asked, "Miss Alicia, was Dashell the only one blackmailing you?"

"Of course he was," she replied with some asperity. "He was the only one who knew."

"You haven't been approached by Waldo Wylde or Madame Norina?"

"Waldo? Young woman, what are you talking about? Madame Norina asked me to invest in her salon, along with the rest of the class, but Waldo Wylde?" Miss Alicia was back to normal. "What on earth has he to do with this?"

"Nothing," Flora said and abruptly stood up. "We must go, Rebecca, now that Miss Alicia is recovered. You will," her attention switched directly to Miss Alicia, "think about what I said?"

"I will think about it," the old woman said, suddenly not looking so old anymore. "I will most certainly think about it."

"Do you think she will?" Rebecca stretched out her legs and leaned back in one of Flora's surprisingly comfortable antique chairs. The ice in her wine spritzer tinkled seductively. "Go after the father, I mean."

"I knew what you meant," Flora replied, sipping from her own drink. "What that woman has suffered, and it's all her own fault. If she'd just had some gumption."

"But the times . . . weren't they awfully censorious back then?"

Flora eyed Rebecca sharply. "Don't talk about 'the times' as if they were ancient history. It wasn't that long ago. And yes, the times were dreadfully puritanical and narrow. But there have been a lot of times and changes since then. Not many of them good, but there have been changes. After all that vulgar hippie idiocy in the late sixties, Miss Alicia's peccadillo would have been small stuff."

"I wonder why she didn't do something then."

"The strongest cages are those of our own making."

"Who said that?"

Flora shrugged. "Some philosopher or other. I read him in college — one of those things you have to learn to get a degree and then never use again." She took a long sip. "It's always the secrets. Keeping secrets is dangerous."

Rebecca was still thinking about cages. She didn't have any secrets — well, one, and Frank Titus could stay a secret as far as she was concerned — but she knew all about cages. She had made herself a good one. Esther had tried to tell her, as had the mandated police department shrink, and her brother, and her few friends, but she hadn't listened. Now her cage was weakened, not broken, and if she weren't careful it would harden again around her.

"Look at Miss Alicia," Flora was going on. "How different her life might have been if she'd only stood up to that man. And Eleanor Anthony. I wonder if Eddie has done what I said."

"Do you think she'll ever come back?"

Flora shrugged. "Depends on why she went away. Maybe she has more secrets."

"I wonder what Laura Tyler's secrets were."

"Maybe she didn't have any. I've certainly seldom heard of any creature leading a more boring, honest, or blameless life."

"Boring, honest, and blameless people," Rebecca said wryly, "seldom get themselves murdered."

"That's why I still say it had to be the gamblers over her son."

"I don't think so. Anyway, there's a memorial service tomorrow."

"I know. Ten A.M. at the Christian Light Methodist Church just off Garland Road. You can pick me up."

"You're awfully sure I'm going."

Flora raised an amused eyebrow. "Aren't you?"

"Yes. Maybe if we can talk to the rest of her family, there'll be some hint, some lead we can use."

"For someone who kept saying she wasn't going to investigate the case you surely have become quite interested."

"And who is to blame for that?"

Looking sublimely innocent, Flora quoted, "Do not burden others with your conscience."

"Who said that?"

"Melkiot. Flora Melkiot."

The first person Rebecca saw in the simple sanctuary of the Christian Light Methodist Church was Detective John Ashdown. He was sitting in the back of the church, trying to be inconspicuous and not really succeeding. He was not happy to see them there.

Flora gave a small sniff and swept past him, all but pulling Rebecca in her wake toward the front pews. The church was almost full, but somehow Flora managed to fit the two of them in the row just behind the family. A small, simple building, the Christian Light Methodist Church did not possess a separate family mourning room.

Not that the family appeared to be mourning all that much. Of course, Rebecca would have bet that the boys would be stoic like their dad, who came from a time and a place where for a real man to show any emotion was "sissified." Emotion was a woman's business, but none of Laura's three daughters-in-law seemed to be showing much emotion either.

A brass urn, plain and square and unadorned, sat on a small table in front of the altar. Apparently Laura Tyler's sons had had her cremated. Remembering the queenly portrait from Phantasy Fotos, Rebecca could only conclude that one of the boys must have picked out the urn. Laura would never have chosen anything so stark.

The service was long; the minister (F. Osgood Chapman, according to the program) must have known Laura Tyler well, because he gave the mourners a long and detailed biography of her life. A biography, Rebecca noted, that ended before Laura's move to the Olympus House. He couldn't gloss over the fact that she had died in the salon there, but a stranger listening might never have known that she purchased a condo and moved away from Garland.

What startled Rebecca even more was that each of her sons rose and, dry-eyed, spoke — what a wonderful mother she had been; what a wonderful wife to their dad; how much their dad had loved and tried to provide for her. Again nothing was said about her bolt from Garland or her striving for a — to her — better life. Rebecca felt intensely sorry for the funny little gray-haired lady; even in death, she was forced to accept the parameters of her life as

406

defined by others rather than being remembered for her individual self. At least the self she had so desperately longed to become.

At any rate, the exercise gave Rebecca a chance to study Larry and the three other sons. They were pretty much as she had expected, which wasn't much; stolid, unimaginative working men who met life head on and reduced it to their terms.

Except for Skeeter. He was as much a changeling in that family as Laura must have been. To begin with, he was as handsome as a movie star and blessed with a charm that could have taken him to the White House. Even as he mouthed the same platitudes about his mother as his brothers had, there was a sense of sparkle and life that had been missing in the others.

Rebecca couldn't help wondering if any of his gambling buddies were lurking in the back of the church.

After the service finally ended, Rebecca watched with dismay as a totally unashamed Flora latched onto Larry and, perforce, the rest of the family. There was a spate of introductions, but she never could quite figure out which name went with which lady and which lady went with which husband. The sons — with the startling exception of apparently wifeless Skeeter — were practically clones of Larry, with either more or less hair and paunch.

In one way the wives were as interchangeable as Legos; solid, hardworking women all teetering on the edge of a middle age that was already not being very kind to them. There were physical differences among the three, of course — one was almost anorexically thin, while another could be described as Stylish Stout only with great charity — but all had a sameness of expression (sour, as if they had been somehow cheated) and taste (mass-market polyester) that banded them together more than their differences of body type could ever pull apart.

Again with the exceptions of Skeeter and Larry, they all looked at Flora and Rebecca as if they had been a particularly distasteful pair of rodents walking across the floor. Rebecca couldn't figure that out; they certainly looked respectable enough for a funeral. Flora was wearing her customary black, today a light silk in a semi-1950s cut with a shirtwaist top and a pleated skirt. Rebecca hadn't been able to face her only black suit — a mid-weight wool with a faint gray pinstripe that would have been suicidal on a hot Dallas summer day — so had opted for a tunic and pants of pale peach linen and some old pawn turquoise beads.

"It was so nice of you to come say good-bye to Mama," Larry was saying. His was the only genuine smile Rebecca had seen in the entire group.

"Yeah," said one of the wives. "At least two of Mama Laura's new friends bothered to come to the funeral. I notice no one else could." The edge in her voice turned the word "new" into an ugly pejorative.

"Just her old friends did," said another. Her voice was harsher, her anger deeper. "The ones Mama Laura was too good for all of a sudden."

"Now, honey . . ." said Ed.

Rebecca thought it was Ed. He and Al looked a great deal alike. So did Larry, for that matter.

"Well, why did she have to sell her pretty house and move into that crackerjack apartment in a building full of people who thought they was so much better'n her?" If there was any emotion in that rough-hewn face, it wasn't grief. It was anger. "She had no call to up and leave everything she'd knowed all her life."

"Why is that?" Rebecca asked in a soft voice.

The woman looked at her with surprise. "Because — because — because Daddy

Edwin had given her everything."

"Perhaps she wanted a change."

"A change from what? And why?" asked the skinny daughter-in-law, readily jumping into the discussion. "She had a good life here."

"Of course she did," Flora said soothingly. "But perhaps there was something here that she wanted to get away from? Something that might have frightened her?"

As if attached by strings, every Tyler head swung to look at Skeeter, who appeared amazingly nonplussed. Apparently he was accustomed to being the family whipping boy.

"Nothing to do with me," he said with a patently charming smile. "Everything in my life is on the up and up."

Rebecca would not have believed him if he had said the sun was shining without checking outside first.

"What would Mama Laura be afraid of? She lived a good life and she knew everyone around. No one here would hurt her," said the fat daughter-in-law. "Everyone loved Mama Laura."

One someone didn't, Rebecca thought.

The tallest of the boys — Ed? — looked pointedly at Rebecca's cane. "Accident?"

Rebecca shook her head. Usually if people

were so tactless as to ask a direct question, she had a nice evasive answer. No more of that. She was going to keep pounding at her weakened cage until she could reclaim all of her life.

"No. I was shot four years ago."

It was like a scream in a crowded room. Although she had spoken softly, all conversation in the Tyler family ceased and again they stared, this time with a kind of horror.

"What an awful experience," Skeeter murmured with just enough feeling to imply that he would be happy to help her get over it.

"My Gawd," muttered the mid-sized wife. "That Dallas is truly a Sodom and Gomorrah. Ain't nobody safe there," she added, as if it were days away instead of a contiguous city with sometimes blurry boundaries. "I swear I don't know why Mama Laura —"

Flora was suddenly busy again, saying all the right platitudes, expressing their pleasure at having known Laura Tyler even if for such a short time and their condolences over her loss. Almost before Rebecca knew it, Flora was sweeping her out of the church and down the blistering sidewalk to where they had left the car.

"We aren't going to the mausoleum for the interment?"

"No, we are not," Flora said. "I want to get home and have a nice glass of iced tea in a quiet room. Mainly I want to get out of here before we get lynched, or whatever it is they do to outsiders in this place."

Rebecca was struggling to keep up with Flora's pace. The sun's heat and brilliance were almost like a physical weight on her shoulders. She waited until they were safely in the car, seatbelts fastened, doors locked, motor running and air conditioning on full blast before speaking. "They didn't seem to like us very much, did they?"

"I think they were afraid of us."

"Afraid?"

Flora leaned back against the headrest and wearily closed her eyes as Rebecca pulled away from the Christian Light Methodist Church and the Tyler family. She waited to speak until they were blocks and blocks away. "Not of us, as individuals, but what we represent. A life that's different. Not better, not worse, but different. Something outside their comprehension. I'm beginning to have a little respect for Laura Tyler. It must have taken a great deal of courage to throw over everything and crawl out of that smug morass of lower-middle-class complacency."

"Ouch. Tell me how you really feel."

"Don't tell me you felt any different."

"Okay, I won't. But no one there killed Laura Tyler." Her mouth a grim line, Rebecca floorboarded the gas and swung the car onto LBJ, the eight-lane-wide racetrack that masqueraded as a freeway as it almost made a circle around Dallas. Even at ten miles over the posted speed limit, she was being passed by everything but skateboarders. Once, during her patrol days, she had actually arrested a skateboarder on the freeway. He had been totally unapologetic.

"I agree. Whatever their faults, the crabgrass set is innocent of her murder. Which leaves someone either at the Olympus House or from someplace else entirely."

"You're still betting on Skeeter's gambling friends, aren't you?"

"Yes."

"If they had done a hit on his mother to get a message to him, he'd either be long gone or in deep hiding. I don't think he'd have come and spoken in the open."

Flora harrumphed. She hated to be outlogicked. "I see your point. But who does that leave? Even that idiot detective was there watching him."

"I think he was watching more than Skeeter Tyler." Rebecca's voice was flat and taut. "When there's a murder, especially an

413

CHAPTER TWENTY-FIVE

The linen pile beside the computer was growing, as if the napkins and tea cloths and dresser sets were breeding out of boredom at being neglected. Rebecca stared at the untidy stack without really seeing it. After leaving Laura Tyler's funeral and delivering a speechlessly indignant Flora Melkiot to the Olympus House, she had returned to the shop with the complete intention of getting some work done. She had left the burden of the shop on Esther for most of the week, and there was nothing more she could do on the case anyway. Dead end. Blank wall. Any number of ways saying she had failed.

The screen went from the neglected and forgotten inventory to the screen saver, a montage of antique prints beneath a floating logo of C & L Antiques. Rebecca didn't even notice.

There had to be something missing, Rebecca knew, some piece that would hold all the disparate elements of the crime together. Something teased at the edge of her brain, something that someone had said, something that hadn't seemed important at the time, something that maybe hadn't been connected with the investigation proper.

Now she knew it was important, and she couldn't remember what it was, or who said it, or where they had been. Or — maybe — even if her tired brain was making it up.

Logic. There wasn't any.

Motive. There wasn't any. Everyone in her old life in Garland had loved Laura Tyler. Very few people at the Olympus House had even met her, no one really knew her, and no one — not one human being they had been able to discover — had wanted to kill her.

But someone had done exactly that.

Rebecca swallowed, took a firm grip on her nerves, and punched in a telephone number dredged up from a long-ago memory. It took six more calls and a lot of talking before she finally got the connection she needed.

"Well, if it isn't the former lady cop. I heard you were getting back into the business. Going private, are you?" Vegas Charlie's voice always sounded more like badly maintained machinery than human speech.

"No. I just knew the lady involved. Both of them." One thing about talking to Vegas Charlie, there were no politenesses or social-form questions required. In spite of his name, it was doubtful he'd ever left the Dallas area for more than a weekend, if at all, but if something were going on in a certain segment of the population, he knew about it and he knew who was interested. This knack of his was sometimes unnerving, but very efficient.

"One of them was not a lady. Ladies do not welsh on their debts. Especially extremely large ones."

"Rather an overreaction, don't you think?"

One could almost hear the creak of Vegas Charlie shrugging. "I have heard that a certain person might have mixed in some personal feelings and taken the suggestions of his employer to an unacceptably extreme level. Such actions are not condoned or encouraged. But she should not have welshed on her debts. Do not gamble if you cannot afford to lose."

So much for Madame Norina. Nora O'Malley of New Jersey. Harsh, but true.

"What have you heard about the other lady?" When talking to Vegas Charlie it was easy to slip into his habit of never really putting a proper name to anything or anyone.

"Nothing that is not in the papers. Such a tragedy."

"I've heard her son was an acquaintance of yours."

"I have many acquaintances. I may have met him on occasion." His voice ground down into a lower gear. "I do hope you are not insinuating —"

"Of course not. I just know that if anything is going on in town, you are the most likely to hear about it. I also know that you would be happy to help catch the monster who did such an awful thing." *I really should go in for diplomacy,* Rebecca thought.

It was common knowledge that Vegas Charlie had more than a few bodies buried in his past, if not actually in his backyard.

"Such monsters give all of us a bad name," he answered, apparently mollified. "But I know nothing. No one of my acquaintance would do such a horrible thing to a poor little old lady. We do not harm family members," he added sanctimoniously.

Which was a lie. Rebecca knew of at least two other cases where family members had been definitely harmed. Harmed, but not killed, she added just to be fair. A broken arm and a small caliber bullet through the fleshy part of the thigh were very different from a lethal drain cleaner cocktail. But in this instance she believed him.

"Her son is a good customer of some acquaintances of mine," Charlie went on, paying out the words slowly, as if they were coins. The conversation was almost over. "From what I hear he is a couple of thousand down at the moment, but as he has been down more many times before, there is no alarm. He is a gentleman. He pays his debts."

"It's good of you to talk to me, Charlie. I appreciate it."

"Keep your nose clean," he said and then hung up abruptly. That was as long as she had ever known him to speak on the telephone, at least with the forces of the law. He had a healthy respect for wiretaps that had frustrated both her and the force intensely for years.

But she had learned what she needed to learn. Skeeter wasn't in the kind of trouble that could earn a hit on his mother. No matter who held Skeeter's paper, Vegas Charlie would have known about it.

Rebecca took a sip of her now-cold coffee and didn't even notice the temperature. Vegas Charlie had said he and his associates were not involved and, even though he was a total scum-bag, she tended to believe him.

He had a reputation for being behind quick and sometimes lethal violence, but he had never been known to kill a debtor's family member, especially a harmless little old lady.

So, that left the Olympus House. The glasses had come up from the kitchen that morning. Madame Norina had been there when they did. Ashdown and his crew had interviewed every employee and found no connection to Laura Tyler. Also, Flora — who was probably much more intimidating a figure to the kitchen help than a mere police detective — had spoken to the staff and everyone swore that the glasses were clean and empty when they left the kitchen.

So, that left Madame and the jewel class, who had been milling about in the salon area and not watching each other. They might have every motive in the world to do each other and their husbands in, but no one — no one! — had had a motive to kill poor little Laura Tyler.

But any of them could have done it and one of them had to have done it. Which?

And why?

Her head was starting to hurt.

Giving up, she saved the linen inventory file, closed it, and opened the case file, reading every word of her notes, including all the singularly unhelpful information she had compiled from her Internet searches. Surely she had made more coherent notes when she was on the force! This was nothing but a jumble of impressions and hearsay and a very few absolute facts.

Getting hard facts had been easier when she had had a badge to back her up.

Grabbing a pen and a legal pad, Rebecca went through the file again, writing down every concrete fact. It made a frightfully short list, so she added more facts as she remembered them.

Death occurred in the early morning exercise class — the jewel class, so named because of the colored glasses from which they drink Madame Norina's Water of Health, a nasty but harmless mineral water — on Monday morning. I was present to deliver Flora Melkiot's earrings. Laura Tyler had just moved into the building, apparently living out a fantasy of becoming a socialite; she had tried to join the jewel class before, but had been turned down. This was her first day in the class. Everyone got their glass, filled it from the cooler, and chugged down the mineral water. Everyone used the same personal glass all the time. Laura Tyler had chosen her glass just days before and it had never been used. The glasses came up clean from the kitchen that morning. Laura Tyler's glass had drain cleaner crystals in the bottom; the taste was not noticed because of the foul mineral water; same likely with appearance, complicated by the brightly colored glass. Death was quick. Ashdown said a square of plastic wrap was found in one of the potted plants; no fingerprints, only smudges.

Jewel Class:

Madame Norina — fake Middle European accent and ambiance; really Nora O'Malley from New Jersey; some history of lightweight grifting, but nothing serious or violent; apparently very serious about becoming a nationally known exercise/ health guru; bad gambling problem; lived in a room in Oak Cliff; always wore a turban, pink exercise suit, and cover-up.

Eleanor Anthony — former hooker; possibly killed a man in Nevada around eight years ago; disappeared; husband was being blackmailed to run for Senate as a puppet by Waldo Wylde because of what she had done; OH sixth floor, lavender glass, pale gray exercise suit.

Isabel Orwell — bitter wife of Roland Orwell, who was leaving her for Ginny Wylde; drinks to excess — has she always done *this, or only since Roland's leaving her?; a perfectionist; Roland fired her maid during their separation; OH ninth floor, tortoiseshell glass, yellow exercise suit, leopard (or some big cat print) scarf around her neck.*

Ginny Wylde — pretty much a tramp; had many affairs with permission of husband Waldo Wylde, neo-fascist media personality; was tired of latest lover Orwell and looking for new man; OH penthouse, red glass, red shiny Lycra exercise suit with rhinestones around the collar. (Cheap-looking, Rebecca added in the margin; she was not referring to the suit's cost.)

Miss Alicia Carruthers — real-estate mogul; very narrowly moraled woman who has spent her life expiating the sin of having had an illegitimate, severely handicapped child whose existence has been kept secret at all costs; blackmailed for over fifty years by child's father, an attorney — she may press charges against him; OH penthouse, yellow glass, navy exercise suit piped in white.

Roland Orwell — husband of Isabel, had an affair with Ginny Wylde and was leaving his wife because of her; investment banker — had given Madame a large loan on very little collateral and that morning before the jewel class was threatening to foreclose; beat up Waldo Wylde; not known if he drank any water, but probably not.

And, because she had to be fair, Rebecca added:

Flora Melkiot — nosy, bossy, meddlesome old woman who is sharp as a tack; widow of jewelry store magnate Morris Melkiot; OH twelfth floor, blue glass, electric blue suit.

Rebecca stared at the list, waiting futilely for inspiration to strike. Somehow in the dim recesses of her brain she knew that she should have heard something from someone that should explain everything. Only thing was, she didn't think she had. Things like that only happened in the last ten minutes of TV shows, not in real life.

She read the list once again. She was looking at the murderer of Laura Tyler; she knew it. She just didn't know which one it was. Or why.

Esther stuck her head into the office. "When you get a minute, can you come out here?"

Startled, Rebecca looked up, frowned, and stood.

"I didn't mean you had to come now."

"It's either that or start throwing things. I'm no good at paperwork, even if it's done on a computer."

A memory flashed in Esther's mind. Jesse had hated paperwork too; it had been a continual if friendly battle between Jesse and Rebecca as to who would write up the reports.

When does it stop hurting? Esther wondered somewhat bleakly. Four years, and the thought of Jesse's death still caused her an almost physical pain.

Esther forced herself to smile indulgently. "That inventory's waited a couple of weeks now; it can wait a little longer."

"I haven't been working on the inventory. I've been working on the case."

"Any ideas?"

"No. Not a one. I could stick a pin in that list and have just as good a case against that person as anyone else. I know it had to be someone on that list, I know it, but there is no reason for any of them to have wanted to kill Laura Tyler. Each other, yes, but Laura Tyler, no. I'm so frustrated I could scream."

"Just be glad Ashdown's responsible for it

and not you."

"I am. But I hate to see a murderer go free." Rebecca's mouth thinned to a hard line. "I hate to see anyone hurt people and break the rules and get away with it."

"Come on. I want your opinion on this display."

Rebecca edged her way around the desk, careful not to topple the ever-growing pile of uninventoried linens. "I owe you an apology. I'm sorry I've been away from the shop so much. It's put too much of a burden on you."

"I don't mind," Esther said with perfect truth. "As I said, I think this case has been good for you. Got you thinking again. And it's not like we've been overrun with business, either."

They stepped into the shop and with a flourish, Esther gestured toward the front window. The translucent Lucite shelves were filled with vividly colored glass — red to the left side, green to the right. The afternoon sun didn't reach into the window itself, but the light was still bright enough to make the various bowls and compotes and plates and glasses and boxes glow as if electrified.

"I was afraid it might look too Christmassy —"

Brilliant red.

Brilliant green.

Rebecca drew in a deep breath.

"— but it's so pretty, and we said we needed a bold splash of color." Esther's voice faded at the blank look on her partner's face. "Rebecca?"

Red.

Green.

RED.

GREEN.

Could it be? Could the answer really be so simple?

"You don't like it?"

"Of course," Rebecca said in awed tones.

"What is wrong with you, girl?" Esther asked, but Rebecca was gone, running for the office. "Rebecca?"

"It looks great!" she shouted, emerging with her purse and keys. "I think I just figured out why Laura Tyler was killed."

Chapter Twenty-Six

An agitated Flora was waiting for her in the Olympus House lobby.

"I came down as soon as you called. What do you mean, you think you know how Laura Tyler was killed? We know how she was killed, with that drain cleaner stuff," Flora blurted without any other greeting.

"Hush! Don't broadcast it. Has Ashdown arrived yet?"

"You called him?"

"Yes. And got a rather pointed lecture about talking on my cell phone while driving, if you can believe it!"

"I can believe anything about that idiot. Suspecting me of being a murderer, when I've been working my brain to the bone to try and help him solve this case. I don't see why you had to call him."

"He's the police, Flora. If I'm right, he'll need to make an arrest."

"We could do a citizen's arrest."

"There is no such thing," Rebecca said and watched Flora's face, which had lit up almost ghoulishly, fall.

"Drat! I do so hate to do all the work and then let him get the credit."

"But you'll have the knowledge of a deed well done."

"Pooh and piffle!" Flora said, then snorted in indignation. "As if that ever did anyone any good."

Ashdown arrived not two minutes later, followed by his shadow Gus Spencer, and Rebecca was delighted to see them. Flora was teasing her to death about the identity of the murderer and how she'd figured it out. She also paid no attention to Rebecca's stated intention of going over it only once.

Actually, Rebecca was afraid to go over her evidence too many times for fear her case would come apart. She herself had picked a dozen holes in it on the way over, but — as tenuous as it was — it was the only solution that made sense.

"Well, Miss Cloudwebb, you say you've solved the case?" Ashdown's tone was both condescending and angry, and it put Rebecca's nerves on edge.

"I think so."

"Well, explain it to me."

Rebecca had been undecided as to

whether she should tell him or show him, but his attitude made the choice for her. "Come with me."

"Oh, come on, Miss Cloudwebb, you aren't going to pull that old late-movie confrontation scene, are you?"

"Why don't I wait down here?" Gus asked. He had already settled himself in one of the comfortably overstuffed couches and unearthed an only slightly squashed Snickers — king size, of course — from the depths of his pockets.

"What? You want to miss the show? Get your butt in gear." Ashdown retorted in acid tones. His expression reflecting the way he was continually put upon, Gus heaved himself up and they both followed the two women to the elevator.

When Rebecca pushed the ninth floor button, Flora looked at her with startled eyes. "You don't mean . . ." she began, but Rebecca shushed her.

Ashdown had not seen or had not looked at which button she pushed. He was frowning and tapping his foot impatiently while Gus picked at the dark brown wrapping of his Snickers bar. "Of course you won't tell anything, will you, Miss Cloudwebb? Got to go for the grandstand play, don't you?"

"Don't take your frustrations out on me,

Detective Ashdown. You should have seen this long before I did."

Ashdown's inarticulate grumble was lost in the whoosh of the doors opening.

The way to the apartment had never seemed longer, and with each step Rebecca felt her heart sink a little further. If she were wrong, she would probably be sued for defamation of character or some such. If she were right, there might not be enough proof, and the murderer would walk because of her meddling.

Why hadn't she simply kept her stupid mouth shut and let the police do their job?

Because the police weren't getting anywhere.

Because she wanted to grandstand. She wanted to show she was just as good a cop as she had ever been.

By now even Ashdown knew where they were going.

"Are you sure, Miss Cloudwebb?"

"As sure as I can be."

"Do you have proof?"

That was the question, and Rebecca didn't answer it. There was no real proof, and she couldn't see any way of getting it. That was why she had to talk to the murderer.

"There are just a few things I need to clarify."

They had to ring the doorbell three times before there was an answer.

"Good afternoon, Mrs. Orwell," Rebecca said with a smile. "May we speak to you for a moment?"

Isabel Orwell was so drunk she could barely stand. In this bloated, unclean wreck there was no resemblance to the sophisticated and elegant woman Rebecca had seen that first day, the unrelenting perfectionist Flora had known. She scrutinized them through eyes swollen almost shut, then nodded slowly and stepped backward, letting them into the apartment.

The apartment smelled rancidly of alcohol and sweat and garbage. It was still monochromatic, but had none of the previous icy perfection. Empty bottles lay ignored on the floor — Jack Daniels, Chivas, Sauza, Wild Turkey, and more. It was as if Isabel was working her way through the liquor cabinet without regard as to brand or variety. Pillows and cushions and even bibelots were flung about, left lying where they fell. Most everything that could be broken was.

"Sorry the place is such a mess," Isabel mumbled. "I'm going to have to move, you know. Because of what Roland did. It's all his fault, you know. Not mine. His fault, his and that whore's."

In for a penny, in for a pound. Rebecca took a deep breath.

"Roland didn't kill Laura Tyler, Mrs. Orwell. You did."

The bleary eyes took a moment, but they finally focused on Rebecca. They didn't move as Isabel took a healthy slug from the nearly empty bottle of Tanqueray she held.

"It was supposed to be Ginny Wylde," she said at last, a thin dribble of gin escaping the corner of her mouth and sliding unnoticed down her neck. "That tramp deserved it, going after Roland and breaking up our marriage. It should have been her, not that funny little woman."

"So you didn't mean to kill Laura Tyler?" Ashdown asked in a gentle voice that didn't even sound like him.

"No!" It was a wail. "I didn't even know her! It was supposed to be Ginny! Ginny should have died. She deserved to die, the little slut. It was supposed to be Ginny." Isabel looked pleadingly at them. "What else was I supposed to do? I just couldn't let her wreck my marriage. A woman has a right to protect her home." She began to sob as she crumpled to the floor in sections like a collapsing toy. "I was just trying to protect my home."

■ ■ ■ ■

"So how did you know?"

Flora glared at the detective. She poured coffee into his cup, even if her expression intimated she would rather pour it into his lap. "Because she's a good detective, that's why."

Rebecca sipped at her coffee. Somehow she had thought she would be elated to solve the case, but she wasn't. It was heartbreaking. Even sitting here in Flora's comfortable living room, part of her was back in the wreck of the Orwells' apartment, watching Isabel Orwell disintegrate before their eyes. By the time the paramedics had arrived she was almost catatonic, with only the rise and fall of her breathing to prove she was alive. Gus had gone with the ambulance to take her to the hospital. Ashdown should have gone immediately to begin the paperwork, but he had questions only Rebecca could answer.

"Esther's window," she said at last. "Esther loves to change things up in the shop. Today she put colored glass in the window. Red on one side, green on the other."

Ashdown frowned. "And that told you Isabel Orwell killed Laura Tyler? I

434

don't get it."

"Isabel Orwell is red-green color blind."

Understanding flashed over Flora's face. "That was why she was so insistent on having the tortoiseshell glass. It was the only one with a pattern."

Rebecca nodded. "It was the only one she could be sure to recognize. Ginny's glass was red, which would have appeared gray to her. She didn't know that Laura Tyler had chosen a green glass."

"And that would have appeared gray to her too. She put the poison in the wrong glass!"

"And she's been trying to forget ever since. That's when her heavy drinking started."

"Okay," Ashdown said slowly, "I can buy that."

"You have to, since Rebecca made her confess for you!" Flora said with asperity.

Ashdown ignored her. "But how did you know she was color blind? She didn't tell you, obviously."

"No, she never would have told anyone. She was terrified of someone finding out."

"Why?" Ashdown asked, obviously confused. "There's nothing wrong with being color blind. It's just a medical condition."

"Medical condition or abnormality? It all

depends on how you look at it. By all accounts Isabel Orwell was a perfectionist, and perfectionists don't admit their faults."

"That's a mighty slim hypothesis to hang a murder charge on."

"Agreed." Rebecca nodded. It had been slim, so much so that she almost hadn't acted on it. "But it was the only thing that made sense. And there were a lot of other things, little things, that didn't mean much by themselves. When Isabel had a maid to look after her clothes, she didn't have to worry, but after Roland fired the maid out of spite, Isabel began showing up in all kinds of weird colors. There was that creepy, no-color apartment. And Ginny's hair."

"Her hair!" Ashdown said. "How?"

"Isabel called Ginny a gray-haired witch. Ginny's hair is red. At first I thought she meant Ginny dyed her hair to cover the gray."

Flora harrumphed. "Ginny Wylde has had hair of many colors, but I've never seen a thread of gray in any of them. One can always tell."

"And to Isabel the red looked gray," Ashdown said slowly. "My God."

"There were a lot of things," Rebecca finished lamely, all too aware of how little she had had to go on: nothing much but a hunch and a memory.

A memory she had buried so deeply it had almost not resurfaced. Frank Titus had been color blind. He had hid it well, and heaven only knew how he had gotten into and stayed on the police force with it, but he had been good at getting what he wanted. They had been together several months before she'd guessed, and even then he had been very reluctant to admit it.

It's always the secrets.

"What will happen to her?" Flora asked.

Ashdown drained his cup and set it on the coffee table. "My personal opinion is that she'll never see the inside of a courtroom. She'll probably spend the rest of her life in a mental ward."

"Seeing what she did to Laura Tyler drove her crazy," Rebecca said. "That's why she was drinking so much. To forget."

"But she was prepared to kill Ginny Wylde like that."

"Ginny deserved it, Detective," Rebecca snapped. "At least in Isabel's mind."

Flora added, "I think that cheating husband of hers deserved it more, but Isabel would never have killed him."

"I wonder," Rebecca murmured.

"I still don't know how you put it together."

"Several things. One thing was something you said, Flora."

"I?" The older woman was startled, then, recovering, asked blithely, "Which thing was that?"

"About secrets. You said something about everyone having a secret — Miss Alicia, Eleanor Anthony, and the rest — but I got to thinking that Isabel Orwell didn't have a secret. At least, not one that we had discovered. One thing I just realized, Detective," Rebecca said and looked the detective squarely in the face, "is that she told us. She told us several times that Ginny should have been the one to die. We just didn't realize at the time that she was confessing."

Ashdown's face went slack. "My God."

"I wonder . . ." Flora said softly. "If Laura Tyler hadn't chosen that green glass, Isabel would have put the crystals in Ginny's glass and Ginny would have died. I wonder if the case would ever have been solved."

"Of course," Ashdown said, but his tone was defensive and subdued. "Of course we would have solved it. Eventually. Oh, have you heard about Waldo Wylde?"

"No."

"He's improving rapidly."

"Of course," Flora sneered.

"According to the press conference held

438

by his adoring and supportive wife. And he's letting her record the speeches he writes for his radio programs. Apparently his ratings have jumped up almost forty percent since he was attacked."

"There's no such thing as bad publicity, I guess," Rebecca said.

"I wonder if the glorious Ginny has picked out her next victim," Flora mused and was startled when the detective reacted. He was skilled enough to keep his face impassive, but his ears flushed a dangerous red.

That, Flora thought, *was a situation to keep an eye on.*

Her attention focused on the empty cup cradled in her hands, Rebecca hadn't noticed. "I wonder if the whole story will ever come out?"

"If the Orwells have a decent defense attorney it will," Ashdown said and then grinned. "I know of one I might even recommend to them."

"Seems like I should say something about the Wyldes flourishing like the green bay tree," Flora murmured. "Roland Orwell, too."

"Evil?" Rebecca touched her lips with a paper napkin as if wiping away the horror of the word and all it implied. "Isn't that a bit much?"

"I don't think so. Think of all that's happened because of one woman's lusts and one stupid man's weakness. How many lives have been ruined or changed or ended prematurely. You can call me old-fashioned and moralistic" — Flora's angry expression told them they had better not dare — "but it isn't right. It just isn't right!"

"Murder never is," Rebecca answered.

ABOUT THE AUTHOR

Also known as Janis Susan May, **Janis Patterson** is a seventh-generation Texan and a third-generation wordsmith. She is one of the founders of Romance Writers of America and has served two terms as Secretary for the SouthWest Region of Mystery Writers of America. She has sold eighteen or so novels and ghostwritten perhaps twice that many books. Formerly an actress and singer, a talent agent and Supervisor of Accessioning for a biogenetic DNA testing lab, Janis has also been editor-in-chief of two multi-magazine publishing groups. She founded and was the original editor of *The Newsletter* of the North Texas Chapter of the American Research Center in Egypt, which for the nine years of her reign was the international organization's only monthly publication. It was through Janis Susan's efforts that *The Newsletter* (later retitled *Menhedj*) was archived as a scholarly reference work in libraries and universities all over the world. Long interested in Egyptology, she was one of the Organizing Committee of the North Texas chapter and was the closing speaker for the ARCE International Conference in Boston in 2005. Janis married for the first time when most of her contemporaries were becoming grandmothers. Her husband, a handsome Naval Reserve Officer several years younger than she, even proposed in a moonlit garden in Egypt. Janis Susan lives in Texas with her husband and an assortment of very spoiled dogs and cats.

CPSIA information can be obtained
at www.ICGtesting.com
Printed in the USA
FFOW020606110313